Praise for Jessica Clare

"The residents of Painted Barrel are just as lovely as ever."
—*Publishers Weekly* (starred review)

"[A] steamy holiday confection that equally delivers heart-warming laughs and heart-melting sighs." —*Booklist*

"Great storytelling. . . . Delightful reading. . . . It's fun and oh-so-hot!"
—*Kirkus Reviews*

"Jessica Clare found a balance in developing the characters and romance with banter, heart, and tension. [She] introduced colorful new characters along with Eli, Cass, Clyde, and the dogs from *All I Want for Christmas Is a Cowboy*."
—Harlequin Junkie

"[Clare is] a romance writing prodigy."
—Heroes and Heartbreakers

"Blazing hot." —*USA Today*

Titles by Jessica Clare

Hex Series

GO HEX YOURSELF
WHAT THE HEX

Wyoming Cowboys

ALL I WANT FOR CHRISTMAS IS A COWBOY
THE COWBOY AND HIS BABY
A COWBOY UNDER THE MISTLETOE
THE COWBOY MEETS HIS MATCH
HER CHRISTMAS COWBOY
THE BACHELOR COWBOY
HOLLY JOLLY COWBOY

Roughneck Billionaires

DIRTY MONEY
DIRTY SCOUNDREL
DIRTY BASTARD

The Billionaire Boys Club

STRANDED WITH A BILLIONAIRE
BEAUTY AND THE BILLIONAIRE
THE WRONG BILLIONAIRE'S BED
ONCE UPON A BILLIONAIRE
ROMANCING THE BILLIONAIRE
ONE NIGHT WITH A BILLIONAIRE
HIS ROYAL PRINCESS
BEAUTY AND THE BILLIONAIRE: THE WEDDING

Billionaires and Bridesmaids

THE BILLIONAIRE AND THE VIRGIN
THE TAMING OF THE BILLIONAIRE
THE BILLIONAIRE TAKES A BRIDE
THE BILLIONAIRE'S FAVORITE MISTAKE
BILLIONAIRE ON THE LOOSE

The Bluebonnet Novels

THE GIRL'S GUIDE TO (MAN)HUNTING
THE CARE AND FEEDING OF AN ALPHA MALE
THE EXPERT'S GUIDE TO DRIVING A MAN WILD
THE VIRGIN'S GUIDE TO MISBEHAVING
THE BILLIONAIRE OF BLUEBONNET

Holly Jolly
Cowboy

JESSICA CLARE

BERKLEY ROMANCE
New York

BERKLEY ROMANCE
Published by Berkley
An imprint of Penguin Random House LLC
penguinrandomhouse.com

Copyright © 2021 by Jessica Clare
Excerpt from *Go Hex Yourself* copyright © 2021 by Jessica Clare
Penguin Random House supports copyright. Copyright fuels creativity, encourages
diverse voices, promotes free speech, and creates a vibrant culture. Thank you for buying
an authorized edition of this book and for complying with copyright laws by not
reproducing, scanning, or distributing any part of it in any form without permission.
You are supporting writers and allowing Penguin Random House to continue to
publish books for every reader.

BERKLEY and the BERKLEY & B colophon are registered trademarks of
Penguin Random House LLC.

ISBN: 9780593641101

Jove mass-market edition / October 2021
Berkley Romance trade paperback edition / September 2023

Printed in the United States of America
3rd Printing

Book design by George Towne

For the jolliest Holly I know, Holly Root!
Thanks for always having my back.

Also for Kristine, who has also baked
her way through the pandemic.
We are sisters in gluten.

CHAPTER ONE

Painted Barrel was all around a decent place for a girl to live, but it was terrible for desserts.

Holly Dawson gazed into the window of the town's lone bakery-slash-doughnut shop. Glazed doughnuts were in the window. Glazed doughnuts, of all things. And apple fritters. A window was there to advertise your wares, to show off what you could do. You didn't put apple fritters in the window, or glazed doughnuts. That was like a cowboy showing that he knew what a horse looked like. They were basics. They were boring.

She passed this window every day, looking for new things. Holly loved baking. It was her favorite hobby, and she dreamed of opening her own pastry and sweets shop someday. Not here, of course. Painted Barrel had less than three hundred people. They had one bar-slash-restaurant and the doughnut shop that also passed as a café. That was it, foodwise, and it really couldn't support more. Holly couldn't afford to open her own place, either.

But she liked to dream. In her dream, it was *her* shop with a window on Main Street, and she'd fill it with all kinds of darling, enticing-to-look-at sweets. Pink cupcakes with chocolate stars on top. Trays of fluffy profiteroles with gooey crème oozing out of them. Mini cakes and fruit-laden tarts. Shortcakes puffed with whipped cream and colorful macarons in every shade. Exciting things. Fun things. Delicious things.

Not glazed doughnuts.

Hands in her pockets, she stared at the window for a minute longer, and then checked her phone for the time. She had a few minutes before she had to be at work. She glanced down the street at Wade's saloon, Painted Barrel's lone restaurant. The parking lot in front of it was empty, other than Wade's truck, so she could afford to dawdle a little. Holly took one last look at the window and headed inside.

The bell clanged, announcing Holly's presence, and the girl behind the counter got off the stool she was sitting on, putting her magazine aside. Geraldine wasn't the most enthusiastic employee, but Holly had heard that she was related to the owner, and that was how she'd gotten the job here despite being a high school dropout. Not that Holly was jealous. Sure, she was a high school dropout, too, and running a sweets shop was her dream. She doubted Geraldine made more than minimum wage and Holly barely stayed afloat with the tips she made at the saloon. So, no, she couldn't have Geraldine's job.

Even if it irked her that she wanted it.

She smiled overbrightly at Geraldine and gazed at the offerings behind the glass. Pigs in a blanket, doughnuts, doughnuts, more doughnuts, and some sad, stale-looking cupcakes shoved to one end. A couple of chocolate chip cookies that were too flat and had clearly been made with the wrong kind of sugar. Figured. Still, now that she was inside, she supposed she should buy something and support local business. "Anything new today?"

Geraldine grinned and leaned on the counter. "You say that every time you come in. Nothing new, no."

Did she? Maybe it was because she always hoped they would see the opportunity right in front of their eyes. "You know, I'm something of a baker myself. I could make some stuff and sell it on consignment if you'd give me a chance."

The look in Geraldine's eyes grew frosty, as it always did every time Holly brought this up. "I'll talk to the boss about it. Again."

Yeah, Holly knew that wasn't going to go anywhere. She'd pitched it multiple times, only to be shot down every time. People didn't like change. She had to try, though. Not only because her baking was something of a source of pride for her, but also because Holly desperately needed the money. "Just let me know. Can I get two cookies?"

Holly took her purchase—Wade would like the sweets—and headed back onto the street. Just in time. There was a truck pulled up in front of the saloon now, likely waiting for the lunch rush, and as she watched, another pulled up, too. A busy day wouldn't be so bad. Hopefully people would be generous with their tips. She doubted it, though. People got stingy during the holidays, which was tough. It was like, because they were spending money on presents, everyone else should go without. Considering Holly lived on tips, it wasn't her favorite time of year, workwise.

She blanched when a third truck pulled up, because she recognized it and the two dogs hanging out in the back of the bed. One was a great big, beautiful Belgian Malinois, and the other was a retriever wearing a bright yellow vest with EMOTIONAL SUPPORT ANIMAL in black lettering along the sides. They both wagged their tails as she walked past, looking for pets. Holly loved animals, but she was not a huge fan of the owner of that truck.

Sure enough, three guys piled out of the truck, all of them wearing hats. One was Jason Clements, the mayor's lanky husband and a real nice guy. She liked him as a customer— he tipped well. Then there was Carson, a guy with salt-and-pepper hair and a grim expression. He worked at Price Ranch—Jason and Sage's ranch—and since most of the guys they hired were ex-military, Holly suspected he'd seen some shit. He was polite, though, which was all she asked.

And then there was the driver. Adam.

He was tall and gorgeous, dressed in jeans and a puffy vest over his long-sleeved shirt, and wore a worn baseball cap over his dark hair instead of a cowboy hat. Thick slashing brows added to the sardonic look on his face, as if he was always laughing at you. And he had the most perfect mouth, framed by a goatee that made him look dangerous and just a bit dashing. Too bad he was a jerk and a shitty tipper.

God, she hated him.

Her day had definitely taken a turn for the worse already. That was another one of the problems with small towns. If you hated someone, it was absolutely impossible to avoid them. And she got paid on tips, which meant she had to be nice. So Holly pasted a smile on her face, held the door open for the others to file in, and sucked it up. "Take a seat anywhere, boys. I'll be with you in a jif."

Adam Calhoun did his best to ignore their waitress as he took off his hat and hung it on a peg near the door. It was clear she loathed him and was pretending for the tip.

He hated that sort of thing, and it just made him want to stiff her even more. She was so obvious about it, too, her smile fake and sweet as she poured cups of coffee and took orders. She didn't even glance at him as she took his down, just focused on her pad as she wrote. She had plenty of smiles for Carson and Jason, though, which just irked him.

It wasn't that he was ugly. Most women thought he was nice-looking. Adam was just vain enough to know that he had a good smile and a decent personality, and that usually let him get the attention of most women he flirted with. Most. Because waitress Holly was probably the prettiest thing in this town—and several others around—and yet she couldn't stand him. He drained his coffee cup while the others ordered and then held it in the air, a silent request for more.

Her eyes flashed with anger momentarily, and it was quickly covered up by that fake smile again. "Be right back."

She hustled off, her round bottom shaking with every step, and okay, he was red-blooded male enough to watch.

"Now you're just baiting her," Jason commented, sipping his own cup.

Maybe he was. There was something about Holly that drove him absolutely up a wall. Maybe it was that she was always all smiles, even when she clearly didn't feel like it. Her clothes were a little tighter than they probably should have been, her festive red sweater practically painted on her lush figure, and her jeans showing off her curves. Her dark brown hair was pulled up into a bouncy long ponytail atop her head and fastened with a big, garish Christmas bow. She looked festive and flirty and it irked him.

Maybe it was that the first time he'd come in, she'd flirted up a storm with him and so he'd tipped well. He'd even come back later that night, after thinking about her all afternoon, only to see her flirting with another customer like she'd done with him, and he'd realized it was all for tips. It made him angry. Made him feel stupid. So he'd left a dollar.

He'd left a dollar ever since, too. Just to make a statement.

He had a dollar sitting in his wallet today, waiting for the opportunity to poke at her again.

Holly brought back the coffee, taking his mug with a cool expression and filling it quickly. "Separate checks today, boys?"

Jason raised a finger before Adam could answer. "One check. I'm paying for lunch today."

"In that case, make my sandwich a double," Adam drawled. "Didn't know it was free."

The waitress's demeanor brightened. "Well, aren't you sweet, Jason Clements." She winked at him. "You want me to pack up a sandwich for your lovely wife, too? The bread's nice and fresh and I can make hers with extra pickles, just as she likes."

Jason nodded. "That's a great idea. Thanks."

"I'll have it ready by the time you leave." She touched Carson's shoulder, then leaned over him to pour his coffee, and Adam found himself staring at her tits. She wasn't shoving them in anyone's face but . . . how did she expect a man to concentrate when she wore a sweater like that? Ridiculous. She patted Carson's shoulder again, then turned and left, swanning her way to another table full of men. A moment later, her bright laughter floated through the saloon, and it made him grit his teeth.

"You're glaring," Jason commented to Adam.

He shook his head. "I bet she forgets my order. That's

all." He leaned back in his chair. "So, what's the special occasion today?" They came into town once or twice a week for lunch if weather—and the work—permitted. Normally they paid for their own, though. Adam didn't mind that. Sure, the boss had married a wealthy woman and could afford to pay, but if Adam couldn't pay for his own sandwiches, he needed a new line of work.

Jason pulled out a couple of red and green envelopes and slid them across the table to both of them. "Sorry about the glitter. Sage wanted a festive envelope." He gestured at them. "I'm giving you your Christmas bonuses early because I need to ask a favor."

Adam picked up his envelope and casually glanced inside. The check was for more than two months' pay. Damn. That was generous. "Whatever the favor is, I'll do it."

"You might want to hear what it is first." He leaned back in his chair, rubbing a hand over his short, military-precision haircut. "Me and Sage decided we're going to take the kids and visit family back east for the holidays. We're going to be gone until after New Year's."

Adam glanced over at Carson, but the man was impassive. He never talked unless directly prompted, and he didn't look as if he had anything to say about this, either. "Kinda a long holiday," Adam ventured. "Something going on?"

Jason rubbed his neck, clearly uneasy. "Sage needs a vacation. She says she doesn't, but I want her to get away for a while. To relax. The stress isn't good for her . . . or the new baby."

Adam blinked at that. "Another baby?" Both of their children were still extremely young. The little one wasn't more than six months old.

His boss grimaced. "It was a surprise, but not that much

of a surprise?" His look grew sheepish. "It's not like we don't know how babies are made. I'd hoped to have more time before the next one, but the universe has other plans."

Carson just snorted.

As in, Jason couldn't keep his hands off his wife. Adam didn't blame him. He'd never met someone more cheerful or kind-natured than Sage Cooper-Clements. She always had a sparkle in her eye and a kind word for everyone. From the day that Adam had walked onto their ranch, she'd made him feel welcome. He could see why Jason loved her.

And as if to prove that a woman could be beautiful and utterly annoying, the waitress returned with another round of coffee. "Sandwiches will be right out." She smiled at Jason, patted Carson's shoulder, and completely ignored Adam. Figured.

Jason seemed oblivious to their waitress's bad attitude. "I know we're leaving early, and we're shorthanded, but I feel this is important. Sage needs a break. It would mean someone working over the holidays, and if you're interested, I can pay extra to make up for the fact that you can't go home." He looked at Carson, then at Adam. "If you've got plans, one of the hands at the Swinging C offered to help out, but I'm hoping we can manage."

Adam shrugged. "I'm not going anywhere." His brother back in Iowa might be a little disappointed that Adam wasn't going to return to the family farm for Christmas, but he was used to Adam not being home. His parents were long gone, and the ex-wife . . . well. There were no good feelings left there. "Happy to stick around."

"Can't," Carson said, voice rusty. "Leaving on the twentieth to visit family. Back on the twenty-seventh."

Adam rubbed at his goatee. "I should be okay for a week on my own, as long as Swinging C is on call if any sort of crisis happens." It'd mean long hours of grueling work, doing the jobs of three men, but extra pay would be nice. Extra pay was always nice.

Jason looked relieved. He rubbed a hand over his shorn hair again. "Excellent. I trust you guys, and right now things are slow. Calving's not for months, so I don't feel too bad about leaving for a while. You have my number if you need anything. And the greenhorn will be here bright and early in January. I'll be back in time to take over training him and then we should be full staff again." He gave Adam a grateful look.

Adam just nodded. He was the one that was grateful. After leaving the Navy, he hadn't known what to do with himself. He'd gone back to the family farm for a time, but his older brother liked things run his way, and Adam had felt useless and restless. It was the same restlessness that had made him decide to leave the Navy, the feeling that perhaps he wasn't meant to be career as he'd thought. He'd no longer enjoyed the rigid daily routine or the endless travel. He'd wanted to stay put. Set down roots. Focus on the next chapter of his life.

He just didn't know what that was.

He'd thought the reason he wanted to leave was his wife, Donna. To spend more time with her, maybe make a family. But the moment he returned home, he realized a few things—he wasn't in love with Donna, she wasn't in love with him, and she hadn't been faithful while he'd been overseas on deployment after deployment.

The divorce had been swift, and Adam had been left even more rudderless than before. He'd reached out to old buddies via email, just looking to fill time, and Jason had offered him a job on his ranch. While Adam had farming experience, ranching cattle was a completely different beast, but Jason and his wife had trained him and given him a place to stay. Now, a year on, he was comfortable in his job and happy. He liked ranching. He liked Wyoming and the frosty mountains. He liked Painted Barrel and its people.

Most of its people, anyhow.

"It's all good," he told his friend. "You and Sage take as long as you need. Me and Carson will handle things, and I'll hold down the fort while he's gone." He grinned at them. "What could go wrong?"

Carson just snorted and knocked on the table, warding off bad luck.

Yeah, it was probably a bad idea to toss that out into the universe. Adam knocked on the table, too, just in case.

"I'm coming, I'm coming," the waitress called out. Holly apparently thought they were knocking to get her attention, and she hustled over, sandwich plates stacked up on her arm. She set down each one in front of the right person, cast Adam a tight look, and then sauntered off again.

Well, Adam wasn't gonna apologize for knocking. Especially not to her. He was tempted to knock again, just to be a jackass, but the sandwich looked too good. He tucked in—and nearly groaned aloud.

The service at Wade's might not be his favorite, but damn, the food was incredible.

CHAPTER TWO

The last customer was gone, the dishes done, and Holly pounded and kneaded her sourdough while Wade cashed out the register and added up the tips. It was a relaxing end to the workday. It allowed Holly to do her favorite thing—baking—and to work some of her frustrations out on the dough. She kneaded it with particular force today, imagining it to be the face of a certain cowboy who'd made her day start off badly, and it had just gone downhill from there.

Knocking on the table to get her attention, as if she were a dog to be called. She jammed her fist into the dough, gritting her teeth. The only reason the tip had been decent was because Jason had paid with his credit card, and Jason was always generous. Even so, when she'd cleared the table, she'd found a single dollar bill left in the spot where Adam Calhoun had been sitting, folded lengthwise. It had made her want to explode with frustration. It was a slap in the face, that damn dollar, a reminder that he thought she was shit at her job.

She should have spit in his sandwich.

Holly flipped the dough again and gave it another rough knead. The gluten in the dough was working, and she was satisfied, so she plopped the dough into a bowl, covered it with Saran Wrap, and tossed it into the fridge to prove overnight. As she cleaned up the flour-covered countertop, she hoped the rest of the tips were decent. Everyone had seemed to be in a bad mood, hurrying through their day, and no amount of cheerfulness from her had been enough. Now she felt drained and tired . . . and she needed to put on her game face for a while yet.

She washed her hands and headed out into the main part of the bar. "Dough's rising for tomorrow. All done with the tips? I need to hustle on home."

Wade smiled at her, pushing an envelope in her direction. "Polly calling in?"

She nodded, tucking the envelope into her pocket without even looking. She'd count her tips later. "She's coming home for the holidays. It'll be nice to see her again."

"Done your Christmas shopping?"

"God, no." Holly laughed. "I figured I'd just bake everyone something. Hope you like fruitcake."

"I hate fruitcake, but I'll absolutely eat yours," Wade told her, and patted his stomach. He was a big, solid man with a bald head and a thick mustache and an intimidating stare. He was also the kindest man she'd ever met, and the most giving. Now, if he'd only let her sell her desserts at the restaurant, they'd be on the same page. Wade ran a bar, though. People wanted sandwiches and burgers, chips and wings. They didn't want petit fours or éclairs or light-as-air confections. If someone did order a dessert, they always wanted that crappy cheesecake that Wade got from a wholesaler.

As a compromise, he let her bake fresh bread for the restaurant, and their sandwiches were always a hit. She supposed it was something. Not much, but something.

"Fruitcake it is," she teased, and they both knew full well that she'd probably make him a deluxe chocolate cake of some kind, the more decadent the better. Fruitcake was just a running joke. She grabbed her coat and flung it around her shoulders, and then waved at him. "See you tomorrow!"

Holly raced out the door, mindful of the time, and shivered as she hustled down Main Street. Most of the buildings here were restored old wooden frame houses from the turn of the century, and it gave Painted Barrel a decidedly Old West look. She was renting a refurbished apartment above the dry cleaner's, because housing was scarce in a town like this, and she didn't need much, not with her little sister, Polly, gone off to college. She climbed the stairs, unlocked the door, and was immediately met by a flying bundle of barking excitement.

"Pumpkin!" she cooed, putting her hands down and scooping up the tiny dog. "Is it time for walkies?"

The little thing yapped in her ear, then showered her face with doggy kisses.

"Come on, then," Holly said. Even though she was tired, her poor little pup had been locked up in the house all day and needed relief. She grabbed the leash, headed back down the stairs, and walked Pumpkin up and down Main Street, even though it was after midnight. The time didn't much matter, she supposed. Painted Barrel was safe no matter the hour.

And she had a fierce guard dog with her. Holly snickered to herself at the thought. Pumpkin was five pounds of fluff, and because the dog loved being pampered, that fluff was normally cut so that Pumpkin resembled the world's cutest teddy bear of a dog. She was the happiest little thing, and Holly adored her. Sure, she was supposed to be her sister's, but Polly's clever, technical brain had never really connected with the needy little Pumpkin, and so Holly had taken her on. Now they were inseparable.

She thought about her sister as Pumpkin daintily picked her way through the crusted snow on the edge of the sidewalk, looking for the perfect spot to do her business. It had been months since she'd seen Polly, and the semester of college was wrapping up. That meant exams for Polly—a very stressful time for her—but it also meant that it was almost time for the semiannual shakedown, aka tuition fees.

Holly had been saving her tips, but it wasn't nearly enough, and college seemed to get more expensive every time she turned around. She'd never complain to Polly, but even the student loans and grants her sister got were barely a drop in the bucket. She should have talked her into going to a cheaper college, or living in a cheaper dorm, but Polly had wanted the full experience, and damn it all, Holly was going to give it to her.

After all, they only had each other.

Once the dog was finished with her walk, Holly headed back up to her apartment and sent her sister a text letting her know that she was available. Immediately, the phone rang, and she picked up the video call.

"Hey there, stranger!" Polly's voice was cheerful despite the late hour. "How was work?"

Holly's heart eased a little at the sight of her sister's happy expression. Polly looked tired, sure, but she also seemed to be thriving at college. She knew it provided her opportunities that small-town Wyoming simply couldn't, and so she was thrilled for her sister, even if it meant putting her own wants and needs aside for a while. Wasn't that always the case, though? Her sister had recently cut her long, straight dark hair into a thick fringe of bangs that framed her glasses neatly and made her look more sophisticated and intelligent than ever. She felt like a proud parent just looking at her. The proud parent of a hipster, sure, but a proud parent nevertheless. "Work was work. Some cowboy came in for lunch and was crappy to me and that seemed to set the mood for the rest of the day, but it's over now." She shrugged. "How's classes?"

Polly's eyes widened. "Oh god, are they rough." Her sister proceeded to ramble on about computer science and coding languages and advanced chemistry and all the things that Holly knew absolutely nothing about. She listened to Polly talk, though, because she just loved hearing how passionate her sister was. Polly adored college and learning, and she studied hard to get decent grades. More than anything, Holly was just glad that her sister was going to be a success. One of them should be, at least.

The dog crawled into Holly's lap as her sister talked about how frustrating one of her professors was and how she'd been taking extra tutoring just to pass the class, and how much time the tutoring ate up. "Which reminds me," Polly said. "My card is empty. Can you put some more funds on it? I had to pay for the tutor and between that and food, I'm dry." She grimaced. "I hate to ask."

"No, it's okay." Holly was expecting it, even if it meant pinching pennies for a while. "I'll take my tips to the bank tomorrow and get them transferred over to you. Give me a day."

"You sure you don't mind? I know tuition's coming up soon."

"All handled," Holly lied. "Don't worry about a thing."

Polly's eyes filled with tears. "Don't think that I don't appreciate you, sis. I'm so lucky to have you. Thank you so much. Now that I'm here . . ." Her voice trailed off. "I'm just so . . . I feel like it's where I'm meant to be." She put a hand to her chest. "I feel like my whole life is ahead of me now, you know?"

No, Holly really didn't know. Ever since their parents died when Holly was seventeen and Polly thirteen, she'd put her life on hold to take care of her sister. She'd gotten two jobs to make ends meet, she'd packed lunches and handled parent-teacher meetings and just . . . handled it all, because Polly needed her and they were all each other had left in the world. Sometimes it felt a little unfair, but that was just how things were and she accepted it. "I'm so glad. I love you, too." She leaned in toward the phone's camera. "And is it cold there? You're wearing a scarf!"

"The weather's actually really nice." Polly fingered the scarf thoughtfully, a hint of a blush on her cheeks. "The scarf was a gift from Sasha."

Oooh, Sasha. The chemistry advisor. It wasn't the first time Polly had mentioned this "Sasha"—and Holly hadn't asked if Sasha was a man or a woman. Didn't matter. Sasha made Polly light up, and that was all that was important as far as Holly was concerned. "So am I going to get to meet Sasha when you come home for the holidays? I'm sure we can squeeze another on the couch."

Polly bit her lip and got quiet. "Actually, that's something I wanted to talk to you about today."

Oh no. A sinking feeling swept over her. Holly kept her voice light, though. She didn't want Polly to feel bad. "Oh?"

"Yeah. There's a two-week informal prep course that starts over the holidays. I think it started as just a lot of students getting together when they couldn't go home and just tutoring one another. It's supposed to be really beneficial and . . ." She chewed on her nail, clearly not wanting to spit the words out. "And since Christmas is just you and me, I thought maybe I'd stay up here and give the prep course a go. I could really use the extra study time. Next semester I'm going to try and take advanced physics, you know, and it's going to be really tricky and—"

Holly just smiled, even though her heart was breaking inside. "Don't worry about it at all, Polly. Really. If you think this will help you with your grades, then go for it. Heck, even if it doesn't, you'll get the chance to make some new friends, right?"

Polly gave her sister a shy look. "That's right. It's just so nice to be able to really talk to people, Hol. To rattle on and on about the things that interest me and no one's going to judge or look at me like I'm boring them."

Holly's heart broke for her sister all over again. Painted Barrel had been rough on a brilliant, shy kid who dreamed of private schools where they taught organic chemistry and higher-end math skills. Painted Barrel was lovely and sweet, but it was a very tiny town and the school's curriculum was very basic. The kids that had gone to school with her brilliant Polly had been more interested in football and school dances and flirting than calculus or STEM. Holly couldn't fault them, either—her favorite class back when she was at school was English, and that was because her teacher would fall asleep at her desk and the kids would pass notes all class long. She'd never been much of a learner, but she knew Polly had felt stifled. "You should absolutely do the prep course. Is it . . . extra? Moneywise?" Not that she had extra, but she'd scrape it together somehow. She'd ask Wade if she could take on more shifts. She'd hit up all the bakeries and doughnut shops within an hour's radius and ask if they needed help over the holidays. She could sell fruit-cakes on Etsy.

She'd figure something out.

"It's not really extra, but I might need a little cash if everyone goes out to eat." Polly bit her lip. "I order cheap, but I still like to go."

"Of course you should go," Holly promised. She knew what it was like to see everyone going off and having a good time without you. "I'll send a little more this time, and you can always just tell me if you need more."

"Are you sure, Holly?" Polly's voice was soft. "I know it's the holidays . . ."

"It is," Holly said brightly. She squeezed Pumpkin against her, ruffling the dog's soft fur with her fingers. She'd be crying into that fur later tonight, but right now, she was holding together really well. "You can come home in the summer and I'll absolutely smother you in big-sister love. Until then, we have our Friday night calls. And because it's the holidays, what should I bake and send to you? What would your dorm like?"

Polly's eyes lit up. "What are those little cheesy cracker things called? That are shaped like stars?"

"Uh, cheese crackers?"

Polly giggled, and Holly's heart warmed. She loved her sister so much. Maybe being apart for Christmas would be a good thing. She'd get in some extra work, send her sister some money, and focus on getting that tuition payment in for January. And she'd bake her heart out.

She'd make it work. She always did.

CHAPTER THREE

Holly was determined to have a good day the next day, which was why it was so damned frustrating when Adam Calhoun was waiting at Wade's the moment she walked up.

He sat on the bench outside the restaurant, his big, fearsome-looking dog at his side. Even if the dog looked intimidating, he still wagged his tail eagerly as she approached. *Good boy*, she thought, though she kept her expression remote. She deliberately ignored him, not saying hello as she let herself into the saloon. She wasn't officially on the clock until she walked through the doors, and it wasn't like he was going out of his way to be nice, either. She set her handbag down behind the counter and hung her coat in the kitchen, said hello to Wade, then headed out to the bar.

And if she was deliberately stalling a bit as she put on her half apron, well, no one had to know.

Adam walked in before she flipped the CLOSED sign

over. It was like he'd gotten tired of waiting. He just sauntered in as if he owned the place, glanced at her, then deliberately turned the sign on the door over. "It's lunch
hours now."

She gritted her teeth. "I know. I was just about to head
over to the door and turn the sign myself, but it looks like
someone was too impatient." She delivered the words with
an ultra-sweet, saccharine smile while mentally shooting
daggers in his direction. "Is there something I can help you
with, sir?"

"Sir?" He arched an eyebrow at her, swaggering up to
the bar like the cocky asshole he was. "Someone's angling
for a tip."

Ugh, this guy. "Yes, I'm sure if I play my cards right, I'll
get a whole dollar from you."

He just smirked at her from under the brim of his baseball cap. "It's a dollar more than you deserve for this kinda
service."

"If you don't like it, you're free to go somewhere else."

"Ain't nowhere else."

Holly gave him a cool smile. "That's not my problem.
Now, did you have an order? Or are you just here to take up
counter space that a paying customer could use?"

Adam turned slowly, pretending to look around the
completely empty bar. Well, sure it was empty. People
would trickle in over the next half hour. Until then, this was
the perfect time for her to work on baking the bread she'd
left proving all night. Of course, she couldn't do that if this
jerk was in her face, making her hate his guts.

"Order?" she asked again, getting out her notepad and
holding her temper.

To her surprise, he pulled out a piece of paper and rattled off a half dozen different sandwiches. Ah. He was get-

ting lunch for everyone. It wasn't so unusual. They had a lot of walk-ins that picked up brown-bag lunches and headed back out. They weren't her favorite, of course. Tips were always better when someone sat down to eat, because then she could charm them with conversation. After six years of working at Wade's, she had that part of her job down pat.

So she took the order and got to work, moving to the far end of the bar. The refrigerator case at the end held cold cuts and sandwich fixings, and she began to busily pull the order together. The sooner she got him out of here, the better.

"Uh, excuse me," came the hated voice down the bar.

Holly looked up from the multiple sandwiches she had lined up and in mid-assembly. "Yes?" Was he going to pick at everything she did?

"You're using the wrong bread." He moved down to where she was working, pointing over the bar. "I want the same bread we had yesterday. On all of 'em. Don't cheap out on me."

Cheap out on him? Holly's spine stiffened. "We're out. We won't have any until this afternoon." The bread she was putting the sandwiches on was perfectly nice, normal bread, and she made a good sandwich. Nobody seemed to care what bread she used, most of the time. Of course this guy would. She didn't know if she was flattered or irritated that he was making such a big deal.

Irritated, she decided when she looked at his stubborn, handsome face. Definitely irritated.

"I think you're lying because you don't like me."

Holly gave him an exasperated look. "Dude, they're sandwiches. Why would I lie about the bread?"

"Because you don't like me," he continued stubbornly.

Well, no, she didn't like him. But she worked in a restaurant. She never sabotaged the food if she had a tiff with a customer, because that was just asking to get fired. "That has nothing to do with your order. You—"

"Is there a problem?" Wade asked, coming out of the back. He wiped his hands with a towel, affecting his mild, cheery "customer" smile.

"Of course not," Holly began.

But Adam—that horrible jerk—nodded. "She's using the wrong bread on the sandwiches. I asked for the other kind specifically."

So they were really going to fight over sandwiches. She sighed heavily. "And as I've explained, the homemade sourdough won't be ready until later this afternoon. We're out."

"How do you know you're out?" the infuriating man asked, arms crossed over his chest.

"Because I'm the one that makes the damn bread," she snapped. "And I haven't made it yet. I'm standing here arguing with you."

"Now, now Holly," Wade said in his gentlest voice. "I'm sure we can all settle this easily." He beamed at Adam Calhoun. "I'm real sorry, but if Holly says we're out, we must be out. Let me make it up to you. I'll throw in some extra cheesecake for everyone with your order. How's that?"

"Fine," Adam said in an exasperated voice. When Wade turned away, she heard Adam mutter, "That shit's like eating glue."

Holly's lips twitched. She wouldn't give him the satisfaction of a smile, even if he was right about the cheesecake. Didn't matter. She still didn't like the jerk. But she made sandwich after sandwich with no more protest, putting extra bacon on like she always did, and wrapped them all up neatly in butcher paper. She even threw in a baked doggy treat for his pup, because he probably needed a bit of extra love if he had this guy for a dad. Wasn't his fault that he had Adam for an owner.

She handed him his order in silence.

He set down a single dollar—creased lengthwise down the middle—on the counter. "For your service." Then he turned and left.

Dear lord, she hated that prick.

Adam was in a foul temper by the time he got back to the Price Ranch. It was just a damn sandwich run. Why was he letting a foul-tempered waitress get the best of him? Next time he'd just send Carson instead of going himself. He'd volunteered because Carson had been mucking stalls—not Adam's favorite task—and Adam's dog, Hannibal, always loved a ride in the truck. So he'd gone. Yeah, well, never again. Now he was in a crap mood, his sandwich sucked, and he was pretty sure that the next time he went to the only eatery in town, he was going to have spit in his food.

He brought the food to the main house, where everyone seemed to be bustling. Sage had one baby on her hip and the other helping her fold laundry. Jason was on the phone, pacing in the kitchen, so Adam just left their food where it was. He'd heard that Sage wasn't thrilled about the idea of leaving town for an entire month and had to be sweet-talked into a vacation. She was probably as prickly as that waitress and—

"Oh, Adam, is that you?"

Adam hid his grimace and turned around to face his boss and the mayor of Painted Barrel, Sage Cooper-Clements. Well, Jason was technically the boss of the day-to-day stuff, but the ranch belonged to Sage's family. And Sage was the sort that liked to try to manage everything. Not in a bad way, just in an endless need to make things run smoothly. She ran the town, too, as mayor for the last year or two, and he'd seen her at every event the town had to offer, as well as looking after her children and helping with the ranch.

Yeah, he supposed she needed a vacation.

But he smiled at her. "Just dropping food off. I'll be out of your hair in a minute."

She put down the laundry she was folding and headed over to him, balancing the baby on her hip as she moved. "I wanted to ask you . . . are you going to the Winter Festival?"

That felt like a loaded question. "I'm pretty sure. Doesn't everyone go? It's next weekend, right?"

Sage nodded brightly, her smile dimpling across her face. "First official weekend in December! Are you bringing a date? Is Carson?"

Alarm bells went off in his head. "I can't speak for Carson, but no, I'm not—"

"I have a friend of a friend who's looking to meet someone in town. She's lonely and just got divorced and is finding it hard to get back into the dating pool, and I thought, well, I know this lovely young man that works for me and I wanted to ask you . . . ?" She trailed off, probably hoping he'd finish her sentence with enthusiasm.

Enthusiasm was not what he was feeling at the moment. Dread was. Adam didn't want to hurt her feelings, but dating some stranger was the last thing he wanted at the moment. Ever since finding out about Donna and the "boyfriend" she had while she was married to Adam, well, it had kinda soured him on relationships. And if he felt lonely, that's what his hand was for. "I'm not looking to date right now."

Sage gave him an apologetic look, adjusting the child on her hip. "I know I'm being nosy, but I thought I'd ask. It never hurts to ask, right?"

"Of course not. And I'm sure there's a few lonely men in town. I'm sure she won't have a hard time finding someone to date." Not unless she had a personality like the sandwich harridan back at the restaurant. No wonder that one was single.

She just sighed and pulled a lock of her long hair out of the baby's mouth. "Jamie's shy. And I know you well and know you're a gentleman. You'd make a lady feel special, which is why I thought I'd ask." She thought for a moment. "How old is Carson?"

"You want me to ask?"

"No, no, it's all right. I was just thinking . . ." She pursed her lips. "It's nothing."

He supposed he should go warn Carson before Sage decided he needed to be managed, too. "I think I'll go eat my sandwich now."

"Oh, of course." Sage chuckled, clearly embarrassed. "Go and eat. I'm sorry to keep you. I'm just trying to get everything in order before we go. You know how it is. How . . . how are you and Carson going to manage with food, by the way? Should I buy groceries for the house?" She gave him a curious look. "Do you cook?"

"No, ma'am. I got used to having someone else handle my meals for me when I was in the Navy," Adam joked. "I'm afraid it's spoiled me. Don't think Carson cooks, either. I'm sure we'll figure something out. If nothing else, we can always do peanut butter and jelly sandwiches for the next while."

"Oh, that hardly seems fair." She bit her lip. "I'll talk to Jason and see what he suggests. There's just not enough time in the day . . ." She checked her watch and sighed. "Which reminds me, I need to head into town."

Sage walked away, pulling out her phone with her free hand and typing as she headed back toward the laundry and her other child, multitasking. Adam took that momentary reprieve and raced out of the house with his sandwich and Carson's. He planned on avoiding Sage up until she left. Not that she wasn't a nice person and great to work for, but the matchmaking suggestion had spooked him.

The last thing Adam needed was a romantic entanglement. He liked being single. He liked being in a relationship with the only person he could count on.

Himself.

CHAPTER FOUR

The dinner rush at Wade's saloon was just about to start when the mayor walked in pushing a stroller. She glanced around the scatter of tables as if looking for someone and then brightened when she fixed on Holly.

Uh-oh. Holly wondered if Sage had come to apologize for her employee's rude behavior earlier. Probably not. Adam was always rude to Holly and it wasn't as if she ran around town blabbing about it. There were a few people in Painted Barrel that weren't great tippers, but she didn't gossip about it. She figured there were reasons, even if it meant stiffing her. Like the James family? The dad had been laid off in the spring, so she reasoned that's why they all came in and ordered cheap and the tips were light. Or elderly Mr. Swanson, who had come in for dinner every day for the last ten years, ordered a tuna melt, and left a few quarters as his tip. He was old and on a fixed income, and maybe to him, the quarters were a good tip. She still treated him as nicely as she did any other customer.

And Adam Calhoun? Well, he was just a jerk at heart.

See, there was always a reason.

But Sage was a sweetheart and always tipped well, so Holly liked her. Everyone in town did. Some people just radiated kindness and a sincere desire to help make the world better, and Sage was one of those people. Holly put down the stack of sticky menus she was cleaning off and smiled at her friend. "Happy holidays! What brings you in?"

The mayor parked her two-seater stroller next to the bar and gave Holly a tired look. "Oh, just finishing up some last-minute work before Jason drags me out of town for a month." She shook her head. "I can't believe he wants a vacation during the Christmas holidays, but I'm pretty sure he needs a break." She brightened. "So, I'm running around like a chicken with its head cut off trying to get everything settled before we head out! Which is why I'm here."

"Oh?" Holly grabbed a disposable cup and filled it with lemonade for Sage, then produced two cellophane-wrapped cookies that she'd baked to sit on the end of the bar. They were snowman-shaped, and she was hoping they'd take off and she could earn a little cash on the side to send to Polly . . . but Sage's kids were too cute to resist.

Sage gave her a grateful look. "You are the best."

"I'm just glad someone likes them. For some reason sweets don't go well with beer." Holly grinned at her. "What can I do for you?"

The mayor set a couple of green flyers on the bar. "Can you pass these out for me? It's something we're going to have in the Winter Festival. Kind of last-minute, but I'm hoping we get some decent entries."

"I'm sure we can do that," Holly assured her. She picked up a flyer and scanned it. Among the carnival games and craft booths listed, the lower half of the flyer was all about a Christmas Baking Contest.

BRING YOUR FAVORITE HOLIDAY CAKE AND WIN A PRIZE! WE'RE LOOKING FOR SOMETHING EXTRA FES-TIVE THAT WILL MAKE OUR EYES LIGHT UP BRIGHTER THAN RUDOLPH'S NOSE! THE JUDGES WILL BE FROM CARLA'S SWEETS, PAINTED BARREL BAKE SHOP, AND MORE. SHOW US YOUR TALENT! ONE ENTRY PER HOUSEHOLD.

Holly read it twice, then looked up at Sage. "Like a bake-off?"

"Yes!" Sage brightened. "The mayor of North Fork loves our festival and suggested it. I think he's a big fan of *The Great British Bake Off*. He wants to be a judge, too. I thought it might be fun. What do you think?"

"I think it'll be amazing." Holly folded up one of the flyers and tucked it into her pocket. A prize would be nice, but more important, it would be a chance to get her baking in front of people and she could really show them her talent. Two bakeries were judging? At least? That was two opportunities she'd be crazy not to take. This was her opportunity to wow people. "I can't wait to see what everyone brings. I'll have to think hard about what I'll make."

Sage looked impressed. "I didn't know you baked."

That stung a little, but it made sense. How would Sage know? It wasn't as if she could show her talents off much, other than a few cookies and the bread here at Wade's. Not to mention, everyone just assumed it was something he ordered, like, well, that damned cheesecake. "I do. I bake all the bread here, actually."

"That's lovely! I wish I was going to be here for the

competition but I'm sure I'll hear all about it when we get back." Sage's expression turned serious. "And while I think about it, I wanted to ask if Wade's does delivery. Or catering?"

Catering? That was a new one for Holly. "We do not, unfortunately. What do you need? Maybe I can ask around?"

Sage grimaced and leaned over to wipe a bit of frosting from the baby's cheek as the little one gnawed on the snowman. "Like I said, we're leaving town for a month, but our ranch hands are staying on to handle things. Normally I make sure that they have food available and I make them sandwiches or casseroles so they don't have to cook for themselves. But with me and Jason leaving, they're going to be shorthanded as well as looking after themselves, so I'm trying to solve the food problem for them. I was hoping I could set up something where you guys would deliver out there, but if you don't, I understand."

Holly bit her lip, thinking. They definitely didn't cater—Wade didn't want to bother, especially since the restaurant kept a brisk pace—but that didn't mean Holly couldn't step in. Heck, this might be the answer to her need for more money. "The saloon doesn't cater but . . . I could maybe cook for your employees on the side?"

The mayor's eyes widened. "Oh, would you?"

"Well, I mostly do baking but I could make some meat pies or casseroles easily. Soup? Do they like soup? And sandwiches, of course."

"They like whatever they don't have to cook," Sage reassured her. "It would be wonderful if you could do that. You'd be an absolute lifesaver and the men would be so grateful."

Somehow, Holly doubted that Adam would be anything

like grateful, but he didn't matter. If she could make some extra money over the holidays, she'd put up with his unpleasantness for a month. "I can absolutely do that for you. It'd have to be after hours since I'm working here, of course, but I don't have any plans for the holidays and was looking for a way to make extra money."

"This is perfect!" Sage looked so relieved. "How much do you think you'd charge?"

Holly had no idea. "I'm really not sure. Whatever you think is reasonable?"

Sage pursed her lips, thinking. "Well, I was going to hire a temporary housekeeper to look after the men while we were gone but I'm having trouble getting someone trustworthy on such short notice. I was willing to pay about a thousand a week to look after things while we were gone, so I guess I'd offer you the same? You can charge the groceries to the ranch, of course. Whatever you need. I'll give you access to our accounts. And I hate the thought of you cooking so late and driving it over. You could stay in the guest room at the main house if that would make things easier?" She tilted her head, gazing at Holly. "What do you think?"

Four thousand dollars?

With groceries paid for and lodging as well? And all she had to do was cook for a couple of cowboys and tidy the place up while Sage and her husband were gone? And she could work at her regular job as well? It was a dream come true. She'd be able to pay for a huge chunk of Polly's tuition without having to rack up another loan. It wouldn't cover everything, but between the grants Polly received and the extra money from Sage, it would be manageable.

For the first time in months, Holly no longer felt like she was drowning. "I'd love to do it. Please let me do it."

Sage chuckled. "You don't have to beg me. You'd be doing me a huge favor. The guys like simple food, and I promise they won't be a bother."

"Um, I don't think Adam likes me particularly much." Holly's entire body felt tense at the confession, but she felt she had to point it out. "Will that be a problem?"

Sage thought for a moment. "I don't think so? I mean, I can just tell him that I've hired someone to do the cooking and housekeeping who will stay at the main house. Your hours probably won't intersect much. Just make sure to leave plenty of food out for them and they'll be happy."

"I will absolutely spoil them rotten," Holly promised, already imagining all the things she'd bake and cook. Thick, hearty stews with fresh crusty bread. Pot roast with all the fixings. Breakfast casseroles and all kinds of baked goodies for the holiday season. She'd go out of her way to smother them in delicious food and baked treats and they wouldn't complain about her at all. And maybe if Sage and her husband needed help again, they'd call on Holly.

Sure, it'd be a lot of extra work, but she loved to cook and bake, and she needed the extra money badly. And if she was staying at Sage's house, she'd save a lot of money on her own utilities. It was a win-win.

"Will it be a problem if I bring my dog?" Holly asked. "She's a Pomeranian but she won't bother anyone."

"It's not a problem. Achilles will be going with us," Sage said, referring to her husband's emotional support dog. "Oh, this is such a load off. Here, give me your email and I'll give you my contact info and you can ask me questions if you need anything." She held out her phone.

Leaning in, Holly gave her the information. Between the job at Sage's place and the Christmas Baking Contest, the holidays were suddenly seeming very exciting. Maybe this was her year after all.

The next day was Holly's day off from work, so she took her little beat-up car and drove out to the Price Ranch. She'd grown up in Painted Barrel, so she was familiar with a lot of the roads in the area, but she didn't visit many of the ranches. No reason to. Even so, she was familiar with them, and a wave of excitement hit her as she drove past the massive gate and headed for Sage and Jason's house. The Price Ranch was the biggest ranch in the area, with a big main house and a row of cabins for the employees. There was an enormous barn, and in one of the distant pastures, she saw one of the cowboys on horseback, nudging the cattle into a pen as a dog danced around his horse's legs.

Holly hoped they stayed busy. She didn't want to hang out with Adam Calhoun. Carson seemed nice enough, but he was so quiet that she knew he wouldn't be coming in just to chitchat. Adam might show up just to make her crazy or to tell Sage she wasn't doing a good job.

She wouldn't give him the chance. She was here to keep house and cook, and she was going to knock both out of the park. He'd be so well-fed in the next month that by the time Sage and Jason got back, he wouldn't have a chance to complain. She was going to rock this, and then maybe Sage would continue to hire her for cooking on the side. The mayor was busy, and it'd be a perfect solution for her—and one that suited Holly, too.

She couldn't get too far ahead of herself, though. Scooping Pumpkin up, she smooched the dog's adorable little head, adjusted Pumpkin's sweater on her tiny body, and then tucked her suitcase under her arm. Holly found the key under the mat that Sage had promised to leave, and she let herself into the mayor's house, feeling a bit like an interloper.

The moment she stepped inside, though, she couldn't help but gawk. This was as far from her cramped little apartment as you could get. Past the rustic foyer filled with family photos, the house opened up into a large main room with massive two-story windows framing an enormous stone fireplace. There was a festive wreath over the mantel, and Christmas-colored throw blankets decorated the two couches facing each other. This looked like something out of an architectural magazine, Holly decided. And she got to live here for the next month? It was unreal.

Sage was too dang nice to give her this opportunity and to trust her with her lovely house for a month.

Holly wandered past the library and what looked like an office, complete with an enormous wood desk and more family photos. Beyond that, she saw the kitchen, and it took her breath away. It was so big that Sage had set up a Christmas tree in one corner, a festive skirt underneath and lights twinkling. There were boxes under the tree, to her surprise, and she peeked at the tags. Two for Carson, two for Adam, and . . . one for her? Holly melted at Sage's thoughtfulness.

She turned her eyes to the kitchen. Everywhere she looked, there was counter space. Counter space and drawers. It was so unlike her own tiny apartment, with one utensil drawer and a square of counter space crowded by her coffeepot and toaster both. How often had she longed to be able to play around in a big kitchen like she could at work? Except here, she could sprawl out for her baking as much as she wanted. Holly touched the massive butcher-block cutting board on the island, then practically swooned over the enormous gas range.

This was a dream.

Pumpkin barked somewhere in the next room, and it woke Holly from her daze. Right. She couldn't moon over someone else's stove. There was so much to do. First, she needed to make a list of what pantry ingredients were here, then plan a menu for the men. She'd have to hustle into town to buy staples, come back, and start cooking. There was a lot she could prep in advance, and some things—like bread—needed extra time for proving. She'd also need to set up in her room where she'd be staying for the next while, and make a list of all the bakes she was going to do for Christmas for everyone and—

Her dog barked again, the sound slightly more urgent.

Right. Okay, first things first, she needed to take Pumpkin for a walk. Then she could get started.

CHAPTER FIVE

It was like the moment they were down a ranch hand, everything went to shit. Jason and his family had left that morning, and Adam and Carson had reassured them that it would all be handled. That everything would be fine. That they could take care of things.

Well, mostly it was Adam speaking and Carson just not saying anything at all. But silence wasn't disagreement, right?

Adam had felt pretty confident in things. The cattle were healthy and the weather was decent. Even if they were down a man, they'd manage. It was all gonna be just fine.

Except by noon they'd found a break in the fence and Carson had to repair it while Adam rounded up the strays that had wandered away. Then one of the horses threw a shoe, which meant it couldn't be ridden, and the bale un-roller they used to spread the hay for the cattle to eat wouldn't start.

Things just kinda went downhill from there. It was normal stuff, of course. Half the time, being a rancher meant you were chasing down problems—missing cattle, sick cattle, broken fences, dried watering holes, you name it. Broken equipment happened. You fixed it and moved on.

But Adam noticed that Carson seemed to be moving slow that day, and his nose was bright red. He sniffed a lot, too, every time Adam was near him.

"You getting sick?" Adam asked as he changed the timing belt on the bale unroller. "Do I need to worry about you bailing out on me?"

Carson just scowled and swiped at his nose.

Right. His coworker wasn't the type to complain, but Adam suspected he was under the weather. He didn't have his normal easiness as he mounted his horse. He moved as if everything ached, and when he sneezed, Adam made up his mind. Carson was definitely catching something.

And that was a problem. One of them sick would be bad, but if Adam caught whatever Carson had, they'd be doubly miserable. The cattle still had to be fed and tended to, even if they were in bed with the flu, so neither could afford to get sick. He needed to go into town and buy some meds to ward that kind of thing off, maybe stock up on vitamin C. By the time they put their horses in the stalls for the day and brushed them down, though, he was tired and hungry.

Maybe he'd just stop by the main house and see if he could scrounge any meds off of them. He'd get some for Carson, too, and maybe some soup.

Carson headed off to his cabin without a word, and Adam finished up in the barn, then reached down to pet Hannibal. "You tired, boy? You hungry?"

The dog danced with excitement around his feet, still full of boundless energy despite spending all afternoon racing after stray cattle. Hannibal had enough energy for four dogs. He'd calm down after he got some chow into him, Adam figured. He slapped his leg, and the dog came to heel at his side. Together, they headed to the main house. The lights were on, so that was good. There was an unfamiliar car parked out front, which meant that the housekeeper that Sage and Jason had hired was still around.

He headed into the back of the house and pulled off his baseball cap, tossing it on a peg. The moment they got inside, Hannibal raced away as if he were on fire, which was kinda odd. He usually only chased small game like that, which had Adam a little worried. Was there a rat in the house? They were out in the country after all. Frowning, he headed deeper into the house, looking for his dog. "Hannibal? Come back, boy."

He found his dog in the main living area, his nose buried in some teddy-bear-looking dog's ass. There was a strange dog here? Adam stared at it in surprise. It was beige, and wearing a festive red collar with a little bell on it. As he watched, Hannibal's tail wagged, and the little dog—couldn't be no more than a couple of pounds—squirmed away from his overeager idiot dog. It took one look at him with those button eyes, yapped brightly, and then bit at Hannibal's leg.

Hannibal just bounced, turned around, and then lowered his head, his butt wagging with excitement. He wanted to play.

"No, Hannibal. Come on." Adam slapped his leg again. "That thing's too little to mess with. You . . ."

He trailed off, because the faint sound of singing was

coming from another room nearby. Female singing. Bad female singing.

Adam called out. "Ma'am? You want to come get your dog?"

No answer. All right, then. He headed toward the kitchen—the source of the off-key singing—and stood in the doorway. Sage's normally tidy—and empty—kitchen was an absolute mess. Mixing bowls of all kinds were spread over the counters, along with containers of flour, sugar, and whatever else was used for baking. There was a pan of something sizzling on the stove, and a woman stood in front of it. At least, he thought it was a woman. Whoever it was wore a green and red hooded sweatshirt with the hood pulled over the head, but the hips that swayed as she sang were definitely female.

And she was singing Christmas carols. Badly.

He watched her for a moment, rather entranced by the way she shook her hips. Whoever this woman was, she had a nice ass. It was round and firm and outlined well in her faded jeans. She shimmied as she stirred something in a saucepan, unable to keep a beat as she sang "Jingle Bell Rock."

"Ma'am?" Adam said loudly.

She continued to ignore him, stirring and pausing to shake her butt. And, okay, he couldn't help but look. It was definitely a very fine butt, and she was very into the music. He'd never seen anything so charming, though he felt a bit like a creeper for watching her jiggle her ass from behind.

"Ma'am?" he said, louder, and knocked on the counter in front of him.

She jumped, making a noise of distress, and the pans on

the stove clattered. As he watched, she fished earbuds out of her ears and turned around to look at him.

And . . . hell.

It was that demon from the damn restaurant.

His lip curled in horror. "What are you doing here?"

She frowned at him, then turned back to the stove and stirred her pots again. "I could ask you the same question. Are you trying to scare the ever-loving shit out of me or am I just lucky?"

"I've been trying to get your attention for the last five minutes. Don't change the subject—what are you doing here?" He crossed his arms over his chest.

Tinny music from her earbuds blared on the counter—more Christmas songs. She turned around to flick them off and scowled at him again. He noticed that she wasn't dressed like she normally was when she worked. Her hair wasn't in a big, bouncy ponytail tied up with a Christmas bow, and she wore no makeup and her sweatshirt was loose and baggy. She was actually prettier like this, much to his disgust. Softer. More approachable.

He still hated her, though.

"If you must know, Sage hired me to cook for you guys while they're gone on vacation. I'm taking care of the house and making sure you guys don't have to look after yourselves." She cast a look over her shoulder. "So get used to seeing me here."

"She hired *you* to cook?" He'd thought Sage had gotten a housekeeper, not this nightmare of a woman.

"Yeah, me." Something beeped and she bent over—her enticing butt in the air again—and then pulled a pie out of the oven and set it on the counter behind her. It was golden brown on top, with little cut-out leaves decorating the crust, and the scent wafting up from the pie was heaven itself. It smelled like steak, or something even better.

Adam rubbed his mouth, realizing just how hungry he was. "What is that?"

She glanced up at him. "Meat pie with potatoes and onions." She shrugged a shoulder. "I like making the crust and it turns out well. Reheats well, too. That work for dinner?"

It smelled amazing, but he couldn't resist needling her. "Maybe I don't eat onions."

"Oh, I'm sorry," she said sarcastically. "I didn't realize you were four. Does Carson eat onions?"

Her tone made him bristle. "He needs chicken noodle soup. He's coming down with a cold and we can't afford for him to get sick. We're already shorthanded as it is."

Holly—that was her name, he remembered—immediately grew sympathetic. "Oh, poor man. I'll get right on it. Give me a few hours and I'll bring him a thermos-full. I just need to make the noodles and cook up some chicken." She looked around the kitchen, wiping her hands with a towel, and then began to pull out more bowls from under one of the counters.

So . . . what about his dinner, then? Adam glanced at the meat pie again. It really did smell amazing, and he was tempted to tuck it under his arm like a football and race back to his cabin with it. Doing that felt like it'd be admitting she was right, though. Right about . . . something. And he was not about to let her get the upper hand. "What am I supposed to eat? If you're in charge of cooking?"

She tossed him a look over her shoulder. "I can make you a peanut butter and jelly sandwich, considering you're four," she said. "Give me a moment and I'll even cut the crusts off for you."

Okay, now she was really getting on his damn nerves.

"I'll eat the damn meat pie if you're going to be such an ass about it. Here I was thinking you were here to cook for us, though. Guess I must have misheard that."

A flash of contrition moved across her face and was swiftly gone. She straightened, gazing at him. "I am supposed to cook for you guys, yes. I didn't know what you wanted, so I made the meat pie. It was one of my dad's favorites in the winter. He was a ranch hand, too." She set the bowls down and gave him a piercing look. "You tell me what you want to eat and I'll make it for you guys. I have a menu planned for this week but it won't do any good for any of us if you don't like what I cook."

As he watched, she set the entire pie atop a mason jar, which seemed odd to him. Then she loosened a key on the side of the pie pan and slid the pie out of the tin. A bit of gravy oozed out of the side and his stomach grumbled again.

"I'll eat the damn pie for tonight," he said again, pulling up one of the barstools at the island and thumping himself down. "But I don't like onions."

"You've made that abundantly clear." Holly put the pie on a plate and cut a thick slice. Hot filling threatened to ooze out of the crust, and the scent of it, like stew and fresh bread all at once, hit him like a brick. She put a fork on the plate and slid it down to him, then turned back to the stove.

He took the fork. "Hope it doesn't taste like onions," he muttered, just because he felt he had to say something. He sounded like a child, even to his own ears. Adam took a big bite and the taste was as good as it smelled. The crust melted on his tongue and the meat was soft and tender, the gravy delectable.

He'd die before he complimented her on her food, though. He ate another bite, and as he did, the tiny dog, which looked just like a stuffed animal, came trotting into the kitchen.

It gave him something else to focus on, at least. "What's your dog doing here?" he asked between bites.

"What, I'm supposed to leave her alone in my apartment for a month?" Holly gave him a disgusted look. "You'd do that to your dog?"

Well, no, he wouldn't do that to his dog. He'd never. Hannibal was his best buddy, a companion who never failed to be excited to see him and was utterly trustworthy. Sometimes it felt like Hannibal was the only one he could depend on. "Didn't know you were staying here," Adam grumbled. "That's why I asked."

As if on cue, Hannibal headed into the kitchen and sat at Adam's feet, wagging his tail and waiting patiently for a bite. "Sorry, bud," he told him. "It's got onions."

"You and the onions," she exclaimed. Holly gave him a frustrated look, then went to a nearby jar and pulled out a couple of dog biscuits. "Give him this, all right? And shut up about the onions."

He took it from her and gave it to Hannibal, who took it delicately from Adam's fingers. He watched as she gave one of the bone-shaped treats to her little runt of a dog, too, and thought about what she said. "You're staying here all month?"

She nodded. "Sage suggested it. And it'll be easier on me to cook for you guys after work if I'm already here. Saves me a few steps." She crossed the kitchen and moved to her purse, pulling out a notepad and pen. "Which reminds me. If you don't like onions, what else will you not eat? I'm trying to make a menu."

Adam took another bite of the delicious meat pie that tasted nothing like onions. He was kinda stuck now, though, wasn't he? He'd only brought the onion thing up to irk her, and he'd be damned if he backed down now. "I don't see why you care, since you're going to be stubborn about this."

"Me?" Holly gave him an outraged look. "You're the one being a dick! I need this job. Just tell me what you want to eat and get out of my damn hair so I can get to work."

For a waitress, she sure was a sour sort. "Service with a smile, just like at the saloon. Can't believe you work off of tips, considering you spend all of your time looking at me like you want to cut my damn balls off."

She scoffed. "Maybe if you tipped something other than a dollar you'd get better service."

"Maybe if I got better service, I'd tip more than a dollar," he countered. He scraped the last bite into his mouth and pushed the plate away. "Just stay out of my way for the next month and I'll stay out of yours."

"Absolutely," Holly said immediately. "Just tell me what you want to eat and we'll make this work. I don't want to spend time around you, either."

"Sandwiches are fine. You can drop 'em off on my doorstep." Adam glanced over at her. "Less I have to see your face, the better."

"Fine!" She wrote with a big flourish in her scratch pad. "Sandwiches for the jerk cowboy and chicken noodle soup for the nice one. I got it."

"Good." He turned around and left, irritated. What was it about that woman that got under his skin so damn quickly? She was here to make his life easier for the next month. He was going to work long hours to handle things while Sage and Jason took their vacation with their kids, and he was going to get paid extra for it. He'd been looking forward to the money.

Now he was going to have to deal with her crap all

month long. He couldn't seem to catch a damn break. When Sage had said she would hire someone to cook meals for them, maybe he should have specified "anyone in the world but Holly."

He hoped she kept her word and stayed out of his hair, at least.

CHAPTER SIX

The next morning, there was a basket on the doorstep of his cabin. Inside it were three brown bags, marked *Breakfast*, *Lunch*, and *Dinner*. Each one had the exact same thing in it—a peanut butter and jelly sandwich with the crusts cut off and an apple.

Man, she was really determined to drive him crazy. He wasn't going to complain, though. In fact, he wasn't going to say shit. He'd eat the sandwich and buy snacks in town if he got hungry, because there was no way he was going to talk to her again. He'd rather starve.

So he said nothing, and when it came time for lunch, he and Carson paused on horseback. He watched as the other man pulled out a slice of the meat pie and a thermos that steamed and smelled delicious.

"That soup?" Adam asked.

Carson grunted and took a swig.

In Carson language, that was a yes. Adam sidled his horse closer and leaned over. Sure enough, Carson's ther-

mos was full of a thick, chunky soup with big, fat noodles.
The meat pie looked good, too, even if it was cold. He nodded at the ranch hand. "What did you have for breakfast?"

Carson shrugged. "Breakfast burrito."

"A burrito?"

"With sausage."

Suddenly Adam's peanut butter and jelly sandwich was
feeling a little insulting.

"And bacon," Carson continued. "And potatoes—"

"Okay, okay," Adam snapped. "I get the picture." He was
going to send a strongly worded note, he decided. He'd demand the same food that Carson was getting. He looked over
at the other man and scowled to himself when he brought out
what looked like an enormous cookie of some kind.

She was doing this to get under Adam's skin. He knew
it, and he hated that it was working. He hated that one day
in with her little game and he was going to bend already.
No, he told himself. He'd hold out. He'd hold out and take
the high road, and the moment Jason or Sage called to
check on how things at the ranch were going, he'd let it slip
that she was being petty. She wanted this job so badly and
the best thing he could do was ruin it for her.

Yeah, that's what he'd do.

Adam glanced over at Carson, eyes narrowed. "What's
for dinner?"

"Chili."

Adam swore. He loved chili.

"And corn bread," Carson added.

He clenched his jaw and choked down the rest of his
sandwich. He could do this. It was just food. It didn't
matter.

But by the time they finished their day, Adam was starving. The small sandwiches weren't enough to satisfy his

appetite after a long day of work. Even now, he still had things to do. There was horse tack that had to be oiled and repaired, and it had been muddy so he needed to make sure the horses' hooves were clean and not gummed up. There was also one of the cattle that was looking a little sickly, so they'd separated it from the herd and put it at the far end of the barn, and he needed to check on it, too.

He had to eat something first, though.

"Come on, Hannibal," he told his dog as he stormed toward the main house. "We're going to demand a real meal from that waitress."

Hannibal just whined but followed at his feet.

Inside the main house, though, no one was home. The tiny little dog of hers came out to greet them, its entire small body shaking with excitement. It jumped at his legs and so he scooped the dog up and headed for the kitchen. It was empty, the counters clean and bare. The whiteboard was set up on a stand facing the doorway with a note on it.

Carson,
There's more chili in the fridge, and more corn bread. Please help yourself! Tomorrow I'll be making chicken spaghetti and garlic bread for your dinner with a custard tart for dessert. Let me know by end of day today if you want any changes. I'm here to serve you!

xo—Holly

PS—Pumpkin is a little beggar! Don't feed her if you come in.

No note addressing him. He guessed she didn't expect him to come back into the house. He'd made it pretty clear he wouldn't, but it was just another irritating thing she did.

Frustrated, Adam went to the fridge, and sure enough, there was a huge batch of chili and the nicest little pieces of corn bread cut into stars of all fucking things.

Why did Carson get special treatment and Adam got sandwiches? Right, because Adam dared to not like onions. With a growl, he pulled the food out of the fridge and tossed it into the microwave. He was going to eat the rest of the damn chili, and if Carson didn't like it, he could have a damned peanut butter and jelly sandwich. He shoved a piece of corn bread into his mouth and it was so light it practically melted on his tongue.

He hated that woman. He hated her a lot.

Her little dog sat at his feet, her entire little teddy-bear body wagging with enthusiasm as she noticed Adam eating. And he got a terrible, mean idea in his head. So he pulled out another piece of corn bread and offered it to the tiny thing. "You want this, girl? You want corn bread? Here, have two . . ."

Pumpkin had vomited everywhere when Holly got home from her late shift at the saloon. It wasn't what she wanted to see after a long day on her feet, and she groaned again when she saw the huge puddles on Sage's pristine carpets. That was going to have to be scrubbed.

"Oh, baby girl," Holly crooned to her dog as she picked her up. "You had a bad day, too, didn't you?"

The dog seemed happy enough now, eager to lick Holly's face (which she avoided). She took Pumpkin out for her nighttime walk, and when they went back inside, she got to work scrubbing the worst of the mess out of the carpets. When that was done, she dragged herself back into the kitchen, yawning, and looked for a note from Carson about the food. There wasn't one, so she assumed that her menu for the next day would be good. A quick peek into the fridge told her that all the chili had been eaten, and all but one piece of corn bread was gone.

She snacked on it herself as she boiled spaghetti noodles and thought about the cake she was going to make for the Winter Festival this Friday. She'd work on it in pieces, she decided. She could prep a lot in advance while she was making meals for the ranch hands and just stick it in the fridge to wait until she had time to assemble. She'd asked for Friday night off, switching shifts with the other waitress at the restaurant so she could have the day to work on her Christmas-themed masterpiece.

Chocolate cake, of course. You couldn't go wrong with chocolate cake. Holly thought about the look. White fondant to make a smooth top, she decided, with a sugar-crystal crust to seem like snow. And she could add fondant snowflakes of red and green for pops of color. The inside of a chocolate cake would be rather boring, though, but she could always bake some cutouts into the shape of holly leaves and pepper them through the batter. When it baked, they'd see holly leaves when they cut it open.

And of course, she'd make it utterly delicious. She'd spread the cake with ganache between the layers so you'd get gooey chocolate decadence in each bite. It wasn't the most Christmasy of flavors, but you really couldn't go wrong with chocolate cake, could you?

Excited, she began to make a list of all the ingredients she'd need.

CHAPTER SEVEN

The next morning, Adam headed into the main house. The basket on his porch step had included the labeled sandwiches again, and he was getting a little tired of the joke. The kitchen was tidy again, and a plate of enormous blueberry muffins was next to the whiteboard. He took one and ate it, reading the menu for the next day. Lunch was another soup for Carson, with fresh bread, and dinner would be homemade fried chicken and twice-baked potatoes.

Damn it, Adam loved fried chicken. It had been a long time since he'd had some, too. He didn't know what a twice-baked potato was, but it sounded good.

Make extra, he wrote on the whiteboard, and then signed it with Carson's name. It'd be something to look forward to at the end of the day tomorrow, at least. He grabbed a few more muffins and went back out to the barn. If Carson noticed that Adam was eating her muffins, he didn't say anything. That was the good thing about Carson—he wasn't much of a talker. Adam knew he was being a hypocrite, but Holly brought out the worst in him.

After all, she was there to make their work easier, right? Except her presence—and the fact that she was starving him—did anything but make his day easier. He had a hard time concentrating on work and his task list when he was wondering what she'd pull next. Surely she wasn't going to feed him peanut butter and jelly for the next month? She was probably waiting for him to apologize first, and then she'd feed him like she was feeding Carson.

Yeah, well, she'd be waiting a while for that apology.

By the end of the day, he was tired and hungry and it had started to snow, so he was cold to boot. Hannibal whined as Adam devoured all of his sandwich and the apple, not sharing it with his dog. He scoured his cabin for snacks, too, but all he found was a couple of breath mints . . . which he also ate. He tried to ignore the rumbling of his gut, too. He was hungry, damn it, but he was also stubborn.

Didn't help that Carson was eating like a king right next to him. It just made the peanut butter and jelly sandwich feel even drier and less appealing.

He snuck in at dinnertime and crept out with the extra servings, feeling like a damned idiot and a thief. He lived there, too. She was supposed to be cooking for him, too. He didn't know why he felt guilty, but he thought about it all night long. He tossed and turned in bed, unable to fall asleep. Visions of fried chicken danced in his head, which was stupid. It was just food.

No, he decided. It was more than food. It was a pissing contest between the two of them, and he'd be damned if he let her win.

Adam got up from bed and checked the clock. One in the morning. Hannibal got excited, running for the door and circling, wagging his tail. "No walks," he groaned, shaking his head at the dog. "It's too late."

Hannibal just got more excited, lowering his head, tail moving a mile a minute.

Well, great. He'd said the W-A-L-K word and now Hannibal thought for sure that they were going for one. With another groan, Adam got to his feet, shoved his boots on, and opened the door. "Make it a quick one."

It was damn cold outside, and Adam crossed his arms over his chest as he stood in the snow like an absolute moron while his dog picked the perfect spot to relieve himself. Hannibal was fussy about this sort of thing—hilarious in a dog as big and brutal as a Belgian Malinois—and when he didn't immediately get down to business, Adam found himself glancing up at the main house. The lights were still on despite the fact that it was late.

Of course, Holly was a waitress and the saloon didn't close until eleven or so. Maybe she was a night owl. Not that he cared.

To his surprise, he saw a light click on upstairs, in one of the rooms. As he stared up at it, he saw a female figure move past the window and pull her shirt over her head. He couldn't see much more than a profile, but what he did see was . . . well, it was impressive.

And it made him ache. How long had it been since Adam had had sex with someone? How long since he'd felt a woman's soft body next to his? Not that he'd ever want to touch Holly the Annoying Waitress. She might have a good body, but she had the heart of a viper as far as he was concerned.

He was not going to admire her form as she moved in front of the window. He was not going to picture her breasts bouncing as she pulled off her bra.

His cock was not stiffening. And he was absolutely not going to go back into his cabin and jerk off to the thought of her. No, sir, he was not. There was a war going on between them, and he was determined to be the victor.

On Thursday, Adam decided that if he saw another peanut butter and jelly sandwich, he was going to scream. The weather was decent for the next few days, so he and Carson were moving the cattle to a less muddy pasture slightly further out. He watched as Hannibal rounded up the last of the cattle, then slid off his horse to close the gate behind them. Now that they had a moment to themselves, it was time for a break. He pulled his lunch sack out of the saddlebag and stared at it in disgust. Then he tossed it down to Hannibal, who wolfed it up with excitement.

"I hate that woman."

Carson just looked over at him from atop his horse with a smirk on his face. He tipped his thermos back and took a long swig; the thing was no doubt filled with all kinds of delicious soup, just like it had been all week. She'd been absolutely spoiling Carson, leaving Adam to chase down the scraps, and he was tired of it. As he watched, Carson took out his brown bag for lunch and unwrapped what looked like a club sandwich on a baguette, smothered in bacon and sliced meat. And . . . were those fresh tomatoes?

Well, now he really was hungry. "Damn woman's trying to starve me to death."

Carson offered him the thermos. "You're both being children."

Adam ignored that. He lifted his chin at Carson. "I can't drink from your thermos if you've got a cold, but I wouldn't mind if you shared that sandwich."

Carson just held the whole thing out to him.

"You sure?" His stomach rumbled. That sandwich looked . . . mighty fine.

"Yeah." Carson shrugged. "She sent a bunch of cookies in my bag, too."

He crammed a mouthful of Carson's sandwich into his face. Didn't matter that it was cold and snowy out and so the sandwich was ice-cold, too. It was still delicious. "Cookies, too? What kind?"

Carson pulled one out to show him. It was a white cookie with sugar-crusted cracks on top, and an enormous chocolate kiss in the center. When Carson held it out to Adam, he took it, too. Carson just shrugged and drank some more of his soup. "Never argue with the kitchen."

Adam snorted. "I'm just supposed to ignore the fact that she's acting like this? She's supposed to be here to feed us."

"She's feeding you what you asked for. Doin' her job. You don't like it, go tell 'er."

Damn it. "Really prefer not to talk to her at all," Adam muttered.

"Children, both of you," Carson said again and drank his soup.

W hen they finished up for the day, Adam took a long, hot shower, played with Hannibal for a bit, and then headed into the main house. He couldn't resist the lure of whatever food she'd been making. And since it was dinnertime, she'd be at work, which meant he could raid the fridge as much as he wanted. Her yappy little dog met him and Hannibal at the door, and he scooped it up and tucked it under his arm as he went into the kitchen. "You're not going to tell on us, are you?"

He thought about feeding the dog again, but he didn't like the thought of making it sick just to get revenge on its owner. He already had regrets from the other day when he'd found out he'd made it puke. The dog wasn't at fault, and it was a cute little thing, gazing up at him with those bright button eyes. He rubbed the small, fluffy head and circled the countertop. "Let's see what your mom left out for us."

There were a few muffins left over from yesterday, and he tossed one down to Hannibal before taking one for himself and eating a big bite. He set it down on the counter and headed for the fridge, but when he opened it up, he didn't see food waiting to be eaten. There were a lot of bowls in there, sure, but they looked like a bunch of junk. One was a big wad of bright red dough, another in white, another in green. What the heck? He poked at the plastic film covering one, wondering if it was something he wasn't familiar with—

"What are you doing?"

Busted. Adam froze, then turned around slowly. His nemesis stood there in her work clothes, her tight red Christmas sweater showing off her curves. She had on the half apron that she wore at the restaurant, and her hair was in its typical high ponytail with the Christmas bow across the top of her head. Today, she had Christmas lights for earrings and bright red lipstick on. She looked festive and sexy . . . and he hated that he'd probably jerk off to the sight of her again tonight.

Her gaze slid to the dog he had tucked under his arm, and she frowned.

"I was looking for something to eat since you're determined to starve me," Adam told her, setting the little rat of a dog down on the ground carefully. "I know you think your joke is funny, but I ain't laughing."

She strode forward, closing the refrigerator door on him. "Don't touch that stuff. It's for a cake I'm making."

Well now, Carson was going to get cake, too? She really knew how to twist the damn knife. "I'm tired of peanut butter and jelly sandwiches." Adam glared at her. "I want real food, and I came in here looking for it. You know, the food you're supposed to be making for us?"

She tossed that ponytail of hers, defiant. "I asked you what you wanted to eat. I'm giving you exactly what you asked for. It's not my fault you're choosing to be stubborn."

He was the one being stubborn? Holly was downright impossible. "Then lemme be clear. Whatever you fix Carson, I want the same. I want the soup. I want the hoagie. I want the cookies."

"No more peanut butter and jelly?" She fluttered her lashes.

"You can include one of those. Hannibal likes 'em."

Her gaze slipped to his dog, who was seated in the corner of the kitchen, watching them argue. As she glanced over, Hannibal's tail began to wag, the traitor. A sweet smile curved her red mouth and she brushed past him over to a cookie jar on the counter. "I made dog biscuits. Hannibal's a good boy and deserves the best." She pulled out a bone-shaped cookie and the dog practically whined with excitement, but remained in his spot.

With a sigh, Adam nodded at Hannibal. "Go on."

The dog immediately went to her feet and sat politely, his tail wagging a mile a minute.

"What a good boy you are," she cooed sweetly to his dog as she gave him the treat.

Adam just shook his head in disgust. Traitor.

She turned back to Adam, her arms crossed under her

breasts. "So you're tired of these little games of yours? Dare I hope you've learned your lesson?"

He stiffened. "You're pushing it, sister—"

"Sister," she sputtered. "What are you, some cartoon villain?"

"I am a man who has been starved for the last few days and I work too long and too hard to put up with your sandwich bullshit." He was tired of her games. He wasn't the one farting around on the job. Adam opened the fridge again and stared at the contents. There was a foil-covered dish at the bottom and he lifted the cover off it. Snowman cookies. Fine. He was hungry enough to eat just about anything. Adam grabbed one and bit the head off.

Of course it was utterly delicious, he thought with disgust. He shoved the entire thing into his mouth and reached for another.

"Hey! You can't eat that!" Holly rushed over to the fridge and slapped his hand before he could pull another out of the container. "Those are for Carson."

Of course they were. "Carson would want me to eat it," he explained around the mouthful.

She put a hand on his chest and pushed, as if she could physically shove him away from the fridge. That was cute, given that she didn't even come up to his chin. The look she gave him was utterly indignant. "No, he wouldn't. His daughter has a wheat allergy so I made those with almond flour. He's supposed to taste them for me and if he likes them, then I'm sending them home with him as a gift."

Almond . . . flour? That was a thing? And . . . wait. Adam finished chewing. "He has a daughter?"

She gave him an exasperated look. "You work with the man. Don't you know? Do you even talk to him?" When he didn't move away from the fridge, she tried to wedge her body in between him and the thing, as if she could protect the cookies from him bodily. "Who did you think he was going to visit for Christmas, you nitwit?"

He scowled at her and racked his brain, trying to think of what Carson had said about the holidays. Visiting . . . someone. Family? It was hard to imagine silent, surly Carson with family, much less a daughter. "I'm not the bad guy here!"

"Really? Because you kind of seem like a dick to me." She pushed him away from the fridge.

He pushed back, just a little, and then her body was wedged against his, her backside pressing against him in the most obvious spots. Adam bit back a groan, because the last thing he wanted was to think about *her* in any way other than irritation. Didn't matter that she fit against him perfectly—she was a monster.

"Are you done being like this?" And he placed his hands on the top of the fridge, caging her there if she chose to keep fighting like an idiot. "Or are you determined to keep going?"

She flung herself backward with force, making both of them stumble.

Her pipsqueak of a dog barked.

Adam caught himself on the island counter and managed to keep his footing. That was . . . a surprise. So was the unearthly glare she was sending in his direction. Why was she so damn mad at him?

"You just have no respect for people's boundaries, do you?" She straightened her sweater with a huff. "Don't eat those cookies. In fact, don't touch anything unless it has your name on it. I have plans for all that stuff, and if you go in there eating everything, it's going to set me back hours."

"Oh, I'm sorry," he said sarcastically. "I thought you were here to cook for us. My mistake."

Holly gave him a dirty look. "I am. But I bought some

of that with my own money and I don't want you touching it. It's for a cake. And I'm doing some baking for Carson, too. Not for you. So just tell me what you want to eat and I'll make it for you. I have . . ." She paused and checked the phone she'd set on the counter. "A little over forty minutes before I have to be back at work."

He wanted to argue some more but . . . he also wanted to eat. "What are you making Carson for dinner?"

"He asked for tacos."

It had been a long time since Adam had had any kind of Mexican food. There wasn't much in this neck of the woods, and Wade's saloon didn't serve anything of the kind. He'd grown up near a family-owned Mexican restaurant that served the best damn food, and sometimes he missed their cooking. Now was one of those times. "Tacos are good. I'll have what he's having." He thought for a moment and then added, "Can we do enchiladas tomorrow night?"

She shook her head. "Tomorrow night is the Winter Festival in town. I'm heading there. Carson is, too."

So much for cooking for him, then. Here he'd asked for something just like she was always preaching, and she'd said no. He rolled his eyes. "Whatever."

She gave him another look of flashing irritation. "Will you leave now? I need to get to work on the food and I can't if you're going to sit here and bother me. I'll bring you a plate when I bring out Carson's food, all right?"

"Suit yourself." Why did he even bother? He'd tried to do things her way, and she'd been just as uncompromising as ever. It bothered him.

CHAPTER EIGHT

The fact that he'd compromised continued to bother him all damn night. Why was it every time he ran into her, no matter the situation, he felt like the one that ended up losing? It ate at him. It ate at him even as he thought about those bright red lips of hers and the way she'd felt pressed up against him in front of the refrigerator.

He hated that his damn cock was hard for *her*. She should have made it wither away, but no, here he was contemplating stroking himself to thoughts of her, just to get it out of his system. He hadn't, though. It would have felt like a betrayal to himself. You didn't jerk off to women you hated, no matter how pretty they were or how rounded their butt was in a pair of jeans.

At least dinner had been decent. She'd left the tray on his doorstep and hadn't bothered to knock to let him know, so when he finally figured out it was there, everything was cold. It was just another way she pricked at him, another way to get his goat and have the upper hand. He'd eaten his cold, delicious tacos and stewed. He wanted to do something to get one over on her. He wanted to get control back, somehow.

He wanted her to feel just a twinge of regret for being an ass to him. Just a twinge.

Which was why he sneaked back into the main house once the horses were settled. He left Hannibal back in his cabin, curled up on his bed, and when her tiny dog came to the back door to greet him, he scooped it up and headed for the kitchen again. She'd been busy, he realized. The sink was full of dishes that had yet to be washed, and dry ingredients were scattered all over the counter. It looked as if she'd been baking again, then had to run off to work. Adam checked his watch. Nine at night. She wouldn't be back for at least two hours, which meant he was free to do as he liked.

"So what have we got tonight, squirt?" he asked the dog, petting the tiny head. "Any new cookies?"

The dog just licked his fingers and nipped at them with excitement.

Adam didn't see anything left out like she normally did. Whenever he raided the kitchen, she always seemed to have something available for him or Carson to eat if they wandered in—well, mostly Carson since he didn't let her know that he was coming in to grab food. Tonight there were no muffins or cookies, no rolls or the small meat and cheese board she'd left out last night and they'd promptly demolished. He guessed she hadn't had a chance to make anything yet—even her whiteboard menu was blank.

And for some reason, that irked him. She was there to feed them, right? Why wasn't she feeding them, then?

He headed over to the refrigerator and opened it. Sure enough, the bowls of colorful baking stuff were all still in there, but she'd added Post-its to each one. The red one said CHERRY FONDANT and the green MINT FONDANT. There were bowls of mixes, too, labeled LAYER ONE and LAYER TWO and so forth. It was all her cake stuff. She'd even removed the cookies he'd eaten earlier.

Well. Glad to see she had her priorities straight. The kitchen had a bunch of cake mixes for her project and nothing for him to actually eat. She was baking all this for Carson and nothing for him? It bugged him. It bugged him so much that he set her little runt of a dog down on the floor with a pat on the head, and then considered the lineup of spices she'd left out. Chiefly, the large shakers of salt and pepper in front of him.

Adam smiled to himself. He pulled one of the bowls out of the fridge and peeled back the covering. It looked like a chocolatey sort of mix, all rich and thick and decadent and absolutely not for him. She'd made that clear.

It was all for Carson and not for him.

An ugly feeling clenched in his gut. He'd been in this position before. In the weeks leading up to their divorce, Donna had started little games to tear him down quietly. She'd wanted Adam to file so she could tell everyone she was the injured party. So she'd made special meals and left them out so Adam could see the scraps, but kept nothing in the fridge. She'd spent all their savings buying presents for her boyfriend. She'd use an entire tank of gas going joyriding, just so when he went in to work the next day, he'd have to fill up. Microaggressions, the therapist had called it.

Well, he could play the microaggression game, too.

If Holly wanted to favor Carson, he could even the playing field. Unscrewing the top off the salt shaker, he dumped half of it into the bowl. He added some pepper, too, just because, and then mixed it all in with a spoon. When his additions couldn't be seen, he covered the bowl again, put it back into the fridge, and pulled out the next one to give it the same treatment. If she was going to treat Carson like he was special and ignore Adam, he was going to teach her a lesson.

Was it a dick move? Yes.

Did she deserve it? Oh yes. She'd started it by baking all kinds of delicious things for Carson and not for him. If you were hired to cook for two people, you couldn't just ignore half of them.

One dick move absolutely deserved another.

As if the restaurant customers knew that Holly was off tomorrow, they were determined to crowd in to Wade's saloon tonight. She was so busy there was no time to breathe, much less take a quick break. Table after table was completely full, and she laughed and charmed her way into decent tips for the evening, but she knew she'd feel it in the morning. Her feet hurt by the time the last customer was ushered out with a to-go box and a smile.

Wade looked just as tired as she was. He sat on a stool behind the bar, shaking his head. "Here I thought the rush would be tomorrow, not tonight."

A little twinge of guilt hit her. She locked the front door, flipping the sign, and peered out into the chilly Wyoming night. Some of the decorations for tomorrow's festival had been hung—wreaths decorated the streetlights and strings of plastic ornaments had been hung high between some of the buildings. Tomorrow it'd be totally decked out, with banners hanging off the buildings and booths everywhere. "You think it'll be busy tomorrow night?"

Wade snorted. "It was last year. Good money, too. Now

that I think about it, I had a lot of people coming in looking for ciders and mulled wine. Maybe I should head by the warehouse tomorrow and stock up in preparation."

"Christmas drinks are a good idea," Holly told him brightly. "You know what would go well with that?"

"Chips and hot dogs?"

She grimaced. "No. I was thinking more like apple tarts or gingerbread men."

He sighed heavily. "Holly—"

"I know, I know." She held up a hand even as she moved toward the first table and began to clear it. "I'm always pitching desserts at you and this is a bar, not a pâtisserie. It's just . . . people are looking for something special. Festive treats, you know? I think it might do well. You could even go simple and do caramel apples with Christmas sprinkles on them. Pull people in that want something a bit more than just snack food."

"And who's going to be here to work with Bonnie if we get slammed?" He crossed his arms over his chest. "You have the day off."

Holly bit her lip, thinking. If he let her do this, she'd be up all night baking. She'd have to run to an all-night grocery store to get last-minute supplies, but . . . well, she was going to be up anyhow, right? Her cake wouldn't assemble itself, and it had to look perfect. She needed to grab at every opportunity afforded her. She could sleep some other time. "I can come in and help out, if you don't mind me swinging out for the baking contest. I'll need to drop off my cake and be around for the judging, but I'm sure I can help out after that." She brought the dishes to the counter. "And I can make the treats—and some mulled wine and hot cider—if you let me set up a special table at the front. I'll man it myself and give you half the profits."

"Half?!"

"Well, it's like you said. If it doesn't work, I won't be all that busy." She tossed her ponytail and grinned at him. "And if it does, we'll both make a pretty penny."

"We'll see," was all he said, but Holly considered it a win. She'd just given herself a boatload of work to do at the very last minute, but it was an opportunity.

And she never turned those down.

It was three in the afternoon—an hour before Wade's saloon opened and two hours before the baking contest began—when Holly realized her two tier-cake wouldn't fit in her car. She couldn't exactly seat-belt it in—the delicate marzipan snowflakes would crumble at the slightest touch and the fondant would show the slightest impression. She couldn't exactly put it in her lap, either, and expect to drive.

Holly was going to have to ask for help.

Groaning, she bit her lip and considered the carload of ingredients she still had to take in. There were the candied "festive" apples she'd made all night long. The gingerbread men. The tiny apple tarts in the shapes of stars. Ingredients for mulled wine and apple cider, plus disposable cups with Christmas themes on them. Napkins. Paper plates.

And of course, her cake. Her double-decker, the size of a small tire, glistening with sugar snow and festive snowflakes cake. The beautiful cake that had turned out so pretty that she didn't even care that she hadn't slept in twenty-four hours. She could sleep later. This was too important.

Which meant that she needed to ask for help, because sitting around wasn't going to get her cake into Painted Barrel in one piece. She considered her small car again, and then left the cake on the countertop and went in search of one of the cowboys.

Holly never ventured out into the actual ranch itself. She kept herself confined to the kitchen of Sage's house and the guest bedroom. Sometimes she went into the laundry room, but she kept all the other doors in the house completely shut. It didn't feel right to intrude on someone else's home, even if she was living there temporarily. She knocked on the doors of the small cabins, but no one answered. Holly checked her phone. She was running low on time. Biting her lip, she headed out to the enormous barn.

To her relief, both men were inside. Carson was doing something in one of the horse stalls, while Adam was . . . doing something with hay and a pitchfork. She didn't know what he was doing, honestly. She didn't know squat about ranching. But she put on her brightest smile, clasped her hands in front of her, and ventured inside. "Hi, guys."

They both paused.

Adam groaned. "Oh no. What do you want?"

She wanted to make a face at him, but she couldn't afford to. So she kept her bright smile up. "Are you two by any chance heading in to the Winter Festival? If so, can I bum a ride?"

"Don't you have a car?" Adam asked, ever surly.

"Well, I do, but my cake won't fit." She continued to smile brightly. "I figured if you guys were going, maybe we could all ride together."

Carson—that sweet, kind man—grunted. When she looked at him blankly, he continued. "Gotta finish chores and then we'll be going."

"I hate to ask . . ." She hesitated.

"But you're going to anyhow, right?" Adam leaned on his pitchfork, the picture of dismissiveness. His beaten-up baseball cap was perched atop his head, his hair sticking out ever so slightly underneath, and when he posed like that, it made his shoulders look impossibly broad. She hated that, because he was probably the most attractive man in their small town.

The most attractive man with the worst attitude, which was why she was going to be permanently single. She could worry about that some other time, though. She just kept smiling brightly, ignoring his rudeness. "I have to have my cake at the baking contest in about forty minutes. I hate to bother you, but it's really important to me."

Adam frowned. "Cake?"

She turned her charms on Carson. "Please, Carson. Please. I know it's an inconvenience, but if my cake does well, it could be a real opportunity for me. Please." She moved to the stall door, where he was standing. "I will bake you a dozen things tomorrow, only take me in to town to-day. I'll pay for gas. I'll pay extra. I just need to get there."

Carson gave her a thoughtful look, then put a gloved hand on her shoulder. "Adam'll take you."

"Say what?" Adam called after them.

"I'll finish up here," Carson said. "You two go on ahead."

Adam looked horrified at the thought, but she didn't care. She'd put up with him. Holly gave him her best pleading look. "Please, Adam. I know we're not friends, but I need this. Please? I'll make you a double plate of enchiladas tomorrow."

He growled low in his throat, tossing aside his pitchfork. "Can't believe I'm going to do this."

"Yay!" She clapped her hands and raced out of the barn.

CHAPTER NINE

Adam was . . . well, he was sweating.

He scowled a little when she insisted on filling up the tiny back seat of his truck with plastic tote after plastic tote of goodies and bags full of things for work, she said. But he sweated even more when she came out of the kitchen with the biggest, prettiest cake he'd ever seen . . . and a look of intense pride and excitement on her face as she held it.

He couldn't tell her.

He swallowed hard, thinking about how much salt and pepper he'd added to the components. How he'd thrown in whatever would blend. How he'd deliberately sabotaged her. She had no idea.

And now she was entering the damn cake in the local festival. A cake that she had clearly spent hours and hours on.

He felt the stirrings of guilt. It was one thing to sabotage a cake she was giving to friends or to Carson. Now he was going to make her look foolish in front of the entire town.

But she looked over at him and gave him a dismissive

glance as she held the cake in front of her. "Are you going to open the car door for me or do you hope I'll magically appear inside somehow?"

Okay, he felt a little less guilty after that. Adam moved to the far side of his truck, opened the door for her, and did a mock bow. "Your majesty."

Holly sniffed haughtily and climbed into the truck, precariously balancing her cake in her arms. He was amazed she managed to get in without damaging the cake, but she settled in with the monster of it on her lap and he shut the door. Right. He'd ruined her cake in secret, but she was still a horrendous human being determined to make his life miserable.

Adam got into his truck on the driver's side, only for her to give him a sour look. "I don't mean to be demanding, but can you hurry? I'm on a tight schedule."

"Didn't realize I was your chauffeur," he drawled, even as he started the truck.

"I just need to get this cake there," she told him. "I'm sorry if I'm being short. It's just . . . it's really important to me. I know you don't understand, but I don't expect you to. It's just . . . important."

"Almost as important as good manners, clearly."

She made a sound of disgust. "Why do I even bother talking to you?"

"Because you need my truck? And my goodwill?"

"I wish I didn't."

"Makes two of us, sweetheart," Adam drawled.

They drove into town in silence. He glanced over at her whenever they hit a bumpy part of the road, but Holly cradled that magnificent-looking cake as if it were made of the most fragile glass. He glanced at her face occasionally, too, just because. She yawned once or twice, and he noticed that despite her normal perky ponytail and bow, she looked worn today. Tired. Given the amount of garbage she was bringing into town with her, he guessed that she'd been hard at work all day.

Yeah, well, he wasn't going to feel sorry for her. The last thing Holly deserved was sympathy.

He parked the truck as close as he could to Main Street, which had been roped off for the festival. Adam glanced over at her. Despite the circles under her eyes, she was buzzing with anticipation. He'd never seen her so damn twitchy. It was still a ways to walk, and that cake was massive. "You need help with that stuff?"

Holly lifted her chin and he could tell from the look on her face that she didn't trust him in the slightest. "Thanks, but no thanks. I'll get the rest of it after I drop this off."

He shrugged and got out of the truck, moving around it to open her door. "Suit yourself. What time do you want to meet up to get out of here?"

"I told my boss I'd work," she answered, huffing as she carefully got out with the massive cake. Count on this difficult woman to make the biggest cake he'd ever seen for a damn town festival. "I'll get a ride back with him."

"Suits me," Adam said dryly. He supposed that was what he got for being friendly.

Holly hesitated. "Thank you, by the way. I appreciate you giving me the ride into town." She offered him a half-assed smile, then turned and raced down the sidewalk as fast as she could with that gargantuan white cake. People stopped and stared as she approached with it, and he could see her smiling even wider for them.

Man, he realized as she approached the baking contest

entry table, she had no idea of the shit show that was about to happen. None at all. His neck prickled with unease, but what was done was done. He left the truck unlocked so she could return, and headed into the festival itself. The school band was playing Christmas carols—badly—and there were kids everywhere with their parents. There were booth games and crafts and snacks to buy, and Adam wasn't into any of it. He halfheartedly strolled past a couple of booths, wondering if it was too early to turn around and go home.

Adam liked Christmas well enough, he supposed, but you needed someone to spend the holiday with. All he had was Carson, who was leaving just before the actual day itself, and Holly, who got on his last damn nerve. So it felt extra silly to be at a holiday festival, when he wasn't feeling particularly festive at all.

"You look like you need a scarf, young man," a woman called out from her booth. He turned and saw an older woman with a frosted globe of hair that stuck out over her coat. She beamed at him and held out a pink knitted scarf. "Maybe a gift for your girlfriend."

He smiled politely but didn't reach for the item. "No girlfriend, but thank you, ma'am."

"No girlfriend?" She pretended to look shocked. "Then you should meet my Stacey! She happens to be alone for the holidays and wouldn't mind a dance or two in the town square with a handsome young man." She gave him another fake-innocent look. "The dancing starts in an hour."

Annnnd this was why he hated small-town festivals. Because if it wasn't full of things he didn't need—craft jams, hand-knitted mittens, and decorative needlework—someone was trying to set him up with their daughter.

He wondered if it was too early to get a beer. Maybe he'd

text Carson and tell him to bring a six-pack if they were going to get through the day.

The day seemed endless.

It really shouldn't have. Holly had gotten her cake in just on time, and the judges had exclaimed over how beautiful it looked. It had filled Holly with such pride as she showed it off. This was her chance to show everyone what she could do. That she wasn't just some local dropout with no skills. She could show them that she had a passion and a talent for baking, and she was happy to share that. Really, the cake couldn't have gone better. She was so pleased with it. She'd seen some of the other entries and they looked fine, but they also looked homemade. Hers was professional quality, and she couldn't wait to see what they had to say about it.

She'd pull aside the judges after the fact and let them know she was looking for work on the side, that she could bake for their shops and they could grow business together. This was her moment. This was the opportunity she'd been waiting for.

Maybe that was why every minute crept past as if it was an hour long.

Work was incredibly busy, too. Her idea for the table of Christmas eats near the door had been a good one. She could barely keep up with the demand for mulled wine and spiced cider. The day was a chilly one, with a promise of snow later that night, and everyone was looking for warm drinks as they milled around outside. She'd commandeered the folding chalkboard they sometimes set out on the sidewalk with the day's offerings, and once the parents came in for a hot beverage, the treats sold themselves. Holly was out of sprinkle-covered caramel apples within an hour, and the gingerbread men were the next to go. She ran out of everything else just before the dinner rush was about to start and moved the table back to the center of the restaurant.

"You staying to help?" Bonnie asked as she passed by, harried.

Holly bit her lip. They really did need help, but wasn't the baking contest supposed to be judged soon? She wanted to find out what the judges thought. She wanted to get a chance to talk to them, and she wouldn't be able to if she was waitressing. On the other hand, the day was getting colder despite the nice weather, and more people were coming in from the festival to have a hot meal. They'd be slammed. It'd be good tips, of course, and that was what drove everything. "Give me fifteen minutes," she said. "I need to check on my entry for the baking contest."

"Hurry if you can," Bonnie said, heading back to the bar with another order.

Right. Well, she had planned on working tonight anyhow. It was just . . . well, she'd wanted a few minutes to bask in the glory of her gorgeous cake. She wanted everyone to see that the entry was hers, and to be impressed by her.

Was it so wrong to want to impress the town? To show them that the high school dropout could actually be good at something? She didn't think so.

Holly pulled off her apron and hung it, switching it out for her coat. The moment she stepped outside, a chill breeze hit her in the face, but she didn't care. There were a ton of people wandering all up and down Main Street, looking at the booths, dancing to Christmas songs in the square, and having fun. If she were off work today, she'd be one of them, but she had too much to do. Brimming with excitement, she crossed the street and headed toward the baking contest tables, where people were feasting on slices of cake and pie. She'd been told that the entries were going to be passed out among the towns-folk if allowed, and she'd agreed to let her cake be part of that. Would she come back to nothing at all?

For a baker, the thought was thrilling.

But when Holly got to the judging tables, her gorgeous cake was still there, mostly intact. It was at the far end of the table. One small slice had been taken out of each layer, and the rest was left alone. As she approached, she saw the cakes had been placed in order of their ranking. Well, that was a good thing, right? Her cake was at the end of the ta-ble, which meant first place, didn't it?

When she got closer, though, she saw a blue ribbon next to an empty pie plate. Red was on a sad-looking red velvet cake next to it, and pink on a tray of brownies. First, sec-ond, and third place.

Her cake was at the far end of the table.

She'd come in . . . last?

Her beautiful cake? The one she'd spent so much time on? A sound of wordless protest escaped her throat.

Next to her, an older woman wearing a JUDGE ribbon smiled, her hands tucked into her puffy coat. "Are you here for a tasting? There's not much left. We had so many lovely entries."

Holly didn't recognize her, which meant she was probably from the next town over. "I . . . I don't understand. Is the judging over?" Holly asked. "Did all the cakes get judged?"

The woman nodded. "It was all quite lovely. There was just one unfortunate entry . . ." She trailed off and gazed at Holly. "Is it yours?" she asked gently. "The white cake?"

Holly nodded, numb. How had she come in last place?

"Oh, my dear." The judge gave her a sympathetic look. "Yours was utterly beautiful. Truly lovely to look at. But . . .

did you taste it?" Her expression was kind. "We think you might have mixed up the sugar with, ah, something else."

How? Holly was always so careful, wasn't she? But all she remembered of last night was a sleepless marathon of dipping apples in caramel, icing gingerbread men, and putting her cake together while she'd made enchiladas for the men for the next day. To say that she was multitasking was an understatement. "I thought I tasted it. I always taste my bakes."

The judge pursed her lips. "I'm sorry. Maybe next year?"

"Maybe so," Holly echoed. It had to be a mistake. Had she made the chocolate too strong? Did they not like her flavorings? She marched to the end of the table and picked up one of the tiny paper plates set out with a sliver of her cake on it. She picked it up, took a bite—

—and immediately spit it out.

Salt. All she tasted was salt.

She must have mixed the ingredients up somehow. She'd grabbed a container of salt instead of sugar—how?—and hadn't paid attention as she baked. She'd spent so many hours perfecting her cake and . . .

It was trash. It was just ruined through her own carelessness. There'd be no conversations with other bakeries, no pride in showing the town her talent, no nothing. As she watched, one of the people wearing a JUDGE ribbon at the far end of the table was talking with the others, and he pantomimed spitting cake into his hand, just as Holly had done a moment ago.

She stared down at the beautiful, hideous-tasting cake that had ruined her opportunities. Then she picked it up, walked to the nearest garbage can, and dumped it inside.

CHAPTER TEN

Carson seemed to enjoy the festival a lot more than Adam did. Once he arrived, they paused at every booth and Carson considered every piece of merchandise as if it were a great treasure that needed to be thoughtfully examined. He bought scarves of every color, along with mittens and some festive repurposed kitchen doodads. He ate a turkey leg and sausage on a stick. He smiled at all the Christmas carols and got his picture taken with Santa— who was at least two decades younger than Carson.

Meanwhile, Adam was miserable.

It wasn't the townspeople. They were nice enough, when they weren't throwing the occasional daughter (or grand-daughter) in front of him and asking for introductions. He'd grown up in a small town and he knew that it was just part of the deal. In a town of only a couple hundred people, you did what you could to meet someone. He was pretty good at deflecting after all this time, and even that wasn't what truly bothered him.

Every time he turned around, he felt like cakes were in his face.

Carson had insisted on stopping by the baking contest tables, where most of the prize-winning entries had already been devoured. Even among the remnants, there'd been no sign of Holly's cake, and Carson had specifically wanted to find it.

"Need to support her," was all he'd said.

When they walked past the tables, Adam had seen the enormous cake poking out of one of the garbage bins, and he felt a little bad. She was being paid to feed him, he reminded himself, and she'd sent nothing but peanut butter and jelly sandwiches. He didn't need to feel sorry for her.

Carson gestured at Wade's saloon, which was packed. "Wanna eat?" And before Adam could answer no, the older ranch hand was heading inside. Adam sighed heavily and followed him in.

The restaurant was busier than Adam had ever seen it. The moment a table cleared, someone new sat down, and they waited in silence—because Carson didn't much like talking and Adam wasn't in the mood—until two spots at the bar cleared.

"We want to sit in Holly's section," Carson declared, frowning at Adam.

"Let's just eat. She's busy," Adam said. "You can talk to her later." He suspected Holly wouldn't want to talk to them anyhow. She was hard at work, flitting between tables with a pot of coffee in one hand and a pitcher of soda in the other. She smiled and seemed cheery, her laughter pealing over the packed restaurant. "She's having a great time."

"Nah. She's sad. I can tell." Carson headed toward the bar, to the two empty seats.

Was she? Adam watched her as they squeezed into their

spots at the bar. She was smiling at a customer, but it didn't seem to quite reach her eyes. Her movements were a little slow, as if she had less time to spend being friendly . . . or less energy. She looked tired, but the moment anyone glanced her way, she put on a bright smile.

They ate a couple of burgers and drank a beer, but the place wasn't slowing down much. If anything, more people were piling in and giving patrons that lingered at the bar dirty looks. They paid their tabs in cash and gave up their seats, and Adam hoped that was the end of it. Instead, Carson cut through the crowd, heading for Holly. Biting back a curse word, Adam followed him in.

"Miss Holly," Carson called as she hauled a huge tray of dirty dishes away from a table.

She turned, that bright smile automatically on her face again even as she tried to place who was calling her. Carson was right. Something seemed off with her tonight. She seemed . . . fragile. Brittle. Even when they were at each other's throats, there was a spirit to her. It was completely gone tonight.

It was just a dumb cake, he told himself. And she'd been rotten to him all week, deliberately so. If she couldn't take the heat, stay out of the kitchen and all that.

She spoke to Carson a moment, her head bent, and then nodded at him. Carson headed back in Adam's direction, and Holly disappeared into the kitchen with the dirty dishes.

"Ready to head back?" Adam asked.

Carson shrugged. "Holly gets off at ten."

He was surprised to hear that. It was barely past eight. "You're going to wait around to give her a ride?"

Carson stared at him. "You're not?"

It sounded like a challenge. He'd been the one to drive

her into town, sure, but she'd made it quite clear that she didn't want a ride. He was about to point that out, too. Instead, what came out was, "Why are you so chatty when it comes to her? Took you a month to say hello to me."

The older man shrugged again. "You're kind of an ass."

Adam laughed at that.

Carson smiled. Just a little. "Reminds me of my daughter." They headed out the door, into the crisp night, just as another group of people headed into the saloon. When the door was shut, Carson continued. "After my wife died, Raina was so busy trying to handle everything and take care of me that she never took a moment for herself." He glanced back into the windows of the saloon. "I see it in her, I guess."

In the space of thirty seconds, his knowledge of Carson had just doubled. He knew the man was no longer married, but he didn't know that his wife had died . . . or that his daughter even had a name. Carson kept to himself most times, but he'd grown strangely attached to Holly. Adam looked into the saloon, but he didn't see what Carson did. All he saw was bright red lips, a cheerful ponytail, and tired, tired eyes.

Huh. Maybe Carson was right. But who was she looking after? He was pretty sure she didn't have kids.

Not that he liked her. Not that he cared about what was going on in a damn irritating waitress's life. He didn't. He just wanted three meals a day like any normal man, and to be left alone. Maybe a polite "hello" now and then from Holly. Was that too much to ask? "I think you're seeing things, if you ask me," Adam said. "When I look at her, I see someone with a mean streak and an ornery disposition."

Carson grinned. "She ain't mean to me."

"Says the man that didn't have to eat peanut butter and jelly for a week."

"It's called being polite." The older man smirked. "You should try it sometime."

"She needs to start it."

Carson just shook his head at Adam. "Don't know what woman wounded you in the past, but that doesn't mean that Holly's like her. Give her a chance."

Adam scowled. He wasn't a woman hater. He liked women just fine. It was that obnoxious waitress he had a hard time with. Everyone else he got along great with. His boss? Lovely lady. The gal that cut his hair? Sweet as pie.

Holly? Colder than a witch's tit.

"Just because you're older than me doesn't mean you have all the answers," he told Carson, his good mood evaporating. "You're welcome to stick around, but I'm not. I'm going back."

The other cowboy nodded. "Check on that sick cow in the barn for me."

"All right."

"And make sure the horses are blanketed. Supposed to be a cold one tonight."

"Okay."

"And do a last check on the herd. I didn't have a chance before coming into town." He thought for a moment. "Probably should cake 'em again, too. Just in case it's colder than we thought."

They took turns giving the cows extra feed—or "cake" nutritional pellets—in the winter, because it meant they'd stay warmer. Still, they loved cake pellets and they got pushy about that kind of thing, following close behind the Gator as it spooled the feed out. It wasn't the best to do at night, either, and not Adam's favorite. This turn was supposed to be Carson's, too. "Anything else?"

Carson rubbed his chin. "Actually . . ."

Adam sighed and put his hands on his hips. "You telling me to stay here so you can go back and work?"

Carson put his cowboy hat on. "Now that you mention it, excellent idea." He gave a quick nod. "Much obliged."

Great.

Adam headed back in and squeezed into a spot at the bar once more. He got a soda, sat down, and waited. There was no one he recognized in the saloon tonight—it was all families or dating couples. He guessed that most single people avoided the carnival. Still, it was packed. Sage would be happy. He knew from Jason that she put a lot of work into making the town's events fun and profitable.

As he sat by himself, he checked his phone, scrolling through his social media. He wasn't much of a fan of that kind of thing, but boredom was hitting hard and both Holly and the other waitress were slammed, so it wasn't like he had anyone else to talk to. He pulled up his ex-wife's profile on a whim and saw her posting a few photos of herself. Curiosity got the better of him and he clicked on them.

The first one was Donna at some sort of vacation resort with a tropical drink in her hand, her face pressed to another guy's cheek. BEST MAN I EVER MET was the caption. Didn't surprise him. The divorce had started amicably and ended not so much, especially once he'd found out she'd been sleeping around for a while. Sure enough, a few more photos back and she had posted a picture of a big, ugly ring eighteen months ago. THANKS, ALIMONY PAYMENTS! YOU'RE GOOD TO THIS GIRL. XOXO LOL.

Well, that was enough for one day. Gritting his teeth,

he deleted the app off his phone. He didn't need that shit in his life, just like he didn't need Donna. He wasn't going to let anyone use him again, ever. The alimony payments were done as of January, and Adam was free and clear.

And he liked being single just fine.

Around nine thirty at night, it was like someone flipped a switch in the restaurant. The crowded place emptied out, leaving no one at the bar but Adam, who was nursing his third cup of coffee at that point.

Holly moved to the bar, a slight frown on her face. "Did Carson leave? He offered me a ride."

"We switched," Adam said. "He had some stuff to do back at the ranch. I'll give you a ride." What, did she think he was just hanging out at the bar because he loved Wade's terrible coffee so much?

Her gaze flicked to him, and she bristled. Adam did, too, expecting another argument, but she just shrugged. "I'll get my coat."

"You done working?" He pulled out a few dollars and tossed them onto the counter.

"Yeah." Holly's expression was carefully neutral. She glanced over at the tip he'd left but said nothing. "Night's pretty much over. I'll tell Wade he can hold my tips for me until tomorrow." She walked away, untying her apron.

All right, then. He finished his coffee and grabbed his keys. Then he paused and stared thoughtfully at the money on the bar. It was something Holly had brought up when she was screeching at him—his tips. Did they all think he was a lousy tipper? Why did he care? He added a few more bucks anyhow, just because it was niggling at the back of his head for some damn reason.

He'd always thought of himself as a decent guy. Maybe

a bit rough around the edges at times, but overall decent. Today, though, he was a cake saboteur and a shitty tipper, and apparently it was bothering him.

They were both quiet as she returned to his side a few moments later, her jacket on. He paused, because other than her purse, there was nothing in her hands. It was a drastic change from earlier today, when she'd had massive containers to bring with her and that ridiculous cake. "You got everything?"

"Everything that can't wait," Holly said in a crisp voice, stuffing her hands in her coat pockets. "Can we go? I'm expecting a phone call."

And there was that sour attitude again, as if he hadn't wasted all night waiting to pick her up. Adam's jaw clenched and he held the door of the saloon open for her. "After you, my lady," he said in a sarcastic voice.

With a toss of that ponytail, she headed out.

They were both silent on the ride home. Adam glanced over at her a few times, but she stared straight ahead, her back stiff, her mouth set in that same stubborn cast it always had when she was around him. He should have let Carson drive her home, he decided. It was clear she disliked him as much as he disliked her.

He sure as hell didn't feel guilty about that cake, or the sight of it in the garbage. Or the fact that she'd worked on it for hours. She was just an unlikable person, he'd decided, and therefore she got what was coming to her.

Wasn't his fault.

Adam kept telling himself that all through the drive back to the ranch. He continued to tell himself that as he pulled up to the house and she opened the door of the truck the moment he threw it in park.

"Thanks." She didn't look at him, but her voice was soft. Small.

And she didn't look at him as she got out and walked carefully toward the house.

He told himself it was nothing. If she'd snarled at him as she got out, he wouldn't feel an ounce of guilt. It was just that wobbly, fragile "thanks" that was eating him up as he headed toward his cabin. He thought about that stupid cake, and the glee he'd felt when he'd added the salt to the mixture, imagining her face screwing up as she ate it. He'd imagined humiliating her in private.

Not in front of the whole town.

Maybe that was the part that was eating at him. It wasn't that she was an absolute jerk, or that she'd spent hours on that cake. She was, and she probably had. It was that she'd been incredibly proud of that cake—the pride evident on her face as she'd carried it toward the judging table—and he'd embarrassed her in front of absolutely everyone. Made her look stupid and incompetent.

That was the part that felt all too familiar. Hadn't Donna done that to him? Hadn't he felt the knowing, sympathetic looks of his buddies on base when he'd returned home, because they'd all known his wife had been catting around while he was overseas? He knew what it felt like to have everyone laughing at you. To have to put your chin up and soldier through despite it all.

Adam knew just how that felt, and it sucked.

That feeling was why he paused at his door, then turned around and headed back toward the main house. The lights were still on, and he imagined she'd be in the kitchen, no doubt whipping up food for them for tomorrow. She'd promised enchiladas, and he suspected that despite all the things he disliked about her, she wasn't one to give up on her word. It added to his guilt, knowing that she would be up late making food for them, just as she'd been up late last night, working on her cake.

He needed to talk to her. He wasn't sure why. To apologize? He wasn't sure if he was ready for that, but he just knew he needed to say something. He'd figure it out when he got inside.

He opened the back door of the house quietly. It was just in case she was asleep, he told himself, though he suspected he already knew the answer to that. The moment he stepped inside, though, he heard sounds.

Sobbing.

Adam's chest felt heavy. He headed toward the kitchen, where the sound of the crying was coming from, and couldn't bring himself to step through and announce his presence. He leaned against the wall, listening in like an asshole.

Holly was crying. Big, great, ugly sobs that ripped from her throat. He thought about how stiff she'd been in the car, but he thought that was just because of his presence. He thought about what Carson had said. About how he could tell she was hurting. Did he suspect what Adam had done? Was that why he'd wanted Adam to drive her home? To give him a chance to apologize?

"I'm s-s-so embarrassed," Holly choked between sobs. "You should have seen the way they were all looking at me."

He froze, wondering if she was talking to him.

A moment later, he heard the tinny sound of a response. A phone call. Right. She'd said she was going to speak to someone. He glanced inside and she was seated on the counter, her face red and blotchy, a phone held up in front of her. A video call, then.

"I normally taste everything," she wailed back to the phone. "I d-don't know why I didn't this time. I guess I was rushing." She sobbed again. "They just looked at me like I was stupid, Pol. That's the worst part." She swiped at her face angrily. "Like they all knew I was that stupid dropout that would amount to nothing. It was awful."

More buzz from the phone. He couldn't make out what the other voice was saying, just Holly's responses.

"You want to know the worst part of it?" Holly said in a small voice, wiping her face with her sleeve like a child. "I was so damn confident." A choked sound escaped her. "I was going to go up to the owners of the other shops—the judges—and tell them I could bake for them. I could make stuff for their stores and we could both make some money on the side, you know? But I fucked it up, Pol. I fucked it up so bad and now if they even look at me, they'll just be like, oh, there's that dumb girl from Painted Barrel that put salt in her cake."

A pause.

Holly's demeanor immediately changed. She shook her head, her expression growing tight. "No, money's fine. I promise. It was just me trying to get a foot in the door, you know? Do you need some cash? For books? Or anything else?" A pause. "Right. Okay. I'll send you some first thing Monday." Another pause. "No, it's not a problem. I promise. Enough about me—I'm just disappointed over a stupid cake." She put on a bright smile, and it was like she'd put on a mask. "Tell me about your week. How are exams coming along?"

Adam stepped away as the conversation changed to what sounded like college stuff. She was sending money to someone, then? He thought about how tight her expression had been when she talked to him, how she'd mentioned that she needed this job.

Money issues? Was that why she was so devastated over the cake? She'd thought of it as a way to earn more funds?

Who was she supporting in college? A boyfriend? A child? A family member?

He didn't know, but he knew who would.

CHAPTER ELEVEN

Y ou sure you need a cut?" Becca asked him as he sat in the chair at her salon. "Still looks pretty short to me." She touched his hair with short, quick flicks, as if testing the length with her hands as well as her eyes.

"Sage and Jason are out of town," he explained. "Just gonna be me and Carson at the ranch over the holidays, and Carson's heading out. I won't have time to sleep, much less get my hair cut, while he's gone." He gave her an easy smile. "Thought I'd get it done before everything hits the fan."

She smiled at him. "Tricky, tricky. All right. Same as usual?"

"Same," he agreed, and she got to work. "You and your husband doing anything for Christmas?" he asked, making small talk. Wouldn't look smart if he just launched right in to quizzing her about Holly.

Becca rattled on about her husband and their daughter, and some pink playhouse thing they'd gotten her for Christmas, but he wasn't much listening. He was too busy waiting for the right moment to pose a question about Holly. "What about you?" Becca asked, flicking on the razor. "Are you going to do something special for Christmas?"

"Working," he told her. "Sage hired the waitress that works over at the saloon to cook for us through Christmas."

"Oh good!" Becca lit up. She put a hand to the back of his head and began to shave his neck. "Holly could use the money."

"That so? Supporting a boyfriend or something?"

The hairdresser shook her head. "Her younger sister. She pays for her to go to college. Poor thing always goes without because she's sending every penny to Polly." She chuckled. "I still can't believe their parents named them Polly and Holly."

"You should give them a tongue lashing," he teased. "That sort of thing is criminal." Criminal, kinda like parents that didn't send their own kid to college and forced her sister to pay for everything. He was sure there was a story there.

She turned the shaver off and asked, "You didn't hear? I guess Holly doesn't talk about it much."

"Hear what?"

"Holly's parents died in a car accident when she was seventeen or eighteen. I don't remember exactly, just that it was a big deal because Holly and Polly had no one to turn to. Holly was old enough to be considered an adult, but they were going to send Polly into foster care. So Holly dropped out of high school, got a job waiting tables to support her sister."

It wasn't what he'd expected to hear. It was also damn impressive. "So she's sending money off to college?"

Becca nodded. "Holly compromises so Polly can have a normal life. Polly's really smart, you know. Valedictorian of her class. I think she wants to major in biochemistry or something along those lines. It's definitely not cheap for Holly, but she never complains."

He thought about how upset she'd been last night.

They just looked at me like I was stupid.

They'll just be like, oh, there's that dumb girl from Painted Barrel that put salt in her cake.

Well, if Adam had felt guilty last night, it was nothing compared to how he felt now. He grimaced. "I don't think she did well in the baking contest yesterday."

Becca's expression grew sympathetic. "Did she not? Poor thing. She's such a good baker. Her food's way better than anything you can get at the doughnut shop." She paused, thinking. "Maybe I'll ask her if she can make some cookies for us for the holidays if I offer to pay. She usually brings everyone in town cookies. It's so sweet."

"I'll mention it to her," Adam said casually. "If you like."

"That'd be lovely. Ask her what she charges." She shook her head, smiling. "Hank's brothers are always eating me out of house and home and it'd be a good idea to have some treats lying around, especially treats I don't have to make. Plus, I'm sure she could use the money."

He thought about how she'd stiffened up when the person on the phone—her sister—had mentioned money. "I'm not sure she'd want charity."

Becca chuckled. "You don't get it. Nothing makes Holly happier than baking. Nothing at all."

Adam was pretty sure he needed to apologize, but he wasn't sure how to go about it. How did you confess that you'd sabotaged someone so badly? But that you'd really only meant to humiliate the one person and not in front of the entire town? No matter how he thought about it, it sounded bad.

So maybe instead of an apology, he needed to make it up to her. Make her feel good about herself somehow.

It took him all day to come up with a plan, but when he finally had it, he congratulated himself on the idea. It was simple, but it'd be effective. Cheered, he watched the main house for the lights to come on. They finally did at midnight, which meant she must have been working again.

She always seemed to be working. Damn. As a ranch hand, he was used to long hours in the cold and how random tasks cropped up out of nowhere, but he'd never seemed to pay attention to the fact that every time he went into Wade's, Holly was there. Did she never take a day off for herself?

Maybe his plan wasn't such a good idea after all. But then he thought about what Becca had said, how Holly loved to bake. He decided to go with it anyhow . . . mostly because he was a rancher and a soldier, not an ideas man. Nervous, he adjusted his cap and headed for the kitchen in the main house.

She was inside, all right, humming a Christmas song to herself as she slapped dough against the counter. Her purse was nearby, her hair still in the bow and ponytail she wore for work, and he saw she'd kicked off her shoes and was standing barefoot in the kitchen. She slammed the dough down, lost in her own little world.

He coughed, and she jumped.

Her little dog ran in, barking at him.

"Jesus, you scared the shit out of me," Holly declared, bracing her hands on the counter.

Adam scooped up her little dog and petted its head, tucking the small, wriggly thing under his arm. "Sorry."

She wiped at her brow with the back of her hand, careful not to get flour on herself. "It's all right. I just didn't expect to see anyone this time of night. What can I do for you? Do you have a request for dinner this week?"

He moved across from her and leaned against the counter. Close, but not too close for her to get antsy, since they always seemed to be antsy around one another. He scratched the little dog's ears and studied her face. "You look tired."

Holly looked surprised at his statement. "Me?" She blinked for a moment, and then went back to her customary bright smile, the one he now knew was for customers. It was the smile that said "I'm fine" when she wasn't fine. "Just been a long day," she said. "Seems to get busier the closer it gets to Christmas."

"I bet." Adam scratched her dog under the chin. "Wade should hire more people."

"Probably, but then we'd make less in tips." She shrugged, her brows furrowing. "Did you . . . come over to ask me about work?"

Yeah, that did seem weird, didn't it? "No, actually. I did want to ask you about food."

"Oh?" She gazed up at him, no smirk on her face, no anger in her eyes, no nothing. She just looked soft and tired and a little worn around the edges.

She also, he noticed, had the warmest brown eyes he'd ever seen, with long lashes that framed them perfectly. Her mouth was full and pink and seemed to be curved in a half smile even when resting. The tip of her nose was just a touch pink, as if she'd come out of the cold, and he realized . . . she was really damn pretty when she wasn't scowling at him.

Really pretty.

She had a smudge of flour on her nose, too, but he didn't point that out. It made Holly seem more approachable, far less like the hissing, spiteful waitress he thought of her as. She tilted her head at him, that ponytail swaying, and he realized she was waiting for him to say something.

Right. "Birthday cake," Adam said. "For me."

Her expression changed from amusement to pleasure. "Oh, is it your birthday this week?"

"Yup," he lied. It was the only logical reason he could think of for her to bake him a cake, though. "On the fifth."

"Tomorrow?"

Shit, was it tomorrow? "Yeah. Tomorrow, I guess. Time got away from me."

She flipped the dough over and kneaded it again with her hands, all the while keeping eye contact with him. "And you want a cake? I can manage that."

He smiled. "That'd be great. My mom always made cake for me when I was a kid. I haven't had it since I left the Navy." Yet another lie. They were all piling together right now, weren't they? His mother had died when he was eight, and his father had bought him some stale sheet cake from the closest grocery store every time his birthday came around. No name on it, no candles, no nothing. Just the bare minimum for a birthday celebration. He was too busy trying to keep the farm running. Might as well go all in on the lies, though. "A cake would be great."

"Any particular kind that you like?" she asked brightly. Her expression seemed lighter, and a hint of a smile played on her lips. "I know you're not a fan of onions, so I guess onion cake is out."

He made a face. "Tell me you're joking and there's no such thing as onion cake."

Holly chuckled. "If there is, I've never heard of it. Carrot cake, yes. Lemon cake, yes. Onion cake, no."

"Thank god." Her dog wiggled in his arms and so he gave the ears one last scratch and then set it down.

"So . . . what kind of cake did your mother make for you?"

He thought for a moment, panicked. He hadn't really thought that far ahead with his lie. "You pick. I'm fine with anything."

She arched an eyebrow at him. "You? Not making demands?"

Adam snorted. "Ha ha. It's true. I'm usually not demanding. Sometimes I'm even capable of decent conversation."

Her lips twitched. "I see." She gave her dough another flip and knead. "Well, let me think. I could make chocolate with chocolate chips? I could make strawberry, or lemon. Pumpkin spice. I could go with a Christmas flavor of some kind. Chocolate mint? Gingerbread?" She tilted her head, thinking. "But I'm guessing you already got hit with a lot of Christmas stuff around your birthday every time, right?"

"Me? Why?"

"Uh, because it's in December?"

Right. He'd been distracted by her lips and thinking about them and not the fact that his real birthday was in July. "Yeah, no Christmas flavors," Adam amended. "Just for a nice change." He paused, then asked, "Pumpkin cake?"

She shrugged. "Some people like weird stuff." With a chuckle, she continued rolling the dough under her hands. "And sometimes a weird flavor combination is a good one."

"Like birthday cake and pumpkin?"

"Well, maybe not that one." Holly laughed again. "But chocolate and pear is a good combination." When he made a face, she giggled. "Okay, not that one, then. I'll think of something sufficiently manly for your cowboyish birthday needs."

For some reason, he liked that little laugh of hers. It was bright and sweet, and he liked that despite the fact that she was tired and sad from the cake situation the other day, she still had a genuine happiness to her spirit. She really did like talking about baking. He tried to think of anything he was that passionate about and drew a blank. The most enthusiasm he ever had was for his dog, Hannibal, and even that darn mutt got on his nerves when he ate Adam's socks.

But for some reason, he really liked Holly's smile. "Well, the cake's only if you have the time. I know you're busy."

Holly shook her head, rolling the dough under one hand and then the other in practiced motions. "I'm off work tomorrow."

It was her only day off and he was demanding that she bake for him? Man, he really was an ass. "If you're off work, the cake can wait—"

"No, it's okay!" She smiled up at him. "I like baking. I don't mind at all. And since I'm off tomorrow, I won't feel the need to rush around. I can relax and enjoy myself. What would you like for dinner?"

He flushed. "Are you asking me on a date?"

Holly blinked up at him and then chuckled again. "Uh, no, I was asking you what you wanted me to cook for you for your birthday."

Now he felt twice as stupid. Here he was on the verge of giving her the I-don't-date speech and she wasn't even asking him out. "Right. Just . . . whatever."

She gave him an exasperated look. "Two 'whatevers' from you and you're being nice to me. Have you been drugged? Did body snatchers take the real Adam away?"

He adjusted his cap, tempted to drag the brim down over his entire face. His cheeks still felt hot with embarrassment. "I'm nice all the time."

"Not to me, you're not," she sang out gaily. "You're a dollar-toting asswipe to me."

"Well, you're not exactly my favorite person, either," he began, and then stopped. He was ready to lash out, but he kept thinking about her crying last night . . . and her bright laughter today. "At any rate, I would love a birthday cake, and I'm going to get out of your hair before I say something stupid." He nodded at her. "Thank you very much."

Her laughter followed him out into the night, and for some reason, it made him smile. Sure, they hated each other most of the time, but he'd rather have her smiling and sharp instead of sad and lost.

And he'd use whatever means necessary to get it.

CHAPTER TWELVE

After the chaos of the last few days, it was a pleasure for Holly to take her time and enjoy herself in Sage's lovely kitchen. Some people might have hated the thought of baking on their day off, but she enjoyed it. She'd slept late that morning and tossed a load of laundry into the washing machine before heading into the kitchen and starting on her projects for the day.

She made some more dough for fresh bread and set it aside to prove, and then began to work on Adam's cake. She still wasn't sure why she hadn't told him to get lost. Maybe she'd been having a vulnerable moment. More likely, she could sympathize with wanting to celebrate a birthday and having no one around but you. How many birthdays had passed her by with no one but Polly or Wade to give her a card or even remember that she was turning a year older?

She could relate. And so she was going to make him an extra-nice cake today . . . and she'd taste every bit of it before constructing the damn thing. Her cheeks still burned with humiliation at the thought of her contest disaster. It was just a onetime thing, she reminded herself. She could cook. She could absolutely bake. She'd just been running on fumes that day and rushing to make everything perfect and it had backfired.

It wouldn't happen again, not that it mattered as far as the contest went. She'd flubbed that one royally. She'd never be able to approach a bakery within fifty miles for a business proposition.

But at least her goodies at the front table of Wade's had gone over well. Her work hadn't been completely for nothing, and she'd been complimented by a lot of people on the baked goods. It was something . . . just not the right something.

So she threw herself into making Adam's cake, if only to prove to herself that she still had it when it came to cakes. That she could make this an absolute dream to eat. And when it was in the oven, she hopped up on the counter and checked her phone for messages. Polly tended to text randomly, sending over memes or complaining about a particular assignment. When she'd first gone off to university, the texts between them had flown fast and thick. Polly missed Holly, and Holly was desperately lonely. Texting back and forth had eased a lot of the pain of the separation.

As Polly had gone into her second year, though, the texts had grown less frequent. Polly had gotten involved in university life, joining clubs and hanging out with fellow students at the library. Holly was thrilled for her, she really was. She'd known that her sister would move on and have a life without her, but she hadn't quite expected it to hurt so much. Each time she checked the text messages and there was nothing new from Polly, she ached a little more. Holly wanted to text her, but she warred with the need. She didn't want to be an overbearing, overprotective sister. More than that, she didn't want Polly to feel guilty at Holly's loneliness and feel as if she had to return home. University was the best thing for Polly, and of that, Holly was absolutely certain.

Even if it did make her a little sad inside. It was that sadness that made her decide to text anyhow.

HOLLY: Good afternoon, sunshine! How's the weather there? You taking it easy today?

POLLY: Hey sis! Day off?

HOLLY: Yeah, I'm baking a cake of course. ☺

POLLY: Gah, again?

HOLLY: Glutton for punishment, that's me. One of the cowboys has a birthday today and asked for a birthday cake. I couldn't refuse! He's here without his family and you know I'm a sucker for that sort of thing.

POLLY: I thought the cowboys were jerks to you? That you were avoiding them?

HOLLY: The older one (Carson) is nice, but very quiet. Very Clint Eastwood. It's the younger one that's kinda a dick . . . and the cake's for him, heh.

POLLY: Oh, Hol . . .

HOLLY: I know, I know. It's just . . . it's a birthday, you know?

POLLY: So get a cake mix! If I know you, you're going to spend six hours working on some elaborate creation he won't even be thankful for.

HOLLY: Oh come on, I will not.

POLLY: What kind of cake then?

HOLLY: Peanut butter chocolate fudge?

POLLY: Uh huh. Sounds too simple for you. What's the frosting?

HOLLY: Actually I'm doing a ganache sandwiched between the layers

HOLLY: And a chopped praline layer for crunch

HOLLY: And a mirror glaze on top

HOLLY: Decorated with more praline on top . . .

HOLLY: I know what you're thinking.

POLLY: I'm thinking my sister doesn't know what the term "day off" means.

POLLY: Or the fact that he won't appreciate it!

HOLLY: But I enjoy making it. He didn't ask for anything specific. It's me that decided to do all that.

POLLY: And it sounds utterly delicious. And I know it will be. It's just . . . take care of yourself, too, okay?

HOLLY: You're one to talk! How are finals?

They texted for a while about Polly's classes and the terrible professor she had in organic chemistry, the cute business major that sat in front of her and played games on his laptop through every lecture, and her tutor, who was several classes ahead of her and a year younger. Polly mentioned a party for a few of the chem students the following weekend, and Holly was thrilled for her. She made a mental note to send her sister a bit more money so she could get new clothes, if needed.

It felt good to connect with her sister, and when Polly eventually signed off to study, Holly focused on the birthday meal she was making for Adam, her spirits light. She'd made the right decision in spending every last penny on Polly's future. At least she had one. Holly was happy where she was at, mostly, and she had plans.

If those plans took a little longer to come to fruition, so be it. She could be patient.

Dinner that night was roasted whole chicken with mashed potatoes, homemade macaroni and cheese, and fresh rolls. Yes, she was absolutely going overboard, but Holly didn't mind. Being in the kitchen helped her think. It was relaxing to pull everything together and know she'd done an amazing job. The smells were heavenly, and while the chicken roasted, she worked on the caramel for her praline.

Holly had just finished putting the mirror glaze and the last few decorations on the cake when the first chicken was ready. She'd learned over the last week that whatever plans she had for food, she needed to double. Carson and Adam both ate far more than she'd anticipated, and so she kept one chicken for Adam's dinner, and one chicken for Carson's. For herself, she'd just have a little bit of macaroni she'd put aside. Once everything was ready, she put it all into individual containers with reheating instructions, carefully placed them in a warming bag, and took the first bag outside to place on Carson's doorstep.

To her surprise, she ran into Adam, who was coming from the barn, Hannibal at his side. It was snowing, big, fat flakes floating down from the gray skies, and she wasn't wearing a coat, so to be caught by him felt foolish. He was dressed warmly, in a puffy lined vest over a thick flannel shirt and gloves, along with that beaten-up old baseball cap.

He frowned at the sight of her, hurrying to her side. "What are you doing out here?"

"Dropping off Carson's dinner," she said, determined not to bristle at his tone. She told herself he didn't mean it as abrasive as it sounded. "I want to make sure it's ready whenever he comes home." She moved toward Carson's cabin, and the meal itself was heavy in her arms. Funny how the cabins seemed close to the house until you had to deliver a big, heavy meal.

She didn't protest when he took the warming bag from her arms. "I can get that," he said. "Carson'll be here soon. He's finishing up in the barn."

"Thank you?" Holly crossed her arms over her chest, shivering as he jogged up to the cabin and put the bag on the doorstep.

Hannibal immediately tried to stick his face into it, and Adam pushed him aside. "Come on, boy. That's for someone else." Adam straightened and turned to her, glancing at his doorstep. "Am I getting peanut butter and jelly again?"

She laughed, the sound a little too braying in the quiet. "Funny."

He gave her an awkward smile, and she realized he wasn't joking. Oh. He really did think he was getting those sad sandwiches again? She felt terrible. For some reason, she was feeling a little fond of Adam that day. Maybe it was because he'd been surprisingly decent to her last night and she'd worked on food for him all day? Or maybe it was because despite her public humiliation, he'd still asked her for a cake, and that was a sign of faith in her baking.

Holly gestured at the main house. "Actually, I was just about to bag yours up and bring it out to the door. Everything's ready to go except the cake. I wanted you to look at it before I cut it up." God, just saying it made her sound like an arrogant idiot. He probably didn't care what it looked like. He just wanted cake. She was the one that wanted to preen with pleasure when he tasted it. How silly of her. "But I can bring it out with the rest, actually . . ."

A boyish grin curved his mouth. "My cake's ready? Really?" When she nodded, he patted his leg, calling Hannibal to heel. "If you don't mind some company, I'll eat at the main house, if that's all right with you."

"Oh." Surprised, she hesitated only for a moment. "Company for dinner would be great, actually. It's been a while since I've had a sit-down meal."

They walked toward the house, Holly noticing that he shortened his long strides to keep pace with her. Hannibal bounded between them with excitement, and Adam gave her a sheepish look. "He's starting to associate the big house with treats. Thinks he's getting fed."

Aw. "Well, I'm sure we can find something suitable for a good boy like him." She cooed at the big dog in a baby voice. "Because you're such a good boy, aren't you?"

Hannibal whined and chased his tail with excitement, which made her laugh all over again.

He glanced over at her, and she wondered if he was bothered by the baby-voice thing. She did that to Pumpkin constantly and it slipped out the moment she saw a wagging tail. "So," Adam said, moving to get the back door before she could touch it. He opened it for her and held it as she stepped inside. "Hope you didn't go to too much effort with the food."

"Define 'too much effort.'"

Adam followed her inside. "Working all day?"

"I'm being paid to work all day on cooking for you guys."

"Yeah, but you said today was your day off, right?" He gave her a rueful look. "Ask a ranch hand how precious that kind of thing is."

"I guess you guys don't get a lot of time off, then?" She headed for the kitchen and saw Pumpkin was in her little bed under the Christmas tree. She lifted her head, smacked her lips, and then went back to sleep. She supposed her return didn't merit excitement to her own pup. She headed for the microwave, where she had Adam's roasted chicken warming. He didn't answer her, and so she turned around.

Adam was in the kitchen, still, Hannibal at his side with his paws up on the counter and tail wagging. She wanted to point out that the dog needed to get down from the counter, but the look on Adam's face distracted her. He was staring at the big, decorative covered cake plate in the center of the island that held his birthday cake. The look on his face was nothing short of utterly flummoxed.

"You okay?" she asked softly.

He rubbed his goatee. "Is . . . that my cake?"

She blinked. "Oh yes. Is it not what you wanted? I'm so sorry. I figured you weren't a confetti-sprinkle kind of guy so I veered away from vanilla cake and went for something a little more decadent." Holly moved toward the island and pulled the top off so he could get a good look at it. "I didn't get birthday candles, though. I might be able to scrounge some up. Sage might have some—"

"It's okay," he said, interrupting. His gaze was glued to the cake. "You made this from scratch? For me?"

"I thought it turned out pretty nice," she admitted, and hoped it didn't sound like boasting. "Do you want to eat dinner first? Your chicken's ready."

He glanced up at her. "Right. Dinner."

"I wasn't sure what you wanted for a birthday dinner so I hope roasted chicken is okay?" Why was she asking what he thought? Normally she didn't give a crap what Adam thought about her cooking. If he didn't like it, she'd make him a sandwich. But here she was, practically groveling for praise. Ugh. This is what happened when you entered into public competitions and got thoroughly thrashed—it destroyed your self-esteem. "There's also mashed potatoes and macaroni and cheese."

"For my birthday?" He still sounded surprised.

"Well, I had to feed you anyhow," Holly teased as she pulled the roast chicken out of the microwave, which was keeping it warm. "I figured you can't go wrong with a chicken dinner." She headed to the table with the chicken, nodding at him. "Come sit down and I'll fix you up with a plate. You want coffee? Soda? Water?"

"Coffee's fine." He pulled off his beat-up hat and ran his hand over his hair, recently shorn shorter than usual. "I just . . . Thanks, Holly. I guess I didn't expect all this."

"Birthdays are important," she told him, even though she was blushing a little at his praise. "I always pulled out all the stops for my sister Polly's birthday when we were growing up so she'd feel special. It's the one day out of the year that's truly yours, and I wanted her to know it. If you have something in particular you ate when you were growing up, let me know in advance and I can make it happen. I haven't cooked everything but I'm willing to give most stuff a try."

Instead of sitting at the table, he began opening cabinet doors. "It's been a long time since someone fussed over me. Kinda forgot how it feels." He pulled out two plates and turned around. "Silverware?"

"That drawer," she said, pointing to the one in question. They worked together to set the table, Holly filling serving bowls with completely inappropriate amounts of macaroni and mashed potatoes. There was a gravy boat too, and butter for the rolls. She didn't think it was too much, but clearly Adam was touched, and it made her feel good.

Even if it was just food, meals were important. You could show someone how much they meant to you with a home-cooked meal. And while they were enemies, sometimes that didn't matter. Sometimes even the enemy needed a nice, hearty meal and a pretty cake to make them feel like they mattered.

Once she poured the coffee, she sat down at the table with him, her hands in her lap. It felt weird to be sitting down with Adam freaking Calhoun. She liked to think of him as "that dick Adam from Price Ranch" and "the jerk that tipped a dollar." She always said most people had a reason for how they acted. Maybe Adam did, too.

So she sipped her coffee and waited for him to serve himself. "You said it's been a long time since someone's fussed over you. You've been here a little over a year, right?"

He nodded, carving both legs off the chicken for himself and then adding a mountain of mashed potatoes to his plate. Men were amazing with how much food they could put away. If she ate half of what he did, she'd be too bloated to wear her jeans and would gain five pounds overnight, but Adam was trim and fit.

Not that she noticed that sort of thing, of course, and then Holly felt weird for even thinking about it.

"I was in the Navy," Adam said. "Did a couple of tours in the Mediterranean. Seaman. Ship maintenance. Petty officer second class. I was thinking about going career, but I had a wife at home and . . ." He trailed off, a frown on his face. "I left her alone for too long at a time, so I didn't re-up when it came time. That was a mistake." His mouth grew hard. "After the divorce, I did a few odd jobs here and there but couldn't find anything I liked. Jason suggested I come out and work for him, so I made the move." He shrugged. "That's all."

"Oh." She had so many questions she wanted to ask, but

it seemed inappropriate. You couldn't exactly quiz your enemy about the divorce he'd casually mentioned, or his naval
career and if he missed it. Once he started eating, she
served herself and tried to think of a polite way to steer the
conversation without seeming obvious. "Is that when you
got Hannibal?"

The dog heard his name and appeared between their
chairs, tail wagging.

"This big lug?" Real affection crept into his voice, and
she watched as he pulled a piece of chicken from the bone
and carefully held it out to the enormous dog. "Gift from
my ex, actually. She got him for me when I was home between deployments. I should have known it wasn't meant to
be between us when it killed me to leave him behind but
not her."

"I get it," Holly said, spooning a bit of macaroni onto her
plate. "There's an innocence to a pet that people don't have.
It's almost like a child because they're so trusting."

"Speaking of children, how come your little runt isn't
here begging for scraps like this one?" Adam asked. He
took a bite of chicken for himself and closed his eyes. "This
is really good."

Holly flushed with pleasure. "Thank you. And she's absolutely a beggar, but I just fed Pumpkin and I imagine
she's sleeping it off now."

"Pumpkin. Of all the things to name a dog." He arched
a brow at her as he took another bite. "Why not just call it
'Snookums' and get it over with?"

She chuckled, eating a forkful of macaroni. "The dog's
actually my sister's. She named her, and she was the one
that started cutting her hair like that. She loved that she
looked like a teddy bear, but she didn't have the patience

for her. I think we were both relieved when her dorm said no pets. Now she's mine and Polly doesn't have to feel like a bad parent."

He smiled again. "Makes sense. You didn't look like the type to name your dog 'Pumpkin' anyhow."

"Oh? And what type do I look like?"

"Depends, are you at the restaurant? If so, Cujo."

She snort-giggled into her macaroni. "You are all wrong. If I was as snarly as you say I am, I wouldn't make any tips. And tips are my livelihood."

"Should be cooking," he told her, taking another huge bite of chicken. "This is amazing."

"Well, it's your birthday." She wanted to preen with pride. "It's hard to mess up roasted chicken."

"You haven't seen Carson in charge of the kitchen, then."

They ate companionably, the conversation flowing easily between them. Most of it was about Sage and Jason and their enormous house and ranch, but that was all right. It was just nice to talk to someone while she sat and ate a relaxing meal. Most of hers were comprised of wolfing down a sandwich as she stood in the back room at the saloon. Or wolfing down a sandwich as she stood at the sink, cooking for the two men.

Really, now that she thought about it, she didn't take much time for herself, did she? Huh.

Adam ate an enormous amount of the food, nearly devouring the entire chicken by himself. She was pleased to see that he was careful and checked any bits that he gave to Hannibal before he handed them over, and he never gave the dog bones. Sure, the big Belgian Malinois was a bit of a beggar, but he'd been trained that way, so she couldn't really fault him for his manners. He always put his paw politely on Adam's leg to let him know he wanted another bite, and Adam always obliged.

She liked that. She liked that he was so good with his dog. It made up for the fact that he was such a raging jerk sometimes.

Once the food was gone, he drained his coffee cup, then leaned back in his chair. "I don't know about you, but I'm ready for dessert."

"Now?" After he'd just stuffed his face full of chicken and most of the sides? She shook her head, amused. "Is your leg hollow?"

"Yours isn't?" he jibed back.

"Let me clear the table and then I'll bring the cake out," Holly told him. "More coffee?"

"More coffee would be great, and it might be my birthday, but it's your day off," Adam said, and got to his feet. "I can clear the table." He plucked one of the dirty plates out of her hand before she could stop him. "You've done plenty."

That was . . . kind of nice of him. But she teased him anyhow, just because. "Well, darn it, there goes my dollar tip."

He smirked at her. "Hey, you deserved every bit of that dollar."

She made a face in his direction. "I'll get the coffee at least." Her steps were light as she headed into the kitchen, and she couldn't stop smiling. It was weird, having a truce between the two of them tonight. Normally they were hissing and spitting at each other like two wildcats, but tonight, it was . . . easy. It was fun.

It was almost like . . . flirting.

The moment it crossed her mind, Holly shoved it right

back out. Adam was not her type. He was just being polite because she'd worked hard to make him a nice dinner, and he was grateful. Their jabs still had a bit of an edge to them, and a lot of their conversation tended to steer clear of anything that could head in the wrong direction.

It was a cease-fire. Nothing more.

CHAPTER THIRTEEN

Adam supposed he should have felt guilty about that dinner.

He'd lied and told Holly it was his birthday, and instead of just pulling together some quick cake and shoving a candle on it, she'd worked in the kitchen all day to make him a heavenly meal and then the most obscenely chocolate cake he'd ever tasted. The thing had peanut butter on the inside, and he'd been surprised at the sly joke.

She'd only winked at him as she'd licked the back of her fork.

Now he was back in his cabin, his belly full and an enormous container of leftover cake on the table . . . and his cock was hard as a rock.

What was his damn problem? He stopped hating Holly for an entire night and suddenly his dick sprang to life?

Adam rubbed the front of his jeans, aching painfully. She was just cooking food. She was just being nice. It didn't mean anything. Except every time he tried to think about anything else, he thought instead about how she'd worn her dark hair down and it had framed her pretty face. He thought about how soft and touchable it looked, and he wondered how it'd feel against his fingers.

He thought about how she'd licked the back of her fork, her tongue darting out to capture a bit of chocolate. He thought about the husky note of her laughter.

And he jerked at his belt, quickly undoing it and taking himself in hand. He stroked his length fast and hard, imagining her pink little tongue flicking over the head of his cock like it had over the fork. He thought of her under him, her dark hair spilling over his pillows. Within moments, Adam came with a groan, the release barreling out of him like a freight train.

Damn.

He lay back on his bed, panting. He didn't understand himself. She was still his enemy, still the annoying woman who'd deliberately given him peanut butter and jelly sandwiches with the crusts cut off, just because she didn't like him. Except tonight . . . he'd kinda liked her sharp sense of humor. She'd made him a big meal and an amazing cake because she'd wanted him to feel special. It hadn't mattered that they were at each other's throats more often than not.

She'd wanted him to feel special on his damn birthday. Not that it really was his birthday.

For all that he disliked Holly . . . she had a kind streak inside her. He thought about how she made sure to take care of Carson, how she had made soup after soup for him so he could fight off his cold. How she was baking cookies for him to take to his daughter. He suspected Holly genuinely liked taking care of people.

He wondered if anyone had ever taken care of her. Probably not, if what Becca had told him was true. That she'd fallen into the role of her sister's caretaker and dropped out of high school so they could stay together. Her sister was in college now, but from what he could tell, she was still determined to take care of her from afar, and now she was focused on him and Carson.

Adam pulled off his shirt and wiped his spend off his chest, grimacing to himself. He hadn't come so hard or so fast since he was a schoolboy. He got up from the bed and glanced over at Hannibal, who was curled up in his own bed in the corner, his favorite chew toy tucked between his paws. Hannibal liked her, too, and his dog didn't like much of anyone other than him. How many times had Donna complained that Hannibal never listened to her? But his big dog was perfectly behaved when it came to Holly.

He headed to the window and peered out. More thick snowflakes were falling, which meant tomorrow was going to be brutal in the saddle. Adam glanced up at the windows to the main house like a pervert, wondering if he'd get a glimpse of her form again. The lights were off, though.

Funny how that disappointed him.

Holly was his enemy, he reminded himself. The last thing he needed was an obsession with a woman just because she'd made him a cake. But . . . it had been nice to not be at each other's throats. It had been even nicer to have dinner with her, to sit down and talk about nothing in particular. Carson never wanted to socialize unless he felt obligated to, like when Jason had brought them to lunch. Or when they were riding together.

Maybe that was it. With only Carson around, Adam was feeling a mite lonely for company. Nothing more.

* * *

The next morning, he woke up with Carson's cold. Groaning, Adam managed to get himself dressed even though everything ached. He felt hot even when he stepped into the snow, and he felt as if he were slogging through molasses as he went through the morning chores.

Carson gave him an odd look as he saddled the horses. "You okay?"

"I caught your cold." Adam shrugged, sweating despite the fact that his breath was freezing in the air. "I'll live."

The other cowboy grunted.

Somehow, Adam was able to get into the saddle. Somehow, he was able to work for several hours, even though his brain felt detached and foggy. Muscle memory, he told himself. Muscle memory would carry him through. He couldn't afford to be sick. People were counting on him. He'd just suffer through.

Lunchtime finally hit and Adam pulled out his meal—a thick sandwich with layers of cheese and meat—and found he didn't have the appetite for it. His thermos held coffee, but it was too hot and the taste was all wrong. He shoved it back into a saddlebag and rode his horse back to the barn. "Think I'll get a head start on spooling that hay."

Carson just looked at him.

He got out the bale unroller and tried to drive it around to the far side of the barn, where the hay was covered with a large tarp to protect it from the worst of the snow. Man, everything felt like effort. He paused, then lowered his head onto the steering wheel and rested. Just for a moment.

Adam woke up to Carson shaking his shoulder, a frown on his face. He sat up, rubbing his mouth. "Sorry. I dozed off."

"You're no good like this," Carson said in that sharp voice of his that brooked no argument. "Go home. Take a nap."

He wanted to protest, but a nap sounded like heaven. That'd be the ticket. He'd sleep for a few hours and then come back refreshed. Nodding, he dragged himself out of the machinery and headed toward his distant cabin. So damn distant. Even Hannibal's playful bouncing couldn't entice a smile from him. He just wanted a nice long nap.

By the time he got to his cabin, he was wiped. He didn't take off his boots or his jacket, just climbed into bed and closed his eyes. Hannibal jumped onto the bed next to him and Adam put an arm around the dog, tucking him against his body. "We'll play later, boy," he mumbled.

For now, sleep.

A dam floated in and out of sleep for what felt like forever. He kept telling himself he needed to get up and help Carson with the chores, but he couldn't manage to drag himself from his slumber. It was like a blanket was over his senses, muffling everything, and all he could do was lie down and sleep.

And sweat. He was pretty sure he was sweating and too tired to wake up and take his clothes off. Too tired to push Hannibal's hot body away.

At some point, there were noises. Hands touched his brow and they were cool and wonderful. He groaned, leaning toward that refreshing touch, but it moved away again. Vaguely, he realized someone was pulling off his boots and socks. It felt good, and he rolled over onto his back, determined to thank whoever it was.

Instead, he was rewarded with a cool, wet towel on his brow.

Damn, that felt good. He groaned, still half-pulled into the darkness of sleep, and reached out for whoever it was. A soft hand brushed his, and then squeezed his fingers. "Just relax," Holly told him gently. "You're sick."

"Need to get up," he mumbled. "Carson—"

"It's all under control," she soothed. "Go back to sleep."

He did, mostly because it was too difficult to answer. His face was too tired. He drifted for a while, vaguely aware of more cool cloths pressed to his brow and those gentle hands tugging at his shirt.

Adam woke up, rubbing his eyes and still feeling like death warmed over. He glanced over at the alarm clock. One in the morning? Jesus. Had he slept all day? Carson was going to kill him. He—

"You're awake?" Holly's voice was a low whisper.

He rolled over—though it felt like effort—and turned to look at her. She sat in the lone chair in his cabin, her phone in hand, and as she put it down, he caught a glimpse of a candy game on the screen. "What . . . what are you doing here?" He rubbed his face. It felt hot and sweaty, just like the rest of him.

"You're sick," she said in a patient voice. "Now that you're awake, I want you to eat a little something and go back to sleep, all right?"

He closed his eyes again. "Not hungry."

"I don't care. I'm your nemesis, remember? I'm here to torture you." Her gentle voice was full of amusement and he felt the bed sink as she sat on the edge of it. "Sit up and drink this, and then I'll let you go back to sleep."

Somehow, Adam managed to sit up. He took the cup she held out to him and took a cautious sip—lukewarm broth. It actually tasted pretty good, and he finished the whole thing before he knew it. She made him drink a cup of water next, and then insisted he get up to use the bathroom before he went back to sleep. When he finally flopped into bed again, she pressed another cool cloth to his face, and he groaned his thanks.

"Hannibal's fed and Carson's got the cattle handled," Holly told him, stroking his brow through the wet fabric. "Just get some sleep and you'll be better in the morning. I'm going back to the house but I'll be by to check on you again in a few hours."

He reached out and grabbed her hand before she could leave. "Thanks," he mumbled. "For a nemesis, you're all right."

Her chuckle echoed in his ears long after she left.

CHAPTER FOURTEEN

The next morning, he felt well rested but still awful. Adam groaned over and over again as he hauled his heavy body out of bed. At some point, Holly had removed his shirt as well as his boots, but he was still covered in sweat and his blankets were soaked and uncomfortable. Hannibal pawed at the front door, desperate to go outside, and Adam shuffled to the door to let him out. A blast of cold air hit, and it felt so good that he closed his eyes and just lingered there for a few minutes.

Being sick sucked.

When he opened his eyes, though, he saw Holly heading across the snowy ground, a bowl in one hand and a mug in the other. He watched her approach, wondering if she was coming to take care of him again today . . . and why he liked it so much.

She gave him a bright smile as she came to the door. "Well, you're upright! That's a good sign."

"You didn't see how long it took me to get this way," he

managed to joke. "To what do I owe the pleasure of my nemesis once more?"

She moved onto the step that led to his door and nudged him with the bowl in her hands. "I'm going to feed Hannibal, get this broth in you, and then I'm driving you to the doctor."

"I don't need to go to the doctor—"

"Well, you certainly can't afford to be like this for the next week," Holly told him in a chirpy voice. "Carson and I figured it'd be best to get you medicated so you can return to work sooner. Now, come away from the door—it's cold out—and drink this." She held the large insulated mug out to him.

Even as he took the mug and sat back down on the edge of the bed, he protested. "I really don't need the doctor."

"Then you won't get a prescription, will you? He'll just give you a nice vitamin D shot and send you on your way, but you're still seeing him this morning. Now, drink up."

It was impossible to argue with her when she was in this sort of mode. The I'll-take-care-of-everything mode came naturally to her, he suspected. After raising her sister and working at the restaurant, she probably just tried to handle everyone that came her way. It should have bothered the hell out of him. Instead, he sipped the broth and watched as she put the bowl down for Hannibal, then poked through his clothing drawers, looking for fresh socks.

Holly turned to look at him. "You want to keep wearing those jeans?"

"I do unless you want to help me strip them off," he drawled.

To his surprise, her cheeks flushed with a hint of color and she tossed the balled-up pair of socks at him. "Looks like you're going to keep wearing them, then."

Seeing her flustered was . . . kinda fun. He scratched at

his stomach and noticed her gaze flicked in that direction. Well, that was . . . interesting. If he wasn't so damned tired and hot, he might have pursued it. As it was, he just wanted to take another nap.

Holly nagged and pushed him around for the next ten minutes, helping him pull a shirt over his head and putting his socks on his feet. If she felt strange kneeling in front of him to help him with his boots, she didn't say anything. Her cheeks were crimson, though, and Adam suspected it wasn't all cold. She stood in front of him and insisted he finish his broth, and then held out his jacket, like he was a child.

She was patient as they headed out to her car, though. Adam was pretty sure he was moving slower than usual, but she didn't make him feel as if she were rushing him. She even flipped up the back seat and patted it so Hannibal could ride with them.

If she wasn't his nemesis, he'd have considered her efforts rather thoughtful.

As it was, she was managing and annoying, but it must have been the sickness that made it all seem amusing and not that bad. In fact, it was kind of cute. It had been a long time since anyone had hovered over him, and Holly was doing exactly that as she drove him to the next town over, then led him into the doctors office. She even signed him in.

"Are you his wife?" the receptionist asked.

"Nope," Holly said, even as she held her hand out to Adam. "Give me your driver's license so I can fill out your paperwork."

The receptionist smiled. "He's lucky to have a girlfriend like you to take care of him, then."

"I'm not his girlfriend," Holly corrected, but her cheeks were flushed again. "I'm his enemy."

"Whatever you want to call it, honey," the receptionist said. "But you'll have to sit in the waiting room with the dog."

An hour later, Adam had two prescriptions to fill and had endured a shot in his ass, and then Holly drove him back to the ranch and insisted on putting him to bed again. "I'll pick up your prescriptions," she told him as she helped him pull his boots off again.

"Carson—"

She shook her head. "Carson wants you to get better. He's handling things and he said if he needs more help, Caleb from the Swinging C offered to come by."

He knew Caleb. He was the only guy in town as quiet as Carson was. Maybe it was something with *C* names. Who knew. He let Holly fuss over him for a bit longer, then lay down for another nap. When he woke up, she was there with fresh soup, a bottle of water, and his medicine. Her hair was in its customary ponytail and he knew she was heading in to work. Did the woman ever stop? he wondered. Probably not. She'd probably break into a hundred pieces if she did.

The next day, he was feeling more like himself. He was able to get up and do some of the chores in the barn, though Carson handled most of the workload. Holly's hovering was less intense, though she kept him in hot soup and warm bread. The day after, he felt like himself again.

Which was a good thing, because Carson had a bomb to drop on him.

"What do you mean, you're leaving tonight?" Adam asked, frowning as he picked mud out of his horse's shoes. Winter was a miserable time. The snow was pretty, but cold, and when it melted, it left muddy sludge everywhere. He was constantly cleaning it off the horses' legs, their hooves, off his own boots, and he had to rotate the cattle to a different pasture when the mud got too churned up and thick around the natural watering hole. Today, they were moving them to a closer pasture with metal troughs because the weather was supposed to be unpleasant over the weekend. If the snow was thick, there was no sense in traipsing all over the hills to try to look after the cattle, not when it was just the two of them.

Carson had a mulish look on his face. He shrugged, flipping a toothpick between his teeth. "Mean what I said."

"I thought you weren't supposed to leave until right before Christmas. That's still almost two weeks away." Not that he couldn't handle it; it was just . . . not what they'd planned.

Carson just gave him a cold look. "Am I ruining your Christmas shopping?"

Adam snorted, picking out a big chunk of mud from Eisenhower's hoof while the horse stood patiently. "No. I ain't doing anything for the holidays and you know it. It's just . . . not great." What could he say? That he wouldn't have anyone to talk to for the next three weeks and it'd be lonely? The only person that would be around was Holly, and she was gone most days until practically midnight.

Not that he wanted to spend time with her, of course. Nemesis and all.

"You can handle it," was all Carson said.

"Of course I can handle it," Adam blustered. "Does Jason know?"

"Jason's fine with it. Talked to him while you were sick."

He had? Why was Adam just now hearing about this? Fighting back a surge of irritation, he set the horse's hoof down and moved to the other side carefully, making sure Eisenhower knew where he was at all times. He tapped the foreleg and the horse obediently raised the new hoof for cleaning. "So you're just going to head off on Christmas holidays early?"

"Yeah."

Adam rolled his eyes. "Well, enjoy yourself, then. I can handle it here."

Carson crossed his arms over his chest and leaned against the stable door. "We'll check the outlying pastures later today, make sure the fences are good. Told the Swinging C I was heading out. They know you might need help."

He snorted. "I won't need help."

"You sound pissed."

"I'm not pissed." Of course, when he said it like that, it did sound kinda pissed. He couldn't win. "I'm really not. Just kinda surprised is all. The work's fine." He pried a large clump of mud out of the horse's hoof. "Just goes by a lot faster when there's someone else to talk to." He patted Eisenhower's leg again and the horse set it down. "That's all."

Carson grunted. They were both silent for a long moment, and then the older cowboy spoke again. "My daughter's getting induced early. Preeclampsia. She's in the hospital right now."

Adam felt like an ass. "Shit, man. I didn't know." Hell, he hadn't even known that the man had a daughter, much less that his daughter was pregnant. "Of course you have to head out. Ignore my bitching. Family comes first."

Carson just nodded. "I'm catching a midnight flight." He eyed Adam. "You gonna be all right here alone with Holly?"

"Why wouldn't I be?"

"Be nice to her."

Now he was starting to get irritated. "I am nice to her."

Carson just grunted.

Did that grunt mean that he didn't believe Adam? Or did it mean something else? Holly could stand up for herself. He was pretty sure that if she thought he was being mean that she wouldn't have gone to such lengths to take care of him when he was sick. Even as he thought about it, though, he wondered. Did she just consider that part of her duties since she'd been hired to look after them? She had introduced herself as his enemy to the receptionist, after all. Maybe she still considered them to be . . . at odds with one another.

He wasn't sure how he felt about that, either, which was strange. Why did the thought of them being foes bother him? Was it the cake he'd sabotaged? Or how kind she'd been while he was sick? Or something else?

CHAPTER FIFTEEN

Holly was just about to head to work when her phone buzzed with an incoming text. She was excited, thinking Polly had reached out, but it was only Becca, who ran the hair salon in town.

BECCA: Hey Hol! Got a moment?

HOLLY: Sure, heading in to work soon. Do I need to set up a hair appointment?

BECCA: Oh, I mean, you could, but that wasn't what I was texting about! Did Adam talk to you about my cookie request?

HOLLY: No . . . what's up?

BECCA: He must have forgot. You know how men are. I'm throwing a party this weekend and I'm trying to pull together refreshments.

BECCA: I thought a couple of trays of cookies would be great and wanted to know what you'd charge.

BECCA: Also before you think you're not invited . . . you are! I just delivered invites out and yours is waiting at the bar. I know I'm late but I hope you can come.

BECCA: And if it's too last minute for the cookies, that's all right, too. I feel bad! I'm not trying to pile onto you at the last moment.

Holly frowned down at her phone. This was exactly the kind of lead she was hoping for—people wanting her to bake for them for money—and she was thrilled about the offer. Yet . . . why hadn't Adam said anything? She'd shown him she loved to cook, and hadn't they been getting along recently? Was this just him being a dick again after everything? Or had he truly forgotten?

She thought for a moment and decided to give him the benefit of the doubt. He'd been sick recently, and between that and his birthday, he'd probably just forgotten. It was a little irritating, but not anything to get upset over.

HOLLY: I would love to make you cookies!

HOLLY: And attend your party! You tell me what you had in mind and I'll be there. ☺

They worked out the details of the order, and Holly quoted a price that would cover the cost of the ingredients, plus a little extra for her work. She felt she didn't have the clout—especially after her public cake disaster—to be able to charge more.

BECCA: Girl, that is far too little $$$. But thank you! I'm excited to see what you bring. ☺

HOLLY: I'll see you Friday night, then. Is it just casual wear? Do I need to bring a gift?

BECCA: There'll be a crazy gift exchange, yes, and a few festive games. Just wrap up something random and fun. Dress code is party attire, but not black tie? AKA wear your nicest gown but your boyfriend doesn't have to wear a tux.

HOLLY: No boyfriend on this end.

BECCA: Can you bring a friend? Just to keep the numbers even? If not, that's ok, but I've got a few holiday games planned that require couples.

HOLLY: I'll see what I can do. ☺

In truth, she had no idea who to bring. Her last boyfriend had been over a year ago and he'd moved away from Painted Barrel. It was a small town and while she knew a lot of people, she'd also fallen off the radar after high school because she'd been so wrapped up in taking care of Polly's needs. She supposed if someone showed up at the saloon tonight she could ask them for a date, but that might lead to weirdness.

Then again, there was always Adam. He owed her a favor after all the nursing she'd done in the last few days. Sure, they were enemies, but she knew for sure he wouldn't have a date, and if nothing else, they could just take one car. That'd make things simple.

She'd been putting up with him for well over a week now. She could put up with him for a night.

Business was slow at Wade's saloon, and Holly's tips were sad and pathetic. She'd scanned her customers, looking for potential "dates," but other than a truck driver stopping through, most of the people at the saloon that night were far too old and far too married.

She was going to be stuck with Adam, she realized.

As if her thoughts had called him, Adam showed up that night in the kitchen. Holly was up late after the day's work, prepping food for the next day's meal. Carson had left her a sweet note, thanking her for the cookies she'd baked late last night so he could bring them to his daughter. She hoped everything turned out okay and made a mental note to text him in a few days and check on things. He'd assured her he wasn't worried, but Carson was hard to read sometimes. There were no messages from Polly, either, which didn't surprise her but still made her feel a little sad.

Maybe all that was why she was happy to see Adam show up. "Hey there," she called out as he walked in. "How are you feeling?"

"Like freshly warmed shit," Adam said, moving to the kitchen island and pulling out a stool to settle in.

"Is that an improvement from yesterday?" she asked, tossing strips of chicken in breadcrumbs. With Carson leaving, it was ruining some of her plans for batch baking big casseroles so they could eat as much as they wanted. She couldn't exactly make huge plates of food for one guy, so she'd try out a few different things to see what he wanted. Tomorrow's menu would be homemade crunchy chicken strips with mashed potatoes and white gravy.

"Slight." Adam gave her a faint smile. He looked tired, his face a little pale, and she knew he was pushing himself hard to get back into the swing of things. He hated being sick. It was something he'd repeated over and over (and over) again when he was half-asleep with his fever. "Carson left tonight."

"Yep, I heard." She laid the chicken strips on a plate, only to see Hannibal's nose getting a little closer to the counter than she'd like. Well, she had a solution for that, too. She glanced over at Adam and nodded. "Will you distract Hannibal with one of those dog cookies I made? They're in the cookie jar."

"You made dog cookies on top of everything else?" His mouth tugged into a reluctant smile, but he grabbed the jar.

"Of course. I can't spoil everyone except the dogs, right? I have to spoil everyone." She went back to breading chicken strips. "And those are made with peanut butter and oatmeal and bacon but no sugar." Holly heard the click of Pumpkin's tiny nails on the floor. "Give one to Pumpkin, too?"

"Naturally." He leaned over and fed both dogs, then turned back to her, watching her work.

"Are you hungry? I was making these for tomorrow but tonight works just as well."

Adam gave her a sheepish look. "I'm always hungry."

"It's a good thing for you that I'm always cooking, then." She cast him a teasing smile over her shoulder, then headed over to the fryer she had plugged in. It was still warming, so she glanced back at him. "Becca texted me today, by the way."

He snapped his fingers. "Cookies. Shit. I totally forgot."

She'd suspected as much. "It's all right. But now you owe me one for sabotaging things." Did he turn pale just then? "You okay?"

"Just hungry." Adam shook his head. "But yeah, I blanked out about the cookie thing. I'm sorry. How do I make it up to you?"

Holly already knew. "You're going to be my date to her Christmas party Friday night."

He made a face. "I am?"

"Don't look so thrilled. And yup. You owe me, and Becca wants everyone to have a date because of party games or something. And I kinda have to go because I'm dropping off the cookies."

"Ah."

"Yeah, don't worry. I'm not madly in love with you." Holly dropped the first chicken strip in, testing the oil, and then glanced over at him. "I'll do my best to leave early but I also don't want to hurt Becca's feelings. So you might be stuck with me for a few hours."

Adam was quiet for a moment. "I guess I do owe you," he finally said. "I just . . . after my ex and I divorced, I vowed to remain single. It's not worth the hassle, you know? And I've been telling everyone that for forever." He paused. "Including Becca."

She fought the urge to roll her eyes. "Calm down, Romeo. It's not like I can't handle a platonic date. It changes nothing between us. And if anyone asks, you can tell them that I'm just using you for sex."

He was silent.

She looked over at him. The expression on his face was definitely weird. Probably still feeling under the weather. "That was a joke."

Adam managed a smile. "Right."

"Don't worry. No one in this room is catching feelings for one another. I figure as long as we're on the same page, we show up, drop the cookies off, drink her wine, smile at a few people, and then call it a day. Easy."

The expression on his face was suspicious, but at least he wasn't declining outright. That was good. She meant every word of what she said, too. They'd show up, hug a few people, make an appearance, and call it a day.

And absolutely, positively avoid all mistletoe.

Holly took pictures of Pumpkin in a Santa hat and sent them to her sister Friday afternoon.

HOLLY: Ho ho ho, your favorite elf says good afternoon!

Polly's answer was slow to come through.

POLLY: You only send me dog pictures when I ask or when you're nervous about something. What's up?

Did she? Was she that obvious? She tried to think back

on other dog pictures she'd sent, but the last one was right before the big baking contest, which she'd flubbed. Hmm.

HOLLY: I'm going to a party tonight. Becca asked me to make cookies for her guests. I'm just killing time until my date arrives.

She hoped that would flush Polly out and force her sister to call. It had been far too long since she'd heard Polly's voice and maybe she was feeling a little lonely. It was two weeks before Christmas and the weather was cold and frosty, the days short, and . . . she missed her family. The ache of missing her parents was one she was used to, but Polly's absence was like a hole in her heart, made worse by the fact that she knew Polly was having a lovely time at university and enjoying herself . . . and for some reason, Holly resented it. Just a little.

And she hated that she resented it, too. It felt . . . unsisterly. She was happy for Polly but . . . she also wanted Polly to miss her. Just a touch. And it felt like Polly didn't.

But that was just Holly being needy. It was the holidays, and she was alone. That was what it was.

POLLY: Who's your date?

HOLLY: The jerk cowboy I'm cooking for. It's platonic, of course. I just didn't want to go by myself and he owed me a favor.

POLLY: What are you wearing? Your red holiday dress? He's going to fall in love with you. ☺

HOLLY: How did you know I was wearing the red dress?

POLLY: Because you only have the one?

Well, that was fair. Wasn't much point in having multiple party dresses when she didn't really party. It was one she'd gotten at a thrift store years ago for Polly's prom that she'd ended up not going to, and ever since, she'd pulled it out for holiday pictures and special occasions. The top part of the dress was tightly fitted and pure, bright red with a square neckline. It dropped to a natural waist and the skirts flared out and twirled around her knees. It felt very retro and glamorous, even if she didn't have a stiff crinoline to wear underneath for fun. She'd paired it with black heels and decided to wear her hair in a Veronica Lake side sweep held back by a clip adorned with a small red Christmas bow.

She told herself she wasn't dressing up to impress anyone, but the truth was, she wanted to make Adam sweat, just a little. Not that she wanted to date him. She just wanted to make him regret that whole I'm-not-interested-in-dating comment he'd thrown out.

As if she was asking him to date her. Whatever. He'd clearly not heard the part where she said he owed her a favor.

Holly took a few pictures of herself with Pumpkin in front of the tree and sent them to her sister. She gave the dog a kiss for being such a good girl, cuddled her for a moment, and then pulled off the hat and set her food bowl out. It was almost time for them to head out for the party and there was no sign of Adam.

If he stood her up, she was going to throw onions into his food for the next lifetime.

The back door opened and her nerves flared. Holly had no idea why she was nervous. She texted a quick goodbye to her sister and then trotted out in her black heels to meet Adam. "About time," she called out as she turned the corner. "Here I thought we were going to be . . ."

She trailed off at the sight of him.

". . . late."

She'd forgotten to tell Adam the dress code. He was dressed in a tuxedo, a black bow tie done expertly at his neck and matching cummerbund. The jacket framed his shoulders perfectly and emphasized just how big he was. Lord have mercy, he really was *big*. As he took a step forward, she couldn't stop staring at his shoulders and arms. He could be a linebacker, she decided, with that build. It probably came from tossing hay and slinging bags of feed but—

"Did I overdress?" he asked, rubbing his newly trimmed goatee. His brows were drawn together in a frown.

"It's fine," she told him, breathless. "I did, too. We'll look like a matching pair."

Adam's mouth curled at the corners, and her heart fluttered at the sight of his smile. "You look . . . nice."

Just like that, her heart plummeted. A grudging "nice" was all she warranted? "Stop, you're killing me with praise," she said dryly. "I'll get a swelled head if this keeps up."

He chuckled. "I meant that better than how it came out. You do look nice, but you always do."

She waved a hand at him, dismissing his words. He'd already made it quite clear he wasn't attracted, and that was fine. As long as they were on the same page, they could still enjoy the evening. If she thought he was smoking hot in a tuxedo, well, that was her problem.

On the bright side, she was showing up with a gorgeous date and heading to a party, so all in all, it was still going to be great.

CHAPTER SIXTEEN

A dam was in a mess of trouble.

He should have known that going to this party with her was going to be a mistake. It was only guilt that made him agree . . . or so he told himself. He'd told himself that even as he'd trimmed his goatee and splashed on after-shave. He'd told himself that as he pulled his tux out of the garment bag. Guilt and a sense of obligation, he told himself as he stared in the mirror, trying to make his tie perfect.

When he saw Holly in that red dress, though, he knew he'd been lying to himself.

She was utterly, stunningly gorgeous. Holly was always pretty, of course, and he noticed her body even when he didn't want to. Here he'd preached all about how he wasn't looking for a relationship or to be with anyone. He wasn't . . . but he hadn't counted on Holly in that dress. Holly, who looked like she'd stepped out of an old-fashioned magazine . . . or his wet dreams. Her hair was loose and shiny, pulled back to reveal one small ear that practically begged to be nibbled on. The bodice of her dress fit her like a second skin, and when she moved, her skirts swished.

Every time they did, he pictured bending her over the couch, pushing those skirts up, and taking her.

Which was not something you pictured about your friends. Adam swallowed. Hard.

She gave him a playful smile as she headed toward the kitchen. "Are we taking your truck? Because I have a bunch of cookies I need to bring with me."

He watched her skirt swish as she moved, and it only emphasized the curve of her hips and her legs in those heels. Had he ever seen her in heels? Normally he was pretty sure she wore sneakers. Maybe those shoes were why his cock was practically standing at attention and he couldn't take his eyes off her.

Just . . . shoes.

Yeah, he sucked at lying to himself.

He headed into the kitchen after her, as always, astonished at the sheer amount of baking she'd gotten done. There were four large containers of cookies, and as he peered over her shoulder, she adjusted them to sit neatly in each box. One was full of gingerbread men, another full of cookies shaped into presents and brightly iced, another one full of stars, and the fourth one just looked like plain chocolate chip.

Adam reached over her shoulder and took one of the chocolate chip ones. "This one fell on the floor."

She laughed and swatted at his hand but didn't stop him. When they stood like this, he could practically smell her hair, could feel the warmth of her body. She was a perfect fit to tuck against him, and if she leaned back, she'd nestle in his arms as if she belonged there. He was probably being a creep standing this close to her, but he couldn't help himself.

He was . . . lost.

She smelled amazing, too. Like warm vanilla and the gentle scent he'd recalled from being sick, the faint perfume that was Holly. Adam shoved the cookie into his mouth and it melted against his tongue. "Good," he managed to say around the mouthful, and managed to tear himself away from her. "Which ones you want me to carry?"

"All of them?" Holly looked up at him and fluttered her lashes in an obvious way. "I've got our presents wrapped and ready and I thought I'd carry those."

"Presents? What presents?"

She snapped a lid onto one plastic container. "Don't panic. Becca told me they were doing some sort of goofy gift exchange, so when I was at the grocery store, I looked down the seasonal gifts aisle. One of us is giving away the ugliest pair of chicken-shaped salt and pepper shakers ever, and the other is giving away a foot massager."

He chuckled. "Those sound terrible."

"Exactly." Holly closed the other cookie boxes and smiled up at him. "Oh, and if you want to drink tonight, I don't mind driving home. I'm used to being the responsible one."

And didn't that just make his heart clench up a little? Was there ever a time when perfect, looking-out-for-everyone-else Holly let herself relax? Was there ever a time she let herself be free?

A tiny plan formed in his mind. "I'm not drinking," he told her.

But if it was up to him, he'd make sure she did. He

wanted her absolutely drunk and having the time of her life. Not because he wanted to laugh at her or humiliate her, but because she deserved to have a friend—just one friend—that had her back and that she could let loose around. She deserved to have someone there to catch her.

For some reason, Adam wanted to be that person.

They drove up to Becca's salon on Main Street, where the party was being held. Like most of the buildings in downtown Painted Barrel, the salon was an old-timey building with a covered porch and two stories. The salon was established in the front of the building, and the apartment Becca shared with her husband, Hank, was in the back of the place. Christmas lights hung off the porch and big decorative snowflakes covered the flocked windows. Inside, he could see a few people standing around, holding drinks. It'd probably just be people from around town—Becca's salon clients and Hank's people from the Swinging C Ranch.

He looked over at Holly, ready to make a quip about a party in a hair salon, but it died on his lips at the look on her face. She was frozen, her face white, her hands nervously smoothing her skirts over and over again. Her gaze was glued to the windows and the party.

"You okay?" Adam asked.

She nodded, and he saw her throat flex as she swallowed. "Just . . . nervous." She licked her lips and gave him a frantic look. "I didn't taste the cookies. I don't know what I was thinking. I should have tasted them but I've made them so many times." She babbled on, clearly anxious. "I should have stopped to taste everything before bringing them out here. What if they're awful? How can I let Becca pay me? How can I present them like I'm proud of them if they're garbage? What if—"

"Stop," he said in a low voice.

Her jaw clamped shut and she looked over at him, her face full of worry, her eyes helpless in the dark.

"The cookie I tasted earlier was the best I've ever eaten," Adam told her quietly. "If you want, we can pull the others out and I will taste each one and tell you if we need to turn around. But we both know they're great."

"I just . . . I don't trust my baking anymore," she told him in a broken little voice. "I thought it was something I could do well but I just don't know anymore."

He needed to tell her. Adam needed to reassure her that she wasn't the problem, that he was. That he'd played a dirty trick on her and ruined her cake. He hadn't known all that she had riding on it. He'd thought it was just a dumb cake, and he regretted his actions now—not that it did any good.

Adam said nothing, though. It was selfish of him, he knew, but he didn't want to ruin the evening. He wanted to stay at her side all night and devour her with his eyes. He wanted to see her get drunk and have a great time. He wanted her to present her cookies and have everyone exclaim over them . . . and that wouldn't happen if he blabbed before they even got to the party.

"Calm down," he said, and it took everything he had not to gather her in his arms and hold her close to comfort her. He didn't know what the fuck was wrong with him—she was his enemy and this was just a temporary truce—but for some reason, he was having a hard time thinking about that tonight.

Tonight, he just wanted to touch her, even though he knew he shouldn't. So he'd settle for watching her have a wonderful time.

She nibbled on one of her red lips, then pulled out one

of the large plastic containers and popped the lid off. Mutely, she held a cookie out to him, her eyes full of worry.

He took it from her and brought it to his mouth, his gaze locked on hers. Chewed. Then held it out to her. "It's amazing."

Holly exhaled, the sigh full of relief. She didn't take the cookie from him, just nibbled on it as he held it. A slight smile touched her face, and she relaxed. "Okay, it tastes fine. I think I was just panicking."

"I've got your back," he told her, even though it was a lie, wasn't it? Because if he really had her back, he'd have never sabotaged her in the first place.

Holly headed into the party with a bright smile on her face, though her nerves were still a little shot. Becca greeted her with excitement, thrilled at the cookies. She hugged Holly twice, beaming, and her daughter, Libby, insisted on trying every single cookie.

Everything was fine. Holly didn't need to worry. Just because she'd messed up once didn't mean that she was a terrible baker. Adam had calmed her nerves, walked her back from the panic she was feeling. She was so darn grateful to him. For a man that didn't want to have a girlfriend, he was already her best date ever.

He looked amazing, she decided, glancing across the room at him after the last of the cookies were laid out and Becca had handed her an envelope. He stood half a head taller than most everyone in the room, and the tuxedo made him look sharp and elegant. Classy. Which was ironic, given that he had a mouth as salty as her own and was at home on the ranch. It was a good thing they'd made it clear that it wasn't a date, because if it was, she'd be preening over how handsome her man was. Oh well. Holly was used to disappointment when it came to dating. It never seemed to work out, and this was just another example of such things.

Not that they had dated. They were enemies. Coworkers forced to endure one another through the holidays.

She turned and glanced around the party. All the faces here were familiar. There were Cass and Eli, who worked at a nearby ranch. Annie and Dustin, her husband. Annie's arms were full of her daughter, Morgan, her belly big with her next one. There was Amy, a local schoolteacher, who was dating Caleb, one of Hank's brothers. There was old Clyde and his wife, Hannah, who ran the town's only hotel. In a town like this, she knew everyone because they all came by the restaurant. She knew who was a good tipper, who was down on his luck, and who had food allergies.

It was like a big family. No wonder she couldn't get a date, she thought with amusement. You didn't date family.

Her gaze landed on Geraldine and her uncle Jonathan, who owned the town's bakery. Hot humiliation flooded through her. Oh god. If they found out she'd made the cookies for the party, they were bound to make a crack or two about it. They'd tell everyone in the room, and then she'd have to endure the teasing and jokes and . . . she didn't think she could.

Holly turned away in a panic, looking for someone to attack with a distracting conversation . . . or just a way to run out of the room. Instead, she saw Adam approaching with a plastic cup in his hand.

"You okay? You look like you saw an ex-boyfriend." Adam arched an eyebrow at her.

Man, did he have to look so damn dashing? She liked seeing him in his regular baseball cap and flannels, but for some reason, with his hair combed into exacting detail like this and his ears sticking out slightly, she couldn't take her eyes off him. "Not an ex," she murmured, moving closer to him. No one would care if she talked to her date, after all. "The owner of the bakery here in town. She's going to call me out on how shitty my cake was at the contest last week."

"If she says anything, I'll provide a distraction," he whispered, leaning in. "How do you feel about me setting the tablecloth on fire?"

She gave a horrified giggle. "I'd hate it, because I worked too hard on those cookies."

"Fair." He pretended to consider his surroundings. "Since we're at a salon, could I fake a hair emergency?"

Now he was just being ridiculous. She kept laughing. "You don't have enough hair."

Adam moved in, as if whispering a secret. "Perhaps that's the emergency."

Holly giggled harder, her hands on the tight bodice of her dress. "Stop, you'll make me split my seams."

"A better emergency than mine," he admitted, giving her that curled-edge, slow smile. He held the cup out to her. "This is for you."

"What is it?"

"Alcoholic eggnog. I'm told it's pretty good."

She paused. "Oh, but I volunteered to be the designated driver since I made you come here and all."

He shook his head and nudged the cup toward her again. "And I've decided that since you took care of me while I was sick, you deserve a night to unwind. I think you should enjoy yourself. I'll handle the driving."

For a nemesis, that was awfully sweet of him. She took the cup and tasted it, and lord, that was divine. She'd never been much of a drinker despite working in a restaurant-slash-tavern. There was just too much to get done every day. But the thought of kicking back and having a few drinks at the party was wonderfully appealing, and she took a larger sip and then smiled up at him.

Adam slung a casual arm over her shoulders, talking in that low voice again so only she could hear. "You might have told me about the dress code for this party."

She chuckled into her cup. It was kinda nice to have his arm around her shoulders, even if it was all for show. "I didn't think you'd show up in black tie. Most guys that live here don't own anything dressier than a clean shirt."

"Then it shows you don't know much about me, do you?" A sly grin curved his mouth. "I'll have you know I have two clean shirts."

Holly sputtered with laughter, nearly spraying eggnog all over the place. She put a hand to her lips, fighting back more laughter. Maybe it was the alcohol, or maybe it was Adam's teasing, but she was suddenly having a lot of fun. "Thank you for coming to this with me," she told him again. "I'm so glad I don't have to stand in a corner by myself."

He cocked his head, glancing down at her. "Why would you be in the corner?"

"Because everyone in this town is married?"

"I'm not."

With a tip of the cup, Holly finished her eggnog and held the empty container out to him. "Yes, but you're also my nemesis, you're divorced, and you've sworn off women, remember?"

"I vaguely remember a few of those," he murmured. "Vaguely." He took the cup from her hand. "A refill?"

"Yes, please." It didn't matter that her date was her enemy and they were just on a truce. She was going to get sloppy drunk and have a grand time, all because she could.

CHAPTER SEVENTEEN

For a woman that worked in a bar, Holly was absolutely a lightweight when it came to her alcohol. By the time she'd downed her second cup of eggnog, her eyes were sparkling and her cheeks were flushed, and she laughed at everything.

Absolutely everything.

Personally, Adam found it charming, and he wasn't the only one. People were casting fond looks in Holly's direction as she approached someone eating a cookie and watched them carefully, as if waiting to be judged on each bite. He couldn't help but notice that a few more people had filed into the party and the place was now wall to wall. A few of the ranch hands from outlying ranches had arrived and he saw a couple of unfamiliar men eyeing his date as she crossed the floor to go drunkenly foist a cookie on someone else.

It was hard not to stare at Holly. She was the most beautiful thing in the room, and he couldn't take his eyes off her. He also felt incredibly protective, and when one of the cowboys started to head in her direction, Adam took her by the arm and gently steered her toward the dance floor, where a few couples were squeezed in and slow dancing near the refreshments.

"Oooh, are we dancing now?" Holly asked, gazing up at him. "I never get to dance."

"Did you want to dance?" He hadn't intended on it, but he couldn't exactly back away now. Not when she was looking at him with such drunken excitement. Normally if a date got smashed, Adam just got annoyed. For some reason, though, on Holly, it was cute. It made him feel protective of her, and he was amused by her antics instead of irked. So he lifted her arm high and twirled her on the floor, her skirts flaring, and she laughed with sheer delight.

He danced with her for as long as she wanted . . . which was about two songs. And then she saw someone eat a cookie, and off she went again. Adam kept close by, a hand on her back, just because he'd promised he'd look after her if she got drunk. He knew he wasn't being completely unselfish, either, as he glared at any man that dared to look at her a little too hard. For some reason, she felt like his, and he didn't like the thought of anyone encroaching on his territory.

"Come on, Adam," Holly said as "Have Yourself a Merry Little Christmas" began to play. "Time to dance!"

"To this?" he asked. The song was slow and somber, Frank Sinatra's voice easily recognizable but not exactly spurring him to dance.

Holly was oblivious. She dragged him over to the designated "dance floor" and then plastered herself to his chest, her cheek resting against his heart. He hesitated for only a moment before taking her in his arms. All around them, people were staring, most with smiles on their faces. He didn't want her to embarrass herself, though. Monday morning regrets were the worst. So he brushed her hair back from her face gently. "You want to drink some water?"

"No. I feel good." She closed her eyes and snuggled up against him. "You're a great dance partner."

He was barely swaying. Barely swaying and yet somehow . . . she felt perfect in his arms. "The bar must be set pretty low."

"On the floor," she agreed.

All of a sudden, she straightened, her gaze locked on something on the ceiling. She grabbed his arms and steered him toward the middle of the room, and he looked up just in time to see mistletoe above his head.

Holly gazed up at him. "Well, now we have to kiss. Christmas rules."

He was pretty sure that was the alcohol talking. She'd sober up and not want anything to do with him—and be incredibly embarrassed that she'd offered. Even if he got all tied up in knots just thinking about it, this lust he felt was purely one-sided and not going to go anywhere. "I'm not sure that's such a good idea—"

"You think too much," Holly declared, sliding a hand to the back of his neck and then dragging him down to press her mouth on his.

Someone catcalled. He ignored it. She did, too. Instead, he was utterly attuned to the softness of her mouth against his. She felt perfect in his arms, like she'd been made for him. Her mouth was sweet, with just a hint of alcohol and eggnog on her breath. And because he was weak when it came to her, Adam held her close and stroked his tongue into her mouth.

She moaned against him, loud and needy.

He froze in place, pulling away. They were still standing in the middle of the dance floor at the crowded party. No doubt several people had heard that sound, and even though it was making his balls ache, he didn't want her to humiliate herself by making out with him while she was drunk. As much as he wanted to clench her against him and kiss the hell out of her, it wouldn't be right.

So he just kissed the tip of her nose and let her go. "I'll get you another drink."

Holly looked up at him, utterly befuddled. Her fingers went to his mouth and she swiped at his lips. "You're wearing my lipstick."

Was he? He rubbed at his mouth and noticed that she had smeared her lips, too. Adam cupped her chin and ran his thumb gently along her lip, smoothing it away. "There. Now you're perfect again."

"Am I perfect?" she breathed, gazing up at him.

Did it matter what he answered? She probably wouldn't remember in the morning, so he could confess whatever he wanted. "You are to me," he told her softly.

Then he stepped away to get her another drink, because if he stuck around and she kept gazing up at him like that, he'd kiss her again. And again. And again.

He was having a hard time remembering why that was a bad idea.

Holly woke up the next morning with a dry mouth and a throbbing headache. She rolled onto her back, squinting up at the sunlight streaming through the blinds. At her side, Pumpkin whined and licked her face, her tiny tail thumping. The little dog had to use the bathroom, but Holly was having difficulty getting out of bed.

Her head felt heavy, and her tongue tasted like ass. She smacked her lips, grimacing, and felt at the thing poking into the side of her head against the pillow. It was her hair bow, and she realized she was still in her party dress from last night, now impossibly wrinkled. She sat up slowly, just in case she was hungover, but it really wasn't too bad. She had vague memories of Adam holding her up as they walked into the kitchen, then sitting her on the counter and feeding her pieces of bread and a glass of water.

She remembered dancing with Adam, and how he'd smelled like spicy aftershave and she'd loved it. She remembered being silly and Adam following her around, a faint smile on his face as he got refill after refill for her. Just like he'd promised, he'd taken good care of her last night, hovering at her side and making sure no one bothered her, and she'd had a wonderful time.

She'd also drunkenly called Polly on FaceTime and tried to get Adam to kiss her again on-screen so she could "show her sister." With a groan, Holly buried her face in her hands. Okay, so she'd embarrassed herself a little. He'd made it quite clear that he wasn't interested but she'd been so drunk and wildly attracted to him that she'd gone and kissed him several times last night. She'd found mistletoe and dragged him under it. They'd sat together when the gift exchange happened and Holly had migrated into his lap, sitting on his knee and pressing kisses to his temple.

Clearly, she was a handsy sort of drunk.

To give Adam credit, he'd shut her down nicely each time. He hadn't taken advantage of her drunkenness. Instead, he'd done just as he'd promised—he'd kept her safe so she could enjoy herself.

Oh, she'd enjoyed herself all right. She wrinkled her nose as she got out of bed, thinking about all the times she'd hovered over someone as they ate one of her cookies, and how she'd demanded to know if they'd liked it or not. God, she'd been annoying.

She owed Adam an apology, for starters . . . and then probably the rest of the town, too, for acting like a fool.

"Come on, Pumpkin," Holly said, putting on her slippers. She paused by the bathroom and swished her mouth out with mouthwash, just because she couldn't stand the taste of it any longer. "Let's get you walked."

When she headed down the stairs, though, she heard a noise in the kitchen. It sounded like dishes clanking, and curious, Holly tiptoed in. Adam was at the stove, holding a frying pan. His baseball cap was on and he was dressed for working outside, in flannel and his cowboy boots. He glanced over at her and grinned at the sight of Holly. "Morning."

"Morning." She rubbed her arms, confused. "Are you . . . cooking?"

"Yup. Badly." He cast her a cocky grin over his shoulder. "Hope you like your eggs burnt and your bacon crispy."

Holly padded over to his side, peering at the food in the skillet. Contrary to what he said, the eggs looked great. "Why are you making breakfast for me?"

"I figured since I made you get drunk, the least I could do was make you food."

"You didn't make me do anything." She nudged him with her elbow. "And I'll be right back. I need to walk the dog."

"You go ahead. I'll keep a plate hot for you." He scraped at the eggs with a spatula as she turned away, and Holly headed outside with Pumpkin, who dove into the snow and then picked her tiny feet up with disdain as she looked for the perfect spot to do her business.

She stood on the step, shivering on the porch in the early morning light. As she did, Holly thought about the man inside who was making her breakfast. He'd obviously been up for a while, and she suspected he was already working. That meant he would have had to come back to the house deliberately to make her food.

That was . . . sweet. Baffling, but sweet. It made her even more embarrassed that she'd mauled him last night. The breakfast was surely an apology, a kind of let-bygones-be-bygones moment. She'd taken care of him while he was sick, so he was doing the same for her.

They were on equal footing now, really.

It made her feel better. Sort of.

It also filled her with a curious sense of disappointment. She'd been drunk, so her memory was foggy, but from what she recalled, he'd felt good against her. His mouth had been that exquisite combination of both firm and kissable, and she'd wanted more.

Heck, she'd woken up this morning wanting more, and that bothered her. He was a jerk. Sometimes. He was rude and obnoxious. Not always, but he could be. He was absolutely the last person in the world she should have wanted to kiss . . .

And yet here she was, a little sad this morning that he'd been the perfect gentleman and hadn't stolen a few more kisses. Lord knew she'd thrown herself at him enough.

When Pumpkin had finished her business, Holly supposed she couldn't delay the inevitable any longer. She scooped up the wet little dog in a towel the moment she got into the entryway and rubbed the worst of the cold from her fur as she headed back toward the kitchen. Adam was still there, seated at the kitchen island with two plates of food ready and a cup of coffee in his hand.

He was looking at his phone but put it down the moment she came inside. "Did you know Carson's a texter?"

That brought a smile to her face. "Actually, yeah. The first day I started here, he texted me and told me to let him know if I needed anything." She headed to the pantry, opened a can of dog food for Pumpkin, and set it out before washing her hands and joining him at the table. "He's very sweet and caring. I think he has a daughter about my age. I think that's why he's always checking up on me."

Adam just shook his head, taking another sip of his coffee. "I think it took the man three months to say five words to me when I first started here. Now I'm getting upwards of ten texts a day about nothing in particular. He even sent me a picture of the sunset over in Malibu."

Holly picked up a fork. "He's just looking after you. He's more of a mother hen than he likes to let on." She fiddled with a bit of egg, unable to look him in the eye. "Thanks, by the way."

"For?" He took a hearty bite of food, apparently unbothered by their role reversal.

"Breakfast? Being my date last night? Letting me get sloppy drunk and not taking advantage?" She waved her fork at the breakfast in front of them. "Doing my job while I slept off a hangover?"

His expression changed to one of concern. "Are you hungover? Do you need some aspirin?"

Holly resisted the urge to poke him with her fork. "I'm the one that's supposed to be taking care of you in this gig, remember?"

To her surprise, Adam rolled his eyes. "Don't start. You know you've been doing a great job."

The praise pleased her, especially because it was unexpected. "Even during peanut butter and jelly week?"

"I'd forgotten all about that," he admitted. "Okay, you're doing a good job this week. We won't talk about last week."

She smiled and ate a few bites of her breakfast. He was tearing through his, so she ended up pushing the rest of her bacon toward him. "Any ideas on what you want for dinner?"

"Don't care. Hot food. That's the only requirement. Bit cold out today."

"It is." Holly picked at her food. It wasn't that it tasted bad; she just couldn't focus on eating. Not when she was wondering if he was horrified that she'd kissed him. She needed to apologize . . . she just had to find the right moment. Once they were done eating, she cleared their plates and turned to look at him.

They stared at each other. No one spoke.

Tension prickled on the back of Holly's neck. "I . . ."

"Yeah?" He watched her with intent, dark eyes.

The apology died in her throat. "I work tonight," she offered. "So I'll leave dinner in the fridge for you with instructions."

Adam's mouth flexed. He took a step toward her, then leaned on the counter. They stood a few paces apart, and yet Holly felt strangely trapped. "That's fine. Anything else?"

Yes, she wanted to say.

No, she wanted to scream.

Holly licked her lips. Time to stop being such a chicken. She took a deep breath and then put on her best smile. "I wanted to say I'm sorry. For last night."

Under the brim of his baseball cap, she could have sworn his brows furrowed, just a little. "Sorry? For what?"

Okay, now her face was getting hot. "For being all over you when you clearly weren't interested." She crossed her arms over her chest, feeling vulnerable and just a hint stupid. "I'm sure I was an absolute nightmare, but you were very kind about it and—"

He took a step forward and pulled his cap off, then set it down. Then Adam took another step forward and braced his hands on the counter she was leaning against, trapping her between his arms. "You were drunk. That doesn't mean I wasn't interested."

Her gaze flicked to his mouth, as full and appealing this morning as it was last night. Oh god, why did she want to kiss him again when she was sober? Was she out of her damn mind? "You . . . We went as friends. You didn't like them—my kisses. And I just—"

"You were drunk," Adam said softly, his gaze locked on hers. "I would never take advantage of a drunk woman, not even if she kissed me. But that doesn't mean that I wasn't interested." He stated it again, cool and calm, as if he were reciting facts.

Goose bumps prickled all over her skin. "O-oh?"

He leaned forward, and sweet lord have mercy, she realized he was going to kiss her again. His mouth lowered toward hers and then he paused, his gaze flicking over her face. "You want me to stop, Holly?" His breath was warm against her cheek and smelled like coffee and sugar. "Say the word."

She was practically panting. "No, I don't want you to stop—"

She couldn't even finish her statement before his mouth was on hers. The kiss was different than last night, she realized. This time, he was kissing her with enthusiasm. His tongue slicked into her mouth, surging against hers in a wicked claim. Holly moaned against him, her hands curling against his shirt as he plundered her mouth, turning her world upside down.

The kiss was over far too soon. He pulled away and gave her a heated look. "What time do you get off work tonight?"

he asked, leaning in. His nose nudged against hers in a gentle brush of skin, and it made her nipples prick in response. "Or do I get you all night?"

Holly blinked, dazed. "I . . . work until eleven thirty or so. We close at ten and then I need to clean up and make dough . . ." She stared at his mouth again.

He moved forward, and instead of kissing her, he just nipped at her lower lip with his teeth. It was the lightest scrape, followed by a lick of his tongue, and lord, she felt her body pulsing in response. "I'll wait for you for dinner. See you tonight."

Then Adam turned and headed out of the kitchen, leaving her weak-kneed and utterly distracted.

CHAPTER EIGHTEEN

Holly thought about that kiss all day.

She was pretty sure it wasn't a good idea. She and Adam bickered more than they got along. He'd quite explicitly said he wasn't looking for a relationship. She knew all that and she still wanted to kiss him again anyhow. The kiss had felt . . . really good. It had felt utterly wonderful, and the way he'd caged her against the counter had made her heart race.

She was attracted to him, if she admitted the truth to herself. Adam was all the things she liked in a guy—handsome, athletic, sharp-witted, and protective. If that sharp wit was sometimes turned against her, well, that could be a problem.

It wasn't as if she had to marry him, though.

He wasn't looking for anything permanent, and really, was she? Holly had too many balls in the air. She rarely had free time to herself, and when she did, she spent it baking or trying to hustle up a few extra dollars to send to Polly.

She worked six days a week, scoring extra shifts as often as possible. She barely had time for herself, much less a relationship.

And she was an adult.

As an adult, if she wanted a no-strings-attached sort of fling, she could absolutely have one, couldn't she? No one needed to know. Carson was gone. Sage and Jason would be out of town for a few more weeks. Polly wasn't coming home for the holidays.

The only one around was Adam.

Really, she was allowed a little bit of fun, she reasoned. She worked hard. Wasn't the saying that you should play hard, too? Maybe she'd "play" with Adam a little. The thought gave her goose bumps.

Work was slow, which she normally hated. Slow meant less tips. But Holly was distracted anyhow, so she didn't mind if less people came in. It was the time of year that people skipped going out to lunch or dinner and saved the money for Christmas gifts. Idly, Holly wondered if she should buy something for Carson for his return . . . or for Adam.

Okay, she was mostly thinking about Adam.

Everyone else in her life was getting baking. Sage and Jason and their family would get their favorite cookies. Becca, Wade, and everyone else would also be getting a large tin of Christmas cookies, all in their favorite flavors and cut into festive shapes. She'd already sent an entire fleet of cookies up to Polly. But if she got something for Adam, would he read more into it than she wanted? Would it irritate him? She was already baking for him, so making his favorite cookies wouldn't seem like a present, and she wasn't the type to knit a scarf or anything. You had to sit for more than five minutes at a time for knitting, and Holly was constantly on the go.

No present, she decided. After all, they were going to do casual. If they never kissed again, fine.

Well, not *really* fine. She'd be irked at his hot-and-cold nature, but she'd get over it.

On her lunch break, instead of heading back to the ranch, she sat in the back room of the restaurant. It was a cowardly move, of course. If she went back, she might run into Adam. What if he was waiting for her to show up so he could explain that the kiss had been a huge mistake and it'd never happen again? That they should just go back to being enemies on a truce or whatever it was that they were at this point.

So she pretended to be super into her phone as she ate a sandwich. She poked at a game she never played, scrolled through an Instagram account she never updated, and eventually gave up and texted her sister.

HOLLY: Hey there, you in class?

POLLY: No! I'm actually on break! Perfect timing, because I was just about to text you.

That made Holly smile, because it was her sister's favorite excuse. Polly was always "just about to text." Holly knew her sister was busy and the day got away from her. As long as Polly was happy, that was all that mattered, even if they didn't communicate as often as Holly would have liked.

HOLLY: No worries, how's class this week?

POLLY: UGHHHH

HOLLY: That good, huh?

POLLY: Let's just say that I'm not confident on my finals.

POLLY: But let's not talk about me. Let's talk about that cute guy you kept trying to get on the video call on Friday night!!! Who was that?

HOLLY: That was my nemesis, Adam. I think I've told you about him? Mr. I Tip a Dollar?

POLLY: Him???? Seriously?

HOLLY: Yeah. He works at the ranch that I'm house-keeping & cooking for.

POLLY: He wasn't acting very nemesis-like.

POLLY: He looked like he wanted to kiss you. Are you guys a thing?

HOLLY: No, I was just drunk and he was being polite. That's it, I swear.

POLLY: Uh huh. I've been drunk before and no one looked at me like that.

HOLLY: Wait, when was this?

POLLY: What? I'm not going to a puritan school, sis. They party here.

POLLY: I promise my grades aren't slipping, though.

POLLY: Don't try to change the subject. For an enemy, you guys looked cozy. I'm just saying. ☺

POLLY: I give you my blessing.

HOLLY: Your blessing?!?

POLLY: Sure. You deserve some happiness. You're so busy taking care of everyone else you never take care of yourself. GET SOME.

POLLY: I gotta run but if you get a chance send some more cookies BYE LOVE YOU!

Dear lord. She couldn't believe that her nerdy, scientific sister had just texted and told her to "get some." Funny how Polly had turned into the party animal and Holly . . . well, Holly was on her way to being that old, crotchety woman that shook her cane at the kids that drove too fast. She wasn't much fun, was she?

Maybe it was time to fix that.

* * *

For Adam, it was a long damn day.

He hadn't minded when Jason and Sage decided to head out of town. He and Carson could hold down the fort, so to speak. As long as there were no emergencies, it was an amount of work that two men could handle, given that it wasn't calving season.

But with Carson gone, he'd underestimated just how much there was to do. He'd started the morning chasing the cattle back into the nearest pasture. They'd leaned on one of the outlying fences until it had fallen over, and then they'd wandered over it, grazing. With Hannibal's help, he'd managed to herd them all back in, but then he'd had to stop and repair the fence. There was feed to be given out. Sick animals to check on. Horses to be tended to. Stalls to be mucked. More feed.

And that was on top of his regular laundry list of chores.

He was still hard at work by the time the sun set and it was dark. The cattle were settled in, all heads counted, and given their last round of hay. Tomorrow, he needed to take inventory on both feed and hay to ensure that they were set, and pull out fresh bales of straw for the horses' stalls.

But that was tomorrow, and he'd think about it then.

He'd been so busy that he hadn't had time to obsess over the fact that he'd kissed Holly that morning. It was only when he dragged himself in from the barn and headed to his cabin that he remembered that he hadn't eaten lunch . . . or dinner.

And that he was supposed to be with her for a midnight dinner. He lifted an arm and smelled himself. Okay, he needed a shower first. He put down some food for Hannibal, who'd helped him move reluctant cattle all afternoon long. "Good boy. Get ready for round two tomorrow."

Adam showered and barely had time to comb his hair back from his face and put on fresh clothing before he glanced at the time. Damn, it was late. And he had to be up before dawn to get moving. The lack of sleep was going to catch up with him . . . eventually. For tonight, though, he didn't care.

Shoving on a pair of snow boots, he yawned as he headed for the main house.

It was quiet as he walked in, and his stomach growled. Adam told himself that it was likely past her bedtime. If she was too tired for dinner, they'd have it some other time. He was exhausted, and she probably was, too. She seemed to work every day of the week, and—

When he turned the corner, Holly was seated on a stool in the kitchen, two plates set out on the bar. She was still wearing her waitressing outfit, her hair pulled up into the tight ponytail and bow, and she sat up a bit straighter when he walked in.

The smile she gave him was bright and nervous. "Hungry?"

She'd been waiting for him. It sent a hot lick of pleasure through his gut to realize that.

Adam took a couple of steps forward and realized the closer he got to her, the more tired she looked. It seemed he wasn't the only one who'd had a long, hard day. Even that perky ponytail of hers was slightly wilted, as if collapsing in exhaustion. She'd set a pretty table for the two of them, but a hard stool didn't look like the most comfortable of spots.

So he picked up the plate she'd left for him and gestured at the living room. "You want to go sit on one of Sage's couches and relax while we eat?"

She bit her lip and picked up her plate, too. "I won't tell if you won't."

They settled in on the plush couches, using one of the

heavy wooden coffee tables to hold their plates. The food—meat loaf and mashed potatoes—was delicious, and he devoured his quickly. She picked at her smaller portion, taking dainty bites, and seemed less enthusiastic about the meal.

"You okay?" he asked.

Holly glanced over at him, a slow smile on her face. "Just tired. For some reason it really hit me today and I'm dragging. When I'm like this, it's hard to muster the energy to eat . . . unless it's sweets. I always have room for sweets." She gave him a wry smile. "Basically I have the appetite of a toddler."

He laughed. "So go get some sweets. I'm sure you have some hanging around the house."

"I actually made a cake yesterday. You want some?"

Adam patted his stomach. "Always."

The cake she'd made that day turned out to be a chocolate pudding cake that was absolute decadence in his mouth. "I'm glad it came out okay. I wasn't sure how the pudding would cook, but I'm happy with it." Holly beamed at him, licking the last bit of frosting off her fork. "You liked it?"

Did he like it? "It's amazing. I'm honestly surprised someone hasn't held you hostage and forced you to bake for them. This stuff's dangerous."

Her face fell. "You'd think that, but I can't seem to perform under pressure."

Shit. Now he was thinking about that cake he'd sabotaged. His mouth glued shut and he thought about confessing, but she looked so damn sad and tired that it felt like a dick move. He could tell her some other time, when it didn't feel like taking potshots at someone that was already heartsore. "I think that's bullshit. You're good. If I was a wealthy millionaire, I'd hire you to make me cake every day."

She laughed. "I would love to do nothing but make cakes for grumpy cowboys all day long instead of standing on my feet at the restaurant."

"Your feet hurt?"

Holly made a face. "Like you wouldn't believe."

Well now, that sounded like an opportunity. He tapped her leg and leaned back on the sofa. "Gimme your foot."

Her eyes narrowed and she gave him a curious glance, but she did as he requested. "Is this a foot massage or a trick?"

"It is absolutely a foot massage," Adam told her. "Why would it be a trick?"

"Because we're enemies?"

He pulled off her sneaker and studied her sock-covered foot. It was small and dainty against his hand, and kinda cute. He wasn't normally a foot sort of guy but he liked hers. He rubbed the arch of her foot and then pressed his thumb under her sole.

Holly's head tilted back, her eyes fluttering closed. "Okay, in this fictional world, if I'm making cakes for cranky cowboys, I'm going to hire you to give me a foot massage every night."

Amused, he kept rubbing. It had been a long time since he'd rubbed a woman's feet and he was rather enjoying her reaction. "This is a very strange world you're suggesting."

"Mmm. That's why I said it's fiction." Her lips curved in a smile. "Besides, I'm sure you're probably good for more than just a foot rub."

"I do a mean back rub, too."

She put a hand to her brow. "Ooh, don't tempt me."

Adam kept rubbing her small foot, content to watch her face. Her eyes were closed as she sprawled on the couch, perched atop several of the throw cushions. Holly looked blissful, and when he rubbed a certain spot or two, he was rewarded with a flicker of pleasure over her face that made lust prick through him. He wasn't massaging her feet to get into bed with her, though. He was . . . Well, shit, why was he rubbing her feet? He had to think about that one. Did he want to get into Holly's bed? Yes, he did, he realized after a moment of self-reflection. But right now, he was more interested in just making her feel good.

She lifted her other foot and extended it his way, and he took the silent cue and switched feet, rubbing it as well. "Better?"

"Much." She sighed deeply, opening her eyes to glance over at him. Her gaze was hooded, and damn if that wasn't sexy. "Do I need to do you next? Is that the trick?"

For some reason, that irked him. That was the second time she'd suggested this was a trick. "Why do you keep thinking there's some sort of trick to this?"

She shrugged. "Because we're enemies?"

He flexed his hand over her foot, rubbing. Her lips parted and it took everything he had not to fling himself on top of Holly and just kiss the daylights out of her. "Is that what we are, then? You still think of me as your enemy?"

"Hard to think of anything during this," Holly admitted, breathless. "But no, I'm not entirely sure what we are. What do you call enemies that kiss?"

So . . . she was thinking about that kiss, too? He set her foot down, then took her hand and pulled her until she was sitting up . . . and tucked right against his side. "You don't call them enemies," he murmured, sliding an arm around her waist.

"No?" Her gaze was soft, sliding to his mouth, and her lips parted again. "What do you call them?"

He didn't know. "I guess 'enemies with benefits' wouldn't make much sense."

"No point in benefiting your enemy," she agreed. Holly slid a hand to the nape of his neck and toyed with the shorn hair there, running her fingers over the stubble. "We must be something else."

"Friends?" he suggested, and boldly tugged her forward. The movement pulled her into his lap, forcing her to straddle him.

She sucked in a breath, both of her arms going around his neck. The look in her eyes was soft with arousal, her lips parted, and the need between them hung in the air. "You kiss all your friends?" she whispered. "Because I sure don't."

He slid a hand along her waist, dragging her even closer to him. He could feel the gentle fan of her breath against his skin, but neither one of them had crossed the gap. Adam planned on kissing her again. Oh yeah, he was going to kiss that pretty mouth over and over again. But he was enjoying himself far too much at the moment to rush things. "I don't much kiss anyone," he murmured. "But I kissed you this morning. So I'm trying to figure out if I like making out with my enemies or if you're a little something . . . special."

Her nails grazed the sensitive skin on the back of his neck. "Which one do you think it is?" She shifted on his lap, her weight pressing down directly over his cock, and damn if that didn't feel incredible. "I've been calling you my nemesis all this time. Should I be calling you something else?"

"You could call me by my name."

The moment the words were out, he regretted them. Adam felt like an idiot when the surprised expression crossed her face. It was too late to take it back, though.

And in the next moment, he didn't want to.

"Adam," Holly breathed. His cock jumped at the word,

and he wanted her to say it again. Just like that. He didn't have to wait long. She leaned in, her lips an inch from his. "Adam."

"Holly." His hand slid to her ass, unable to resist the temptation of it. God, she felt good, too. Her butt looked nice in jeans, but touching it made him realize just how soft and rounded it was. How perfect. She fit against him perfectly, perched atop his lap, like she was meant to be in his arms.

Her gaze darted from his eyes to his mouth. "What are we doing?"

"I'm kissing my enemy," he murmured, and closed the distance between them. His lips met hers, and he felt her suck in a breath. Their first kiss was openmouthed and just a little awkward, as if neither of them had quite realized the other was going to go through with it. But kissing Holly had suddenly become very important to him, and so he kissed her again, taking his time with her soft mouth.

She made a soft, whimpering sound in her throat.

It only stoked the fire inside him. With a groan, he put a hand to the back of her neck and held her against him, their mouths meeting again for kiss after kiss. Each one felt like a light, playful press of lips, a quick tasting of the other person. It wasn't enough for him, though. He needed more of her.

The problem was that kissing Holly once or twice was never going to be enough. He was realizing that now. Everything about her was perfect—from the taste of her as her tongue dipped into his mouth to the way she reacted. The way she felt in his arms. The way she boldly kissed him back, as if she was just as hungry for him as he was for her. Kissing Holly was going to be an obsession with him—he could tell already.

The way her sweet little tongue flicked against his was magic. The way she yielded when he took control of the kiss. The soft noises of pleasure she made, as if she couldn't believe that she liked the kiss so much. All of it drove him absolutely wild.

And tonight was only the beginning, he decided.

Adam pulled away reluctantly, gazing up at her. Her eyes were soft and dazed, her mouth full and pink from their kissing. The temptation to kiss her again in that moment was overwhelming, but he knew if he sampled the pleasure of her mouth again, he wouldn't be able to stop. Not tonight.

And he wasn't about to rush things between them. Not when he was enjoying their push-pull relationship so much. So he just smiled up at her. "That was adequate."

It took a moment for his words to register. Then she made a sound of outrage in her throat and swatted at his chest. "Adequate, huh? I'll show you adequate."

"Tomorrow," he told her, and let his voice communicate his promise.

She gave another gaspy half breath. "Tomorrow, then."

CHAPTER NINETEEN

For the next week, Holly's schedule seemed to be the same every day.

Wake up.

Start on her baking and cooking.

Lunch with Adam, followed by an intense kissing session.

Work at the restaurant until close. Go home.

A late, late dinner with Adam, followed by yet another intense kissing session.

Sleep. Rinse and repeat.

It was . . . a lot of fun, too. They had an unspoken agreement of nothing but kissing, it seemed, because neither of them pushed for more. Maybe it was the fact that both of their schedules were intensely busy, and each moment together felt stolen. It was nice, though, to meet up, talk about nothing and everything, and end with a passionate kissing and make-out session.

It was nice to have no expectations of Adam, too. She

knew what she was getting into when she kissed him. She knew it meant nothing at all, that it was just pure fun. And for some reason, that made it ever so slightly naughty and even more fun. It helped that Adam knew how to kiss. He could spend an eternity just nibbling on her lips, caressing her with his mouth, until they were both panting and full of need.

Then they'd just head home for the night. Was it an odd situation? Absolutely. He was swamped with Carson being gone, though, and every time she saw him, he'd just finished an intensely busy day. So why push for anything more? It wasn't as if she was drowning in free time, either. Between the restaurant and running things at the ranch, her day was full.

As each day passed, she began to look forward to their meals—and the kissing—more and more. Holly wasn't sure what would happen when Sage and Jason returned and she was no longer working at the ranch. They'd probably drift apart, she and Adam, and only see each other when he came in to Wade's for a sandwich.

The thought made her sad, because she was growing to really enjoy his company. Not just the intense kissing, but his sharp sense of humor, too. If it was fleeting, though, so be it. She knew what she was getting into. It wasn't going to last, so she was going to enjoy every last minute of it.

CARSON: Did you check the northeast pasture?

CARSON: The fences there were leaning last time I checked, make sure the cattle aren't rubbing up against it.

CARSON: And check on #34. I know she kicks a lot but she wasn't looking so spry when I left.

Adam contemplated his phone and wondered if he could

fling it into the nearest cattle pond. Most of the time, he could keep up with the endless backlog of things that had to be done on the ranch. The most important thing was making sure the cattle were fed and safe. Smaller things could pile up now and then, though he had texted the Watson brothers over at Swinging C and offered to pay them if they'd help him with some of the barn chores. They'd agreed and asked for some of Holly's cookies, which she was thrilled to volunteer.

It was a lot to handle every day, and Carson's daily texts of things to add to Adam's list didn't help. Carson was still in California, of course, but he was determined to armchair quarterback the ranch from afar. Every day, Adam got a text or two from Carson of things to check on, or reminders to change an oil filter on the Gator, the four-wheeler they used for day-to-day work. There were horse blankets to be aired out, pastures to be rotated, food to be switched up if the cattle's dung didn't show enough protein . . . it was a never-ending list.

Adam tried to keep up with it, he really did, but he found himself heading in to the ranch for lunch even when he didn't have the time. And he was staying up late so he could have dinner with Holly after she got off work. The food was always great, but he was lying to himself if he pretended it was for anything other than her kisses. He'd have eaten another week of peanut butter and jelly sandwiches if it meant Holly would sit on his lap every night and kiss him until they were both dazed.

He was becoming addicted to that woman. When he woke up in the morning, he was hard and aching, and he'd jerk off in the shower to thoughts of Holly and her soft mouth. He found himself showing up earlier at the main house, just because he was anxious to see her. Tonight, though, that wouldn't be possible. Two of the cattle in the herd were sick, with thick nasal discharge, and of course it was two of the more ornery ones. Good mothers when they had calves, but annoying as hell the rest of the time. They refused to be separated from the herd, and so it took some time for him and Hannibal to eventually pull them away from the others and get them sequestered in the barn. Once they were there, he went back and spent the next few hours staring at cattle noses to see if any others were showing signs of illness. If he had an entire outbreak in the herd, everything was going to turn upside down.

He had a call into Doc Parson, the local vet, who came by later that night to check on things. The doc was confident that it wasn't a major outbreak, but he gave Adam instructions to keep the sick ones sequestered and if there were more outbreaks, he'd have to give antibiotics to the entire herd.

Adam wasn't much looking forward to that.

By the time the vet left, it was late. The horses still had to be taken care of, though, and Adam began brushing his down, mentally running through the list of chores he still had to accomplish before Holly got in from work, and what he could put off until tomorrow. He was so focused on getting things done that he lost track of time.

"Knock-knock?" came a familiar voice.

Adam looked up to see Holly in the doorway of the barn. She smiled at him and came forward, wearing her long coat and jeans, still in her work uniform. He glanced at his phone for the time. Shit, it was late. "It's been a bit of a day."

"I bet. Everything all right?"

He nodded. "Nothing I can't handle. You might have to eat without me, though. I don't know how long I'll be here.

I need to finish putting down straw and some bedding in these stalls." He'd skipped it yesterday to buy time with her and it was catching up to him.

"Can I help?" Holly shoved her hands in her pockets, moving closer. "I've ridden a horse once. I'm sure I'm an expert now." Her voice was light with teasing.

He wanted to tell her no, but truth was, he was tired, and he'd been looking forward to spending time with her all day—time that was rapidly getting away from him. So Adam paused, thinking. "If you can move those two out of their stalls, I can get work done a bit faster."

"I can do that," she told him brightly, and opened the door to the first stall, reaching for the halter of the big quarter horse. He turned away for a moment, picking up a bag of bedding.

Then he heard a sickening thud.

Adam whirled around, terror knotting in his throat. "Holly?" He couldn't see her head in the stall. He raced forward, tossing down the bedding and rushing to the stall. Sure enough, she was on the ground, covered in hay, her face contorted as she clutched her leg. "What happened?"

"Kicked me," she managed tightly as the horse danced far too close to her, nostrils flaring. "I might not be much help after all." Her voice sounded as if it was on the verge of breaking.

Blood was roaring in his ears. He knew he should chastise her—horses kicked when someone handled them wrong—but he couldn't find it in his heart to yell at her. She was in pain and all he wanted to do was make it go away. He took the halter of the stomping, agitated horse and led it out of the stall, careful to put himself between her and the horse. When it was safely out of the way, he moved back to her side, dropping to his knees. "Where does it hurt?"

"My pride and my leg," she said, trying to smile.

She had her hands tightly clasped over one calf, and blood pounded in his ears. She could have a broken bone, a shattered leg. Horse kicks were dangerous. He should have known better than to ask her to help. Holly was a waitress, not a rancher. Just because she thought she could handle herself didn't mean she could.

Adam ran a hand down his face. "Do you think you can stand? Should I call an ambulance?"

"I'm okay," she promised him, trying to smile. "Just feeling stupid."

He helped her get to her feet, and to his relief, she could stand. She grimaced with pain when she put weight on her leg, so he looped an arm around her waist and put another behind her knees, bridal-carrying her out of the barn.

Holly whimpered a small protest. "Really, I'm fine."

Adam ignored that. Hannibal raced around them in dizzying circles, no doubt thinking they were playing a game. He carried her to the house, pausing only at the door so he could let them in, and then carried her over the threshold and set her gently on one of the couches in the living room. The house smelled like warm vanilla and fried chicken and his stomach growled. He ignored it, too.

Nothing mattered until he was sure Holly was all right.

He gently laid her legs out on the sofa, running a hand over her jeans as she shrugged off her coat. "I'm going to take your shoes off."

"It's really all right, Adam—"

She went silent at the look he shot her.

Adam carefully sat at the end of the sofa, propping one of her sneakers up on his leg. He undid the laces and eased it off, caressing her ankle and running his fingers up the leg of her jeans as far as he could, looking for broken skin.

He'd seen some nasty horse kicks in his day. Hell, all he could think about was the time his older brother had gotten kicked so hard it split the skin and he'd had to have ten stitches. Inwardly, he wondered where the closest hospital was, in case he had to take Holly there. Casper? Sheridan?

Holly hissed with pain as his fingers grazed the swell of her calf. That did it. He set her legs down—carefully, so carefully—onto the sofa and then began to unbutton her jeans. "We're getting these off of you. I need to see what your leg looks like."

She didn't protest. All she did was whimper and lifted her hips so he could slide the denim down her body. A moment later, he had the jeans off her and ran his hand over one soft, far-too-fragile calf. A bruise was darkening on the side. He kept stroking her leg and her knee, making sure that she didn't flinch with pain as he touched her. Other than the bruise on the meat of her calf, everything seemed to be intact. No swelling, no breaks.

He felt like he could breathe again. Jesus. "You're lucky. I think it was just a warning kick."

"So lucky," she said sarcastically, putting a hand over her eyes. "I feel stupid. I'm sorry. I was trying to help."

"Your heart was in the right place, even if the rest of you clearly wasn't." He rubbed her good leg absently. "I have to go finish in the barn. Stay here?"

She nodded, eyes closing.

He practically raced out of the house, aware of the loose horse and everything he still had to get done. He had to take care of the barn, and yet . . . he needed to tend to Holly. To his relief, when he returned to the barn, the horse was standing nearby, nosing at an empty feed pouch. He put him in a fresh stall, and then quickly got to work.

An hour later, he returned to the house. It had taken

forever to finish up, and he worried Holly would have disobeyed and put pressure on her leg while he was gone. When he entered the house, wiping his freshly-washed hands clean, he was relieved to see that she was in the same spot he'd left her, eyes closed and curled up on the couch. "How's it feel? Can I get you anything?"

"I should be asking you that," Holly confessed. She sat up, wincing at her leg. "You want me to make you something for dinner?"

He frowned. "You don't need to take care of me."

"That's literally my job." She stood up. "You—"

As was their custom, he pulled her into his lap like he did every night. He did it without thinking, mostly because he wanted her off that leg and to take care of herself. Of course, once she settled in against him, his arms were full of gorgeous, sexy Holly in nothing but her panties and T-shirt.

Holly seemed to realize it at the same time he did. "Oh," she breathed, her hands sliding to his shoulders. "Adam, I should get up."

"I kinda like you where you are," he murmured, his hand stroking up and down her back. "Just don't let me bump that leg of yours. In fact, I should probably get up and get you some cream for it."

"I kinda like you where you are," Holly retorted, wiggling on his lap. She moved in just a little closer, her mouth hovering near his. "Though you're probably hungry."

"Ravenous," he agreed, and leaned in to kiss her lightly. "Utterly, completely, ravenous." He punctuated each word with a kiss. "Starving."

Holly made a soft noise in her throat, her hands sliding to his thick flannel shirt. To his surprise, she slipped her fingers underneath the material, grazing his skin. "I want to touch you tonight," she told him between hot, fierce kisses. Her mouth pressed against his with ferocious need. "Or is that too much to ask of my enemy?"

He groaned, cupping her face in his hands. She felt so dainty against him, her jaw small and fragile as he cradled it with his much larger palms. "Only if I get to touch you. I'll avoid the leg, though." He nipped at her lower lip. "Promise."

"I know you will." She flicked her tongue lightly against his open mouth in a flirty gesture. "You'll make me feel good. You always do."

It made him want to puff up with pride, that simple statement. It also made him want to please her even more. He pulled the bow free from her hair—the silly Christmas bow she loved to wear as she waitressed—and then pulled her ponytail free. Her thick, dark hair shook loose, falling about her shoulders in a cascade he longed to touch. He buried his hands there as he kissed her again, claiming her mouth with a hot, deep stroke of his tongue.

Holly moaned, her fingers moving to the buttons of his shirt. "Off. I want this off you. I want to touch you all over."

Oh damn, he wanted that, too. He leaned back, tearing at his own clothing, ripping it over his head and tossing it aside until he was shirtless before her. Holly's gaze locked onto his chest, and she let out a fascinated breath as she placed a palm over one pectoral. "You're not smooth," she told him. "Why did I think you'd be smooth?"

"Dunno. You don't like chest hair?" He had a fair amount across his pectorals and trailing down to his navel, but he'd never given it much thought.

"I like it," she confessed, skimming her fingers over his skin. "I like it a lot. It's just surprising to me."

He grunted, half wondering if her mental images of him

were of some scrawny, hairless boy instead of the real him. "Sorry, not going to shave my chest."

She giggled. "I don't expect you to. Can't I comment on your chest hair without you getting all prickly on me?"

"Guess not."

Holly twisted her fingers against a bit of that chest hair and smirked up at him. "Wuss."

"Please." He grabbed the hem of her shirt. "You know what this means. I need to check you for chest hair now."

She laughed, shaking her head. "You think I have chest hair?"

"I won't know unless I see, will I?" He waggled his brows at her and nudged at the shirt, giving her plenty of opportunity to stop him. Instead, she took the hem from his hands and pulled the entire thing over her head on her own, sitting up straight and proud in his lap. She was utterly beautiful, too. He knew how she was built because she liked to wear tight sweaters when she waitressed, showing off all her curves, but seeing her in only a bra and panties was different somehow. She was softer, curvier, sexier. Her breasts heaved with excited breaths as she watched him, as if she knew just how good she looked and was waiting for a compliment.

The sight of her had taken his breath away, though, and had snatched all his words with it. Reverently, Adam slid his hand over her pale stomach. It wasn't completely flat, with just a hint of roundness to it, showing that she was soft all over. It was a look he decided he liked. No, he *loved*. He loved that glorious feminine softness to her body, and how she knew how beautiful she looked. "Definitely no chest hair."

She leaned in, stroking the back of his neck in that teasing way he loved. "Should you look closer? Just to check?"

Well now, how could he resist that? "My eyes aren't so good. I should probably use my hands just to be certain."

Her eyes widened, and then a smile curved her lips. She arched her back, subtly daring him.

Damn, but he liked this woman. He never thought having an enemy would be so . . . enticing. Adam eased one of the straps down her shoulder as she rubbed her hand against his chest. Her breathing sped up as he peeled the cup of her bra away, exposing one creamy breast with a pale pink nipple.

Gorgeous.

Reverently, he stroked the delicate skin, the creamy swell of her cleavage. He slid his thumb along the curve of her breast, heading for the tip, and then circled the nipple with light, airy touches.

Holly moaned, moving forward and pressing her brow to his. "Adam."

"Everything feels good here," he said in a soft voice, cupping her breast. "Feels perfect. You're gorgeous, Holly. Just gorgeous." He brushed his nose against hers, then gave her another teasing kiss. "Makes me want to taste you everywhere."

She trembled against him in response. "No one's stopping you."

That wasn't exactly encouragement, either. He licked at her mouth, savoring the way she shuddered against him, as if she felt too much every time they kissed. As he teased her mouth, he traced small circles around her nipple over and over again, loving how it puckered and tightened at his touch. "Am I moving too fast for you, though? Should I slow down?"

Holly made a sound of protest. "If you do, I think I might burn your food for tomorrow."

"Can't have that." Not that he cared about the food. At this moment, all he cared about was getting one of those juicy, ripe nipples into his mouth. He lowered his head as he cupped her breast, feeding her up to his lips. He felt her hands tighten against him, felt her body tense . . . and then she pressed her body up against him, seeking more.

He was only too happy to give it.

With a groan, Adam lost control. He peppered her skin with kisses, nipping and sucking at the swell of her breast. He licked the tip, loving the way she gasped and clung to him in response. And when he felt he'd teased her enough, he sucked on the tip, then teased it with his tongue. The sounds she made were beautiful, too. He loved how she squirmed urgently, even as she pulled on his head and demanded more. Her breath was coming in short, shallow rasps, and when he reached for her other breast to tease in tandem with his mouth, he thought she'd come undone.

Her thighs squeezed against his hips, and she raked her nails down his arm, panting. "Please, Adam. Oh, please."

With a low growl, he wrapped his arms around her waist and turned them carefully on the sofa, laying her beneath him. He loved the little whimpering noises that escaped her throat as he tore her bra down to her belly, exposing both breasts. This time there was no impediment and he lavished attention on them, switching from one breast to the other until they were both flushed pink and she was wild underneath him.

"I need you," Holly said, the sound so needy and delicious that it only spurred him on. He moved up to kiss her soft mouth again, hungrily claiming her. She arched her hips against the thigh he had between her legs. She needed him?

Well now, he couldn't have her needy.

Ignoring the throbbing ache of his cock and the hunger

in his own body, he kissed Holly again, murmuring her name. He brushed a hand down her belly, past the discarded bra, past the enticing dip of her navel, and didn't stop at the waistband of her panties. He dipped below the fabric, seeking her heat.

Breath hissed out from between his teeth as he touched her. Holly was utterly soaked.

She moaned against his mouth, her nails digging into his shoulders even as she spread her legs wider, inviting his touch. He kissed her with languid, reverent kisses as he traced her folds, learning her body. She was so soft and wet here, so very pettable, the curls over her sex a delightful contrast to the smooth, hot skin underneath. He found the little bud of her clit and teased it with a careful graze of his finger.

And he loved the way she jumped when he did.

Her gaze locked to his, Holly clung to him as he rubbed teasing circles around her clit, working her to a fever pitch. She arched against him, meeting his hand, her lips parted in a wordless cry as he worked her body. Maybe he was greedy, but it wasn't quite enough. Not quite. He wanted her to lose all control. So he slid that slick finger down her folds, pushing into the core of her, and rested his thumb against her clit. Adam pumped into her, watching her face tighten with need, watching the hunger sweep over her as she came closer and closer to her release.

When it rocked through her, it took them both by surprise. She keened his name, her nails digging half circles into his skin. He didn't feel the pain, though. All he could feel was Holly's body clenching tight around his finger, the shudders of her release, the rush of wetness as she came hard against his hand.

As he kissed her, Adam drank in the smile on her face,

the sated look in her gorgeous eyes, and he started to worry that quick interludes on the couch weren't going to be enough.

They already weren't enough for him. Right now, he wanted nothing more than to fling Holly over his shoulder like a caveman and drag her out to his cabin. He wanted to throw her down into his bed and kiss her everywhere. He wanted to make her come again. And again. And again. Dozens of times, until she was begging for mercy, and then they'd both give in to the need.

He was ignoring his own need tonight. Partly because she was injured, and partly because he was afraid that if he claimed her like he really wanted, he'd never be able to let her go.

And he wasn't sure Holly would want to be claimed by him. Not when they were "enemies." Not when he'd deliberately sabotaged a cake that had meant so much to her.

He still needed to tell her about that cake. Just . . . not when she was freshly sated under him, clinging to him as if he was the best thing in the world.

Not yet. Sure, it was selfish, but it was something Adam was starting to get used to, that feeling. He didn't care how selfish it was as long as it kept her in his arms for a little longer.

CHAPTER TWENTY

Thank goodness the next day was Holly's day off. She couldn't concentrate on anything after last night. Her leg throbbed in a reminder that she'd been in serious danger, but the knowledge of that paled in light of what had happened afterward. Adam had removed her pants and she'd straddled him as they made out. He'd slipped his hand into her panties and worked her until she'd came against his fingers, hard.

And she'd loved every moment of it. So much for being enemies.

She lounged in bed, her hand between her thighs, where her body still throbbed. Holly knew she should get up and start the day, but it was nice to just daydream for a few, imagining Adam's hands on her, his mouth on hers as his hand worked her to orgasm. It had been a long time since she'd had sex, and even longer since a man had made her orgasm.

Now she was like a junkie needing a fix. She couldn't

think of anything but touching him again. Of opening the door to his cabin and crawling into his bed and riding him like the wanton, needy woman she was.

Except the sun was up and he probably wasn't even in bed. So . . . there was that.

Lord, she needed a distraction. Holly pulled herself from bed, walked the dog, and headed down to the kitchen. She'd bake something, she decided. Something chocolatey and delicious and difficult to make so she could focus on a distraction. She needed to make dinner, too. Lasagna? Chicken Parm? She wondered which one he'd like more.

Of course . . . she could always text him.

Her heart pounded like a schoolgirl's at the thought. Why did texting him feel so darn personal? He'd had his fingers in her panties—inside *her*—yesterday. Texting was nothing. And yet . . . it felt like a lot. She didn't want to seem needy. He'd laugh if she fell in love with him or something stupid like that.

Even so . . .

Holly picked up her phone. Stared at it, thinking. Sage had given her both Carson's and Adam's numbers when she'd left, just in case she needed to communicate with them about anything. While Carson never seemed to stop texting about anything and everything, Adam had never texted her. Would it be too pushy? Would it ruin their easy flirtation?

Of course, was it even easy anymore if he'd fingered her until she came? Ugh, she didn't know, and she hated that she didn't know. Frustrated, she texted her boss instead, asking if he needed her to come in. Maybe if she was working, she wouldn't obsess over Adam and his big, strong hands.

When her boss texted back, though, he told her he didn't

need the extra help. Holly groaned, slumping on the couch and staring morosely at her phone.

She'd just text him, she decided. Texts were no big deal. Everyone texted.

HOLLY: Hey there.

Shit. Did she sound too flirty? Too needy? Too *I'm desperate for dick*? She quickly typed some more, as if that could somehow fix things.

HOLLY: I'm heading to the grocery store.

HOLLY: Soon. I mean, I'm not there yet. I'm just going soon.

HOLLY: I wanted to see if we were doing dinner tonight?

HOLLY: Not that we have to, of course. I just wanted to see if you wanted to have dinner like we have this week.

HOLLY: I was thinking Chicken Parmigiana or maybe a homemade lasagna.

HOLLY: That's why I texted.

HOLLY: I'm going to make a cake, too. I was thinking Black Forest. Do you have any feelings on cherries?

She almost typed more, and then stopped herself, horrified at the wall of text she was sending in his direction. Good lord, what was wrong with her? Holly pressed a hand to her forehead, cringing at all the texts. She was coming across as an absolute nut job, wasn't she? If he wasn't going to run away screaming before, he sure was now.

The text that came in surprised her with how quickly he responded.

ADAM: Today's your day off, right? Relax. Take a break.

ADAM: Whatever is easiest. Sandwiches are fine. It doesn't have to be anything crazy. We can just hang out.

Like an idiot, she absolutely melted over his texts. He wanted her to relax? To take a break? Didn't he realize that she needed a project to distract her because she didn't want to be alone with her thoughts?

Because all of those thoughts were entirely about jumping his bones? She thought for a minute, and then texted him again.

HOLLY: Sandwiches it is . . . but I'll make the bread fresh.

HOLLY: And I'll still make a cake, but I'll only do one tier.

ADAM: Jesus woman, do you even know the meaning of the word relax? Lol.

HOLLY: Are you kidding? That IS relaxing for me.

HOLLY: Are you buried today? Should I leave you alone?

ADAM: It's all good. Just checking the cattle for runny noses.

HOLLY: Er, okay.

ADAM: I'll explain when I come in for lunch. Be there in about an hour.

HOLLY: Ok!

An hour. Shit! She had an hour to get ready. With a nervous flutter of her hand to her hair, Holly raced off the couch and headed for the shower. It wasn't a date, she told herself . . . but that didn't mean she wasn't going to shave her legs and fix her hair.

You know, just in case.

Holly cleaned up and blow-dried her hair. She put on a pair of jeans and a sweatshirt, because she didn't want to look like she was trying too hard . . . but then she stripped them off, put on her prettiest bra and matching panties, and then dressed again. If things progressed between them, she wanted to be ready. Was she going to sleep with Adam, no strings attached? If he could give her an orgasm like he did yesterday, she absolutely would.

After all, she was an adult. She was allowed to have meaningless sex, right? Right.

She was a little bit nervous when she headed down to the kitchen, though. Of course she was. If he pulled her against him and lifted that cocky eyebrow like he did just before he kissed her in that sexy way of his, she was absolutely going to fling herself at him.

She'd just covered her bread dough so it could prove when he stepped into the kitchen, Hannibal at his heels. Holly paused in her work, drinking in the sight of him. Why did he get better-looking every time she glanced in his direction? Why did the sight of his scruffy baseball cap perched atop his head fill her with such affection?

He slowly grinned at the sight of her, sending a hot flush roaring through her system. "Hey there."

"Hi." God, now she was all tongue-tied like an idiot.

"Sleep well?"

Holly could feel a blush heating her cheeks. After that orgasm? Yeah, she'd slept well. "Like a baby. Hungry?"

"Always." He moved toward the bar and sat in his regular stool. When she moved close, setting down a plate with a thick sandwich on it, he grabbed her by the waist and dragged her into his lap. Adam buried his face against her neck, holding her tight. "Mm. You smell good."

She practically squirmed with pleasure at his words. "Thanks," she teased. "It's this newfangled thing called soap."

"Soap. Huh." He didn't rise to her bait. "You'll have to show me how to use it sometime."

And of course, now she was picturing running her hands all over his suds-covered body, exploring his muscles with a washcloth, and Holly had to bite back a moan. He kept one arm wrapped around her waist as he picked up half his sandwich and took a big bite. She watched him eat, and when he offered her a bite, she shook her head. "Busy day?"

"They're all busy," he said around a mouthful of turkey. He shrugged. "Just gotta get used to it until Carson and Jason come back."

She patted the arm around her waist. "They'll be back soon enough and then you won't have to suffer with my cooking anymore." She said the words in a light voice, but funny enough, it didn't feel light, saying that. It felt weird. Strange. A little sad. Her stay as housekeeper and cook was half over and she wasn't ready for it to end. At all.

He snorted even as he took another bite of food. "Your cooking is not suffering. It's the opposite."

"Funny, you only ever tipped a dollar in the past."

Adam set down the rest of his sandwich and buried his face against her neck again. "I said your cooking wasn't the problem. Didn't say anything about that sassy attitude of yours."

And he nipped at her neck, his teeth grazing her skin.

It was probably supposed to be a mock bite, a tease to make her jump into the playful banter head-on. Instead, it sent hot need surging through her body, and Holly let out a soft whimper.

Adam stilled. Slowly, he pressed his mouth to her neck, kissing her. He moved up to her ear, his lips brushing against her earlobe, and then he nipped her there, too. "Have you been thinking about last night?"

She let out a shuddering breath, clutching the hand at her waist. "Yes."

"Me too." His voice was low and soft, a caress in her ears. "Thought about you all night and how you came around my fingers. How pretty you were. And I woke up hard and aching because I needed you."

That might have been the most exciting thing Holly'd ever heard. She sucked in a breath, tilting her head back so he could kiss her ear and neck as much as he wanted. "Did you . . . solve your own problem?"

"You mean, did I jerk off?"

She nodded.

"Yeah. In the shower. Didn't do much for me, though. I kept thinking about touching you all morning, and I think I might be more worked up now than I was before." He pressed a kiss to her earlobe, and then ran his tongue along the edge. "Question is, do we want to keep flirting around or do we want to take things to the next level?"

"What do you want to do?" she asked, breathless. She was curious to hear his answer.

"I want what you want," Adam told her. "If you don't want to take things further . . . well, I guess I'd rather know sooner than later so I don't make you uncomfortable."

He was . . . serious? Did he think she was uncomfortable sitting on his leg, or when he had his hand in her panties yesterday? While she was panting out his name? It was sweet of him to make sure, but Holly wanted to shake him just a little. Didn't he realize how badly she wanted him?

"You're asking what I want?" she echoed. "You don't think that's obvious?"

"If I thought it was obvious, would I have asked?"

Her mouth twitched with amusement. She couldn't decide if this was sweet of him or utterly clueless. "What I want," she began slowly, "is for us to enjoy each other. No more, no less. And I guess my idea of enjoyment is a little more flexible than yours—"

Adam stood up abruptly, thumping her onto her feet.

Holly turned to look at him, and in the next moment, she

was over his shoulder, her stomach pressing down on his shoulder.

"Where's your room?" he asked, turning around slowly.

She burst into laughter. The man was wasting no time. Giggling, she sat up, pulled his cap off his head and tossed it to the ground. "Up the stairs and down the hall."

"Good." He headed in the direction that she'd gestured, his hand possessively on her backside, and Holly couldn't stop laughing. Okay, so much for wondering if he liked her or not. She guessed he did. Smiling, she gave a wiggle and was rewarded with a playful swat across her denim-covered butt. "Behave, you naughty girl."

"If you think this is naughty, you are in for a real surprise," she taunted back.

"This day is just sounding better and better."

CHAPTER TWENTY-ONE

Adam headed through the doorway and into the room she'd been staying in for the last few weeks. Upside down, she saw her tiny Pomeranian curled up in her dog bed, her tail thumping slightly. No doubt she thought Holly and Adam were playing games. In the next moment, Adam set her down on the bed carefully and leaned forward, trapping her between his arms. He kissed Holly lightly, his lips full of promise, and then grinned at her. "I'm gonna move the dog into the hallway, if that's all right with you."

She nodded.

He winked at her, then grabbed the dog's bed and slid it out the door, murmuring a few words of praise at Pumpkin before shutting the door. He turned back to her once that was done, a wry expression on his face. "Didn't want my ass getting bit."

Holly pretended to pout. "There go all my plans."

His eyes flared with heat. Adam moved toward the bed

as she lay back, propped up on her elbows. "Were you planning on biting my ass, then?"

She tilted her head in a flirty manner, loving the way he was devouring her with his gaze. "I like to leave my options on the table."

"That so? What all options are on this table?" His big hands rubbed over her hips, pulling her down to the edge of the bed and sliding between her spread legs. He hiked one leg around his hip and leaned in, covering her so he could kiss her again. In contrast with his teasing words, his mouth was hungry and intense. Adam's tongue brushed against hers, and when she made a soft sound of pleasure, the kiss grew hotter, wetter. Fiercer.

Soon, she was clinging to the front of his shirt, her legs locked around him as his weight pressed down on her. God, he felt good against her. And when he bit lightly on her lower lip, it sent a quiver of pleasure straight through her, heat pulsing between her thighs.

Adam's lips played over hers, a kiss that was both flirty and intense all at once. "You didn't answer me."

She looked up at him, utterly dazed. "I forgot the question."

"How," he began, pressing a kiss to the corner of her mouth, "do you see this going today?" Each word was punctuated by a small kiss in a different spot on her face—her nose, her chin, her jaw.

He was asking her—again—what she wanted. As if he wanted to be utterly certain that he wasn't pushing her into anything.

Well, she obviously needed to make it clearer for him. "I'm not on the pill but I have an IUD. Condoms aren't necessary unless you're not clean. Are you?"

"As a whistle," he promised, moving back up to her mouth

again. His hand slid between them, and he cupped a hand blatantly between her thighs, pressing against the denim that covered her sex. "You're beautiful, you know that?"

She loved hearing the reverent way he said it. "Easy for you to say when you've got your hands on my kitty," she teased, oddly nervous.

"It's true. I think that's the one reason you get on my nerves so much. You're so damned pretty and with that sassy mouth, you just drive me crazy with wanting you."

Holly moaned as he dragged his thumb heavily across her folds, pressing down through the denim, making her feel the stroke of his hand. It felt good, and yet it was a tease, because it wasn't nearly enough.

"Should I get you naked?" he asked, voice like rich honey. "Or should I just rub you right here until you come?" And he pushed against her again, making her feel the denim, the seam that ran between her legs.

"Naked," Holly panted. "Let's do naked."

"A woman after my own heart." Adam leaned over her to kiss her again, and Holly clung to his shoulders, greedy. She kissed him with all the need that was racing through her, her mouth frantic on his. Adam rubbed her mound with his hand as his tongue played against hers, until she was practically whimpering against him, her hips arching to add to the friction. If he was going to get her naked, he was certainly taking his sweet time.

When he finally reached for the button on her jeans, Holly wanted to cry with relief. She lifted her hips, frantically pulling at her clothing in her haste to get him touching her bare skin. God, she wanted that more than anything.

Adam was determined to make her crazy, though. He sat up, his hands moving ever so slowly over her clothing, taking his sweet time to pull one shoe off her foot, then the other. One sock, then the other. Then he carefully pulled the jeans down her legs, and Holly wanted to swear out loud with how long he was taking. The pyramids had been built faster than this man was moving, she decided, and sat up to help him.

He immediately put a hand on her shoulder, easing her back down on the bed. "Don't be impatient," he chided. "I'm savoring this."

She squirmed on the bed as he finally freed one of her legs from the jeans. "Can you savor a little faster?"

"Do you even know what savor means?" He arched that sexy eyebrow at her and she wasn't sure if she wanted to reach up and kiss the hell out of him or claw at his eyes in frustration. "Savor means you take your time. Savor means you enjoy things . . . slowly."

And he tugged the other leg of her jeans off, tossing them down to the floor. His gaze fell on her panties—the prettiest ones she owned, a lacy, pale blue satin pair with lace roses dancing across the material—and he rubbed his mouth. "These are pretty."

"Thanks. I'm told they look great on the floor."

Adam's cocky grin flashed. "That's such a waste. You're wearing these for my enjoyment, aren't you?" He put a hand to one knee and pushed it to the side and back, spreading her thighs wide as he stepped just a little closer once more. "Let me enjoy."

He stroked her pussy through the silky fabric, and she moaned. It was one thing for him to touch her through the thick fabric of the denim, and another entirely for him to skate those fingers up and down the gusset of her panties. She could feel everything—how thick his fingers were, how wet she was—and when he dragged one fingertip up to her clit, Holly nearly came off the bed.

"You tease," she panted.

He let one of his big hands glide down the inside of her thigh. "Me a tease? If I was a tease, I'd do something more like this, wouldn't I?" And then Adam bent over, pushing her thighs wide, and pressed his mouth directly against her panties.

Oh god. Holly whimpered, reaching for his head. She held on to him as he licked her through the slinky fabric, his tongue moving over her slit with just the barest hint of pressure. It felt so good and yet it still wasn't enough. She wanted more.

"Please, Adam," she panted.

"So greedy," he murmured. "Rushing me along when I'm trying to enjoy myself." He nuzzled his mouth against her mound, and she moaned, her hands flexing on his head. She wanted to touch him everywhere, but it was impossible with him between her thighs. All she could do was frantically drag her fingers over that short hair of his and plead for him to give her more. "Greedy," he said again in a low voice, his breath fanning over her skin. "But I guess it makes me greedy, too."

He pulled the fabric of her panties aside, exposing her pussy. Holly whimpered, and was rewarded in the next moment when his mouth descended on her skin. This time there was nothing between them, and his lips were scorching against her flesh. He gripped her legs, easing them over his shoulders as he knelt between her thighs and licked her. His tongue trailed over her from the entrance to her core all the way up to her clit, as if he was exploring her body with it alone. Then he swirled the tip of his tongue over her clit and leaned in to suck on it.

Her legs jerked, and Holly cried out. The jolt of him there felt so damn good. He latched on and suddenly there was no more teasing between them. It was all intensity as Adam licked and sucked at her clit, holding her trapped against his face as he worked her with lips and tongue. It had been a long time since anyone had touched her like this, but it had never felt so good. Adam knew exactly what he was doing, and he watched her cues to make sure that he was hitting the right spots. When she began whimpering, he didn't let up. He only added a finger, stroking it deep inside her.

The next thing she knew, he was rubbing against a spot inside her inner walls that felt like it was sending lightning through her veins. Oh god, their first time together and he'd already found her G-spot? He was going to destroy her for all other men. "Adam," she moaned, clinging to him as he teased that perfect spot inside her. "I'm going to come."

He didn't speak.

He didn't let up, either. He just kept sucking on her clit, teasing her, and Holly's body quaked and trembled. She was so close, and he knew it and was determined to drive her over the edge. His mouth was hot and frantic on her, that finger deep inside her endlessly teasing.

When she came moments later, stars danced before her eyes.

Adam lifted his head slowly, pressing kisses along the inside of her thigh as he slid his fingers free. He rubbed his goatee against her leg as she came back to herself. Holly let out a long, gusty sigh and gave him a sated smile. "That was amazing."

"I agree." He grazed his teeth along her skin, watching her with a hungry expression from between her legs. "You're beautiful, you know that?"

Her cheeks heated. It was one thing to have a guy tell her she was pretty, another entirely when he was between her thighs, nipping at her skin just moments after he'd made her come with his tongue. There was no teasing on his face, either. No cocky eyebrow, no wicked smile. Just pure, honest truth.

It made her completely and utterly flustered. They weren't supposed to be having moments like this when they were having a fling. That was off-limits. So she planted her foot on his shoulder and nudged him. "Can I see you naked now?"

"So demanding." That cocky grin was back, and the moment broken. He got to his feet, stripping off his shirt in quick, fluid motions that took her breath away. When his chest was bared, she let out a happy little sigh, gazing up at him. He had big, strong arms and a taut body she could spend hours looking at.

His hands went to his belt, and she sat up on the bed, wanting to get a better look. Eager? Sure. Greedy? Absolutely. But these were the parts she was dying to see, and Holly wanted to see everything.

Adam tugged his pants down, revealing boxer briefs that clung to his strong thighs, and a package that took her breath away. No wonder Adam was such a confident pain in the ass. The man was absolutely packing.

"You're staring," he said as he kicked his boots off and then lowered his jeans the rest of the way off his legs. "Do I meet your approval?"

"I was just noticing you're not a boxers guy. I thought for sure you'd be," Holly deflected.

He shook his head. "Too much jiggling. Doubt any cowboy's a boxers guy. You need your nuts held tight when you're riding a horse."

"A phrase I never thought I'd hear." She chuckled and pulled her sweatshirt over her head, revealing her matching bra and her shameless intentions. She knew by the way his eyes lit up that he'd guessed that she'd worn this specifically for him today. She'd planned on them having sex.

And now he couldn't stop grinning.

She perched on the bed, watching as he stripped off his socks and then reached for the band of his underwear. There was no teasing this time as he pulled them down, too. No coy, flirty moves. He shucked them as if they were a nuisance he couldn't wait to get rid of.

Then Adam was naked and glorious in front of her. His cock thrust into the air, proud and arching, and curved just slightly to one side. The head of him was prominent and flushed a deep shade with his arousal, the tip wet. He looked big and thick and oh lord, it was going to feel amazing. Holly bit back a whimper of need and patted the side of her bed, indicating he should join her.

The moment he did, she lay on her back atop the blankets, watching with pleasure as he moved over her. His face was inches above hers and his hand skimmed over her skin as he leaned in for a kiss. "Hi again, beautiful," he murmured, just as his lips grazed hers.

It took everything she had not to wriggle with pleasure like a puppy at the compliment.

They kissed for a few moments, teasing with light nips before Adam moved to her neck and began to kiss her there. "How attached are you to this bra and panty set?" he asked between kisses. "Because I'd love to see you without it. I want to feel all of you naked beneath me."

"I want that, too." When he rolled off of her, she sat up and undid the hooks at her back, then cast the bra aside. The panties meant a little more wiggling around on the bed, but soon enough, she kicked them off and snuggled back in against his side, facing him. His cock brushed against her skin, hard and urgent, but Adam didn't seem as if he was in a rush. He ran a hand through her hair, watching her, and then brushed it back off her shoulders. She'd never met anyone like him, someone who didn't rush in bed, trying to get his release as quickly as possible. Adam was far more interested in being thorough, in the pleasure of the moment overall and not just the moment when he came.

She loved that. She loved that he made her feel just as beautiful as he said she was. He made her feel adored.

"Look at how pretty you are," he breathed, cupping one of her breasts. His thumb teased over the tip and it instantly hardened. "I could just stare at you all day long and not get enough."

"Guess that wouldn't be great for the cattle," she teased, and then moaned when he rubbed her nipple.

"Who's thinking about cattle right now?"

Well, that was a good point. She kissed him again, her hand on his cheek as he continued to tease and pluck at her nipple as they kissed. Her need was surging through her again, threatening to spill over. She was panting as they broke from their kiss and he rolled on top of her, pushing her thighs apart.

Their eyes met, and Holly felt so vulnerable in that moment. It felt intensely personal to gaze at him as he pressed the head of his cock against her entrance and then slowly, exquisitely fed it inside her. Her lips parted and she was frozen in place, locked against him in every way as he inched forward.

"Beautiful," Adam whispered again, and then gave a small thrust. His hips rested against hers, and she realized he'd pushed all the way inside her. He felt big, but in a good way, she decided. Like he was stretching her body, letting her accommodate him.

She wrapped her arms around him, and Adam bent his head, pressing against her neck as he drew back and then surged deep again. It felt good, like he was filling all the hollow spaces she didn't know she had. She lifted her knees, hooking her legs around his hips so he could thrust deeper, and he started a slow, steady rhythm.

Holly dug her nails into his skin as he pumped inside her. Her world had shrunk down, the only thing that mattered the feel of his body covering hers, driving into hers. His movements started out languid, as if he were testing things, seeing how she'd respond. When she moaned and tried to drag him closer, Adam's movements sped up. The leisurely rhythm changed to something shorter, more urgent. His hips began to snap in a fierce, brutal rhythm that made hot pleasure spiral through her belly.

She was close to coming again, and it shocked her. "Adam," she whimpered. "Adam, I think . . . I need . . . wait . . ."

He growled in her ear like a wild animal, burying his face against her throat even as he sucked on her neck. Holly cried out, lifting her hips to meet his, and he locked an arm around her shoulder, anchoring her to increase the delicious friction between them. He was losing control, and she worried he'd leave her hanging.

She shouldn't have worried. His hand left her shoulder, roaming down between their wildly moving bodies, and he paused, finding her clit. When he did, she cried out. Then he resumed his rhythm, pounding into her until she screamed her release, her entire body tensing as she came. Hot quivers shook through her limbs as he stroked into her, his movements growing ragged. Then Adam let out a low groan, shuddering over her as he came.

Holly trailed a hand up and down his spine as he caught his breath, feeling dazed and more than just a little sated. Two hard, delicious orgasms for her? Lord, she'd take it. That was amazing. She wanted to wrap her arms around him and squeeze him tight against her, keeping him in her bed for hours on end. She wondered how long they'd have in this moment before reality stepped in and he had to return to work.

A tinny sound came from downstairs—the kitchen. Her phone was ringing. Holly groaned. "I bet that's Polly."

Adam pressed a kiss to her neck before reluctantly sliding off her. She expected him to jump out of bed, but instead, he tugged her against him, twining his legs with hers. "It can wait for a few."

Well, if he wanted to cuddle, it wasn't like she was going to object. Smiling, Holly snuggled down against his damp chest, breathing in his scent. He smelled like sex and sweat and it had never been so damn appealing before. "I might not catch her again if I wait," she said, but she didn't make any effort to get up. "Polly's hard to get ahold of."

"Then she needs to try harder," Adam told her, smoothing a tendril of hair back from her face. "You're doing everything for her. The least she could do is call you back."

She studied him, curious. "How do you know what I'm doing for Polly?" She'd mentioned her sister around him a few times, but she'd never gone into details. "What have you heard?"

He captured a lock of her hair between his fingers, rubbing it. "I might have quizzed Becca about you."

"You what?"

He shrugged. "Just . . . curious. That's all. She said you

dropped out of high school to get a job and take care of your sister. And that you're paying for her college. That true?"

Holly nodded. "Anyone would have done the same for their family."

"Would they?" He sounded skeptical. "I heard that you were sending her every penny you had, too."

"College isn't cheap," Holly said evasively. "And Polly needs to focus on her studies. I don't mind."

"I mind," he grumbled. "You're killing yourself working day and night trying to make things easy for her. She could get a part-time job at least and ease some of the burden. It's not like making coffees or working at a bookstore for ten hours a week would kill her."

She said nothing, frowning. He didn't understand.

"Is she coming for the holidays?" Adam asked, tugging on that lock of hair. "I promise to hold all my nagging until then."

He wanted to meet her sister? It made her ache a little inside. "Actually, Polly's not coming down for the holidays. She's staying for a student tutoring thing. Which reminds me . . . I need to bake some more cookies and send them to her." And send some more money, but he didn't need to know that. She wiggled against him, trying to break free from his embrace. "I should probably get up."

To her surprise, he rolled onto her again, pinning her with his weight. "You're mad, aren't you? Why are you mad?"

"I'm not mad!"

His gaze searched hers. "You're mad," he declared again, and she wondered if it'd be rude to kick him so soon after great sex. Adam grinned down at her and then planted another kiss on her mouth. "Don't get upset. Someone's gotta look after you."

"Is that what all this grumbling is?" she muttered. "Looking after me?"

"Is it wrong for me to think she should try harder? You're always the one calling her from what I've seen." He pressed another kiss to her lips. "I'm not trying to rock the boat. I just think these sorts of things are a two-way street. She's your sister, you're giving your life up for her, and the least she could do is call a bit more often if she's not coming home for the holidays." He leaned in and whispered in her ear. "And she'd better give you a hell of a Christmas gift."

Holly chuckled. "Are you this bossy with all the women in your life? No wonder you're single."

His laughing expression died, and Holly wanted to kick herself. Ugh. Why did she have to go and say that? "I'm single," he began slowly. "Because when I was stationed overseas—"

"Adam," she began, interrupting. "You don't have to explain."

He continued on as if she hadn't spoken, taking her hand in his and lacing his fingers with hers. "—I missed my wife and my dog. I was tired of doing tours in strange places and hanging out with the guys all the time. I was tired of ships and oceans and military life. So I came home and found her in bed with an old friend of mine. It happens a lot in the military. Guys come home to find out that their wives weren't all that interested in staying faithful." He shrugged. "So that's why I'm single."

She felt awful. No wonder he was so prickly about such things. "Well," she told him brightly, trying to lighten the mood. "It wasn't because you're bad in bed."

A slow smile curved his beautiful mouth. "No?"

"I can complain about a lot of things about you, Adam

Calhoun, but your performance is not one of them." Holly smiled up at him. "In that respect you did just fine."

"Just fine, eh?" He shook his head. "That's faint praise, 'just fine.'"

She rolled her eyes even as her phone rang again. Neither of them bothered to get up. Instead, Holly teased him back. "What, do you want me to call you a cock god? To tell you that you've dicked me better than anyone has ever dicked me before?"

"I mean, 'cock god' has a nice ring to it," Adam said, pretending to consider it. "Maybe 'Lord of My Orgasms' will work, too."

"More like 'Lord of the Inflated Ego.'"

"You weren't saying my ego was inflated when you were screaming my name a few minutes ago." He leaned down and nipped at her ear. "You liked my big ego then. You liked all my big things."

Holly giggled, even as his movements made her all breathless again. This man was going to make her crazy . . . in all the best ways. "You—"

Her phone chirped with a voicemail.

That made her pause. Polly never left a voicemail. She'd have just texted instead, or sent an email. "Adam." She nudged at his shoulder. "I need to check that call."

He sighed heavily and gave her one last kiss, this one on the tip of her nose. "You and your responsibilities. I should probably head back out myself, too. The cattle aren't going to take care of themselves, more's the pity."

She hesitated, and for a long moment, she didn't want him to leave. It was strange, but it felt like if he left her bed in this moment, he might never come back. She wasn't ready for that yet. "What about tonight?" she asked, breathless.

Adam rolled off the bed. "What about tonight?"

Holly watched him as he moved toward her small bathroom, no doubt to clean up before dressing again. The water turned on, and she could only see the shadow of him in the doorway. "Do you want me to leave your dinner on your step?"

He leaned back, frowning out at her. "You trying to get rid of me, waitress?"

A relieved smile crossed her face. "Waitress? After all we've been through?"

"It's not like I know your last name. 'Holly Whatserface' just doesn't have the same ring to it."

She made a noise of protest. "It's Dawson, you nitwit. I can't believe you don't know my name. I know yours!"

"If it was on your name tag, I would have known it, beautiful." He seemed unruffled by her outrage, finishing up in the bathroom and then tossing the towel in the laundry basket. He strolled back out to her, buck naked, and planted a kiss on her mouth. "Can't be mad over that, can you? Or was I supposed to steal your wallet and memorize your identity?"

"I guess not," she grumbled, that kiss mollifying her. "And I'm not trying to get rid of you."

"Good, because I'll be back later tonight. Wouldn't mind something a little sweet to go with my dinner again."

"Cake?" she asked absently, watching him step into his underwear. She wasn't staring at his butt like a creeper, she really wasn't. It was just . . . it was an awfully nice butt. That was all.

He straightened and grinned over at her. "I was thinking more like pussy."

"Oh my god. You're the worst."

"Five minutes ago you said I was the best."

"That was before I realized your ego was the size of Mars."

He chuckled, picking up his discarded socks. "Not quite that big." Adam glanced over at her. "We on for tonight?"

She felt her cheeks get pink all over again. Funny how she could be embarrassed despite the fact that she was in bed, naked, after sleeping with him, and yet his blatant suggestions got her all flustered. "Tonight, yes."

Adam moved over to the bed and gave her a lingering kiss, his tongue sweeping against hers in such a delicious, languid way she forgot about everything all over again. "Can't wait," he murmured. "And you should probably get that phone."

Phone? She blinked up at him, confused.

Oh. Her *phone*. Right.

Holly jumped out of bed, wrapping the sheet around her as Adam laughed. She cast him a mock-annoyed look as she opened the door, and Pumpkin practically danced with excitement at Holly's return. "Come on, girl," she told the dog as she headed for the kitchen. She'd last had her phone on the counter, she was pretty sure.

Yup. There it was, right next to a grocery list she'd been making. Holly picked it up.

Two missed calls. A voicemail. Seven text messages.

Her stomach dropped and she unlocked her phone quickly, looking through the list of texts as they lined up across her phone. Her mouth went dry. A cold chill swept down her arms. She stared down at the phone mutely, unable to comprehend what she'd just read. Over and over again, she read the series of texts. She read the voicemail transcription next, then went back to the texts, still having trouble digesting it all.

"Everything okay?"

She looked at Adam. His baseball cap was back on his head and he tucked his shirt into his jeans. His mouth was flushed red from their lovemaking, and for some reason she found that impossibly endearing. That, and the look of concern on his face.

"It's work," she said, numb.

"They want you to come in? On your day off?" A scowl flashed over his face.

"No," Holly said slowly. "It burned down."

CHAPTER TWENTY-TWO

An hour later, Holly drove slowly into town. Pumpkin was in the seat next to her, wearing a doggy seat belt and gazing eagerly at Holly, as if this was going to be a fun, exciting trip. Pumpkin loved car rides, mostly because Holly rewarded her with treats every time. It wasn't as if she could see out the windows of the car. She just liked the attention. Holly should have left her home, but the dog was emotional support, and Holly figured she'd need it today.

Even if she was new to Painted Barrel, she would have been able to find the restaurant. Fire trucks and police cars were up and down Main Street, and she saw a familiar police officer directing traffic away from the smoking mess at the end of the street. Holly parked one street over at the feed store and picked up Pumpkin, rubbing the dog's round little head as she walked the block over to her place of work.

It was strange to head downtown, to see the cheerful Christmas decorations lining the street and the wreaths hanging from light posts, the trees covered with big plastic ornaments, and smell the smoke on the wind. Another police car zipped past, one from a nearby town, and she watched as it headed in the same direction as all the others.

Holly was numb all over again as she moved toward the building that had once been her place of employment. The scent of smoke was overwhelming here. Like most of Painted Barrel's downtown, Wade's saloon had been established in the downstairs of an old-fashioned building. The upstairs had always been used for storage as long as she'd worked there, the entire bottom floor converted to the dining area, bar, and kitchen. A wooden sign had hung over the doorway like an old-timey placard announcing the location.

Today, it was nothing but scorch marks. Holly clutched Pumpkin tighter as she approached. The old, weathered building was half-gone, the upstairs nothing but a husk. All the windows of the restaurant were gone, and inside Holly could see nothing but ash and smoking tables. The bar was there, but it looked like just a charred heap of wood, and the bottles of alcohol that normally lined the mirror behind the bar were all smashed. Christmas garlands were melted into sad drips along the sagging, burnt porch of the saloon.

It was a nightmare.

She tried to stand out of the way as firemen moved in and out of the wreckage. People were standing on the street, watching, and she knew most of their faces. The postman was there. The dry cleaner. The owner of the bakery. Hannah at the inn. She didn't talk to anyone, though. She couldn't. There was a knot in her throat that felt like it was as big as a boulder.

Because as she stared at the shell of her workplace, Holly couldn't help but wonder what was going to happen to her now.

"Holly!"

A familiar voice called her, and she turned to look. Wade and Bonnie, the other waitress that worked at Wade's, were standing below a Christmas wreath hanging from one of the light poles. Holly crossed the street to join them. She hugged them both, her little dog licking Wade's tear-stained face with so much excitement that she let Wade hold Pumpkin for a minute. He looked like he needed the emotional support more than she did. She was relieved to see both of them, but a hint of worry hit her as she studied their faces. "Where's Silas?" He was the cook that worked at the back of the restaurant. "Is he okay?"

Wade nodded, clutching Pumpkin against his wide chest. "He breathed some smoke so they took him to Casper to stay overnight at the hospital."

"Oh god. I'll bake him some cookies." Holly bit her lip. Silas was a lovely, kind elderly man with a wife and a grown daughter who lived in the next town over. "And you two are okay?"

Wade nodded as Bonnie patted him on the shoulder. "It was just all so fast. I didn't have time to do more than grab the previous day's receipts and get out."

"What happened?" It felt rude to ask, but she had to know.

"Wiring," Bonnie said. "You know how we're always joking that the microwave makes a noise like it's dying? Turns out it was. Something sparked behind it and the next thing we knew, the whole back wall went up."

And the microwave was steps away from the fryer, with all that oil. Ugh. Holly swallowed hard. "I'm just glad you're both okay. What can I do to help?"

Wade shook his head. "Not a lot to do. It's gonna take months to rebuild." Fresh tears started down his face.

Oh god. Months. "Maybe to-go orders?" Holly suggested. "We could drive them around . . ."

"The place is still smoking, Holly," Bonnie chided her, putting a hand on Wade's back. "It's going to take him days just to handle all the claims. Let's give him a chance to catch his breath, all right?"

"Of course." Holly felt awful. "I'm sorry. I'm just trying to help."

"I know. I know." Wade gave her a teary smile. "When I have things figured out, you and Bonnie—and Silas—will be the first ones I call, I promise. For now . . ." He gestured at the restaurant and a fresh plume of smoke drifted into the air.

"Right. Of course. Well, if you need anything, Wade, you call me. You know I'm here for you." It felt useless to say such things, but she didn't know what else to do.

"I . . . I can't pay you this week," Wade said, handing back her dog and swiping at his eyes. "I grabbed the till but there was nothing in it. We hadn't opened yet."

"Oh," Holly breathed. "Of course not." She knew that there would be only a little money in the till in the morning, just enough to make change. The real money came at night, when people went to the bar, and when they tipped. "Don't worry. I'm sure we can apply for unemployment or something. It'll be fine."

Bonnie nodded, rubbing Wade's back again. Her face was pinched, and Holly knew she was worried, too. Bonnie was a single mom with three young kids. She counted on her check, and she needed that income just as bad as Holly did.

Thank god for the cooking job at the ranch. It would

save her from being completely destitute if it took Wade's a little time to reopen, but now she didn't know how she was going to pay for Polly's schooling in the spring.

Honestly, she didn't know how she was going to pay for anything. The sick feeling in the pit of her stomach grew and grew, even as cheerful Christmas music drifted over the street.

Holly stayed with Wade and Bonnie for a while, but it became obvious that there was nothing she could do, and she was just in the way. She headed to her apartment, picked up fresh clothes, and allowed herself a small cry. Just a small one, because weeping over a job wouldn't change anything.

She'd just have to figure out how to make things work until the restaurant opened again.

So she pasted a smile on her face and drove back to Sage's big, sprawling ranch. She set Pumpkin down in her favorite bed, went into the kitchen, and decided that she might as well get some baking projects started since she had some free time. Her sourdough starter that she kept in a jar at the back of the restaurant would have been burned up with everything else, so she tossed some flour and warm water into a jar and set it aside to start. She made dough for two different types of bread and set them aside to rise. She made cookies. When the cookies were in the oven, she started on a cake. Lemon cake, she decided, because she wasn't much in a Christmas mood at the moment.

It wasn't that she needed the food. She wasn't hungry at all. What she needed was a distraction. Holly kept her hands busy, and as the long, awful day drifted into night, the counter was filled with baked goods. She made yeasty, cheddar-filled rolls. She made two types of cookies—chocolate chip and snickerdoodle. She made the lemon cake with a light buttercream frosting. She made fried chicken and mashed potatoes for Adam, with homemade cream gravy, and put it all in the microwave to stay warm.

Then she started making muffins. She could save a few for Adam, she figured, and bring the rest over to Wade. He'd need cheering up. Bonnie, too. Thinking about Bonnie and her kids made Holly pull out new bowls and a fresh batch of flour. The kids would probably like a cake, too, she reckoned. Maybe something red velvet? Strawberry?

She'd make both, she decided. Both couldn't hurt. Wade would probably want a cake, too, and he liked carrot. She reached for another set of bowls.

"What's all this?"

Holly jerked in surprise, turning around to look at Adam. He stood in the doorway of the kitchen, staring in surprise at the array of baked goods she'd laid out on the table. She followed his gaze to the trays of cookies and rolls, the muffins and the cake. They covered every inch of the counter. All right, it did look like a lot. "I'm baking."

He tore his gaze away from the tableau and looked at her. Really looked. "You all right, beautiful?"

Hearing the endearment made her melt, just a little. She offered him a wobbly smile. "No. That's why I'm baking."

Adam moved to her side and pulled the newest mixing bowl out of her grasp. He took her hands in his and met her gaze. "You didn't text me to tell me what was going on. Bad news with the restaurant?"

She nodded, unable to speak for a moment. "It's gone. Wade's going to have to file claims and, well, it'll take a few months for him to rebuild. In the meantime, I've got to file for unemployment, I think." Holly forced a bright smile to her face. "And I'm baking because Wade's going to have a lot on his plate for the next few days, and Bonnie's got kids to think about, and—"

"And you needed to stay busy," he guessed. "Are you all right?"

"Nope," she said, even as she smiled that bright, fake smile. "But I'll keep on going, because that's what I always do."

She tried to pull her hands free, but he wouldn't let her go. Instead, he tugged her closer and then wrapped his arms around her. "You're allowed to have a day where you scream at the universe, you know. You can be strong tomorrow." Adam rubbed her back. "Tonight you can be just as angry as you want to be."

Holly leaned against him, resting her cheek on his chest. She wasn't angry. Not exactly. She felt . . . hollow. Unsurprised. Sometimes it felt as if the entire universe was working against her. As if the moment she got a leg up on things or found a bit of happiness, life contrived to tear it all out of her grasp again. She was going to use the extra money from working at the ranch through the holidays to get ahead on Polly's student loans for the spring and now she couldn't. Now she'd need that money just to get through the next few months.

Life was always one step forward, two back. It just made her . . . tired. She'd muddle through. She always did. But sometimes it felt like a lot. "I'm okay," she said again softly. "Are you hungry?"

He rubbed her back, his hands moving over her spine. "It can wait if you need to hug it out."

It felt good to be hugged, even if she initially bristled at the thought. It wasn't that she was against hugging, really. It was that she'd crumble. That wasn't who she was. Holly picked herself up and went on, because no one else was going to. She didn't have time to crumble. Crumbling didn't pay the bills. Even so . . . Adam's arms around her felt pretty nice. She slid her hands under his shirt, seeking warm skin, and sighed with pleasure when she touched him.

Maybe a good cry wasn't what she needed.

She pulled back and gazed up at him, need in her eyes. "How fast can you eat?"

Adam groaned and kissed her, hard. "That what you want?" When she nodded, he picked her up by the hips and carried her out of the kitchen. "I can eat afterward."

Holly wrapped her arms around his neck and let him carry her away from her problems, even if it was only for a little while.

A short time later, they had made love, showered together, and eaten. Or rather, Adam had eaten. Holly hadn't been all that hungry. She'd picked at a few bites of food, lost in thought. Adam hadn't liked how quiet she was, so he'd dragged her back to bed and they'd made love one more time before he wrapped himself around her and went to sleep in bed next to her.

And she was too distracted to enjoy the sight of him in bed with her. Hannibal was curled up in Pumpkin's bed, with the tiny dog tucked against his hip. It was cozy and nice and yet . . . she couldn't stop thinking about money. How was she going to make everything work? How could she keep Polly at university if she couldn't afford her tuition? Heck, how could she keep her own apartment if she didn't have money coming in? Painted Barrel was a small town and a lot of the businesses were family owned. She didn't know of anyone that was hiring.

Worry flooded through her. Maybe unemployment would be enough to cover her through the lean period.

CHAPTER TWENTY-THREE

Unemployment was going to pay Holly exactly $193.00 a week.

Holly hung the phone up, sick to her stomach. She'd thought the week couldn't possibly get any worse than the moment when the restaurant had burned down, leaving her without a job. Boy, she'd really underestimated that one. She'd called the unemployment agency to see what kind of compensation she could get, but because she was a tipped employee, it wasn't much.

Wade had called her a few days later, explaining that he was temporarily filling sandwich orders and delivering them to customers that put in requests. Holly was delighted to hear that—at least it was some work, right?

Except Wade couldn't afford to pay both Holly and Bonnie, and Bonnie had three kids, so he'd rehired her instead.

"You understand, don't you, Holly?" Wade sounded so sad. "She needs the money badly."

"It's fine," Holly said brightly, even though she wanted

to fling the phone away. She understood. She really did. Bonnie did need the job and her kids were young. It was just . . . Holly needed money, too.

"Do you think you could bake some bread for me?" Wade had asked. "I'll pay you by the loaf and people love your bread."

"I'll think about it." It was a nice gesture, but it wouldn't be enough, of course. Baking a few loaves of bread for money on the side wouldn't cover her grocery bill, much less her rent. She'd had a few people from town asking around about baking, too. Becca had wanted Christmas cookies to set out in her salon and a friend of hers was having an office party and wanted cookies with the company logo on them.

Holly had told them no.

Maybe part of it was the pity aspect. Holly was used to scraping herself off the ground and moving on. There was no room in her world for self-pity, and so she just soldiered on. The fact that people were putting in orders for her baking reeked of pity. They all knew her cake at the baking competition had been a mess. They knew she was now hard up for money. This was their way of giving her charity.

She wouldn't take it.

Not only was it charity, but it was dangerous charity. She still wanted to open her own business someday. She still had dreams of running her own bakery, and she couldn't afford to sabotage it now just because she was hard up for cash. What if she made another mistake and word got around that silly, stupid dropout Holly Dawson had baked another terrible cake and passed it off for money? Even the pity orders would dry up then.

She couldn't bake for money. Not now. Not when she doubted herself.

Polly had sent her sympathetic texts and love from afar, of course. Polly felt bad for her. Everyone did. She'd been short with her sister on a phone conversation because she hadn't wanted to talk about money issues, so as a way of apology, she'd decided to bake some more cookies to ship to her. The postage would take a bite out of her limited bank account, but her sister deserved to have a bit of home as the holidays approached, didn't she?

So Holly had baked Polly's favorite—maple walnut shortbread with a glazed icing. Or she'd tried to. The first batch had been in the oven when the unemployment office had called back, and Holly had been on the phone with them for so long that the cookies had burned. The second batch had a funny consistency when she'd pulled them out of the oven, and she'd tasted one, only to find that something in the ingredients had turned.

She'd thrown away the entire lot and turned off the oven, heading upstairs to hug her dog for a while.

When Adam had come in after a long day, he'd immediately noticed her mood. Holly had said nothing, but he'd known. He'd come into her room, curled up behind her on the bed, and just hugged her.

"Who do I need to hurt?" he asked.

For some reason, that made her smile. Not that she wanted him to hurt someone, just that he'd immediately had her back, no questions asked. So she'd told him about her day, about her failed baking attempts, the annoyance with the unemployment office, and a litany of small hurts that had just made her want to hide away from the world and never come out.

Adam had listened to everything and hugged her again. "I have an idea," he said. "What if I put out a message to the other ranchers in the area that Wade's doing this to you?

Painted Barrel's a ranch town and everyone loves you. No one would want to see you get screwed over. I bet we could pull away all his business. You could make sandwiches on the side and he'd regret not bringing you back."

She squeezed his hand, utterly touched that he'd go to so much work just to make her happy. "I don't want Wade to fail. He and Bonnie need money just as much as I do. It's just a bad situation all around."

"Yeah, but you're my girl. I want to fix it for you."

And that made her turn around in bed and kiss him silly. Because for the first time in her life, someone had Holly's back. It was the best feeling in the world.

S omething was wrong with Holly.

In the days since the restaurant had burned down, Holly had changed. The first day or two, she'd been a whirling dervish of cooking, and every time he entered the main house, Adam was assaulted by a variety of smells. She'd made bread, rolls, muffins, bagels, cakes, cookies, and every kind of pie he could think of. Every inch of counter space had been covered with baked goods.

Then, it had abruptly stopped.

Adam had come home one night—funny how returning to Holly every day had turned into coming home—and found batches of cookies in the garbage and Holly in bed, curled around her dog. He'd hugged her while she told him all about her terrible day, and he'd vowed to get revenge on the townsfolk that were making her sad.

She'd smiled and kissed him silly, and Adam had hoped he'd fixed things, but the light in her was fading, day by day, and he couldn't figure out how to fix it.

On the surface, everything between them seemed fine.

Holly never cried. She never railed against her unemployed situation or complained. Every time he came in from the barn, she'd made sure that he had a hot meal waiting. They ended up in bed together every night.

And yet . . . something was wrong. Something was off. She wasn't her normal self, and he noticed it, because he noticed everything about her.

As the Christmas holiday crept closer, Adam noticed that Holly seemed more and more withdrawn, even though she did her best to hide it. The meals turned into more of the same every day. Breakfast was eggs and toast. Lunch was a soup and a sandwich. Dinner was a casserole of some kind. And really, it was fine. He'd have eaten more peanut butter and jelly every day if it was because she was busy or occupied. But he knew Holly well enough now to know that her lack of baking was an indication of a deeper problem.

And he had no idea how to fix it.

Every time he tried to get her to open up, she distracted him. It was usually with kisses or flirty looks, and he had to admit that he was rather vulnerable to those. It took him a few days to realize that she was doing it on purpose, too. That she tended to be really interested in sex the moment he brought up employment, or baking. Once he realized what she was doing, he let it slide for a few more days because he was hoping she'd break out of the funk.

After all, Adam knew what it was like to feel as if the careful plans you had for yourself were completely up-ended. Sometimes you needed to regroup and figure out what you wanted to do with yourself. All he knew was that he wanted to be there for her when she figured it out.

* * *

Four days before Christmas, one of the fences broke again and Adam had three cattle missing. He called Caleb over at the Swinging C, and the man helped him rustle up his runners while Adam repaired the fence. With Caleb's help, he also moved the cattle to another pasture, caked them, and settled them in for the weather that was supposed to come in that night. By the time Adam was done for the day, thick, fat snowflakes were falling from the night sky, and the temperature had dropped. Even Hannibal wasn't enjoying himself, picking through the snow with flicks of his paws.

Adam was exhausted, and all he wanted was to hold Holly close, breathe in the scent of her hair, and tuck her body against his. He wanted to hear her soft voice, wanted to listen to her tease him. He wanted her to put her cold feet on his legs and giggle with delight at the outraged sounds he made.

Even though the days were long lately—damn long— somehow knowing that Holly was waiting for him made everything better. Always did.

When he got inside the main house—he'd been spending more time there than in his own damn place lately— Holly was curled up on one of the couches, a magazine in her hands, her dog tucked against her feet. She lit up at the sight of him, a genuine smile on her face. "Hey, stranger. How was your day?"

"Long." He moved to her as she got to her feet and he kissed her in greeting. Funny how they'd fallen into a "married couple" sort of routine and . . . he kinda loved it. If you had asked him a year ago about sitting near the fire while talking about his day, he'd have thought you were insane. Now it was his favorite part of the day, that time unwinding with Holly.

Well, that and the sex.

She wound her arms around his neck and lifted her face in a request for a kiss, and he was all too happy to oblige. Adam's mouth covered hers, hot and hungry. She tasted good, like hot cocoa and sweet sugar, and he made a noise of appreciation, dragging her closer against him. "Dinner's delicious."

Holly chuckled. "I'm not dinner."

"Coulda fooled me." He nibbled on her lower lip for a moment longer, and then reluctantly drew away. "Sorry I'm late."

Her smile became a little too bright, a little too forced. "Oh, it's not like I have to wake up for work, right?"

Damn it, he'd fucked up. He tried not to remind her about work but sometimes it came up anyhow. "Well, I appreciate you staying up for me."

"Come on. I'll feed you dinner." She took his hand and pulled him toward the kitchen. "You and Hannibal both."

"It smells good," he offered, pulling his cap off his head and tossing it down.

"Beef stew," Holly said. "But no bread, sorry. Just stew."

That comment about the bread pricked at him. "Did it not turn out?"

"No, just didn't feel like making it." That too-bright tone was back in her voice, a sure sign she was hiding her emotions. "Sit down and I'll fix you a bowl."

He did, watching her as she moved around the kitchen. The place was tidy, of course—Holly always cleaned up after herself—but there were no telltale bowls of dough left out to grow overnight. There were no baked goods sitting around, waiting to be tasted. The cake plate on the center of the bar was empty, and it was never empty.

And Holly was wearing that too-bright smile on her face as she handed him a bowl of stew and then set down a bowl of dog food for Hannibal.

Adam picked at the stew, eating a few bites. "Delicious. Thank you."

"Don't thank me. That's my job. My only one right now. I'd better do it well." She managed a chuckle.

He felt even worse. His job was to make her smile, to make her forget all her troubles, and he was doing a piss-poor job of that, wasn't he? He wanted to protect her from the world, which was damn weird, because he knew Holly could take care of herself. And yet . . . when she was sad like this, he wanted her to know that he was there for her. That he had her back. That he'd take care of her if she needed it.

So he ate quickly, shoving delicious chunks of stew into his mouth as fast as possible, because he wanted to spend time with her, to distract her from her worries.

Holly watched him eat, her chin resting on her hand, a look of amusement on her face as he shoveled food into his mouth. "So were you able to get the cattle rounded up? Everything good now?"

He nodded. "Caleb was a big help. Didn't realize how behind I was on everything until he showed up." He didn't want to launch into a diatribe about how rough his day had been, not when her mood was so quick to swing to sadness. "Glad it's done, though. Now I get to spend the rest of the evening with you."

She picked up her phone, glancing at the time. "The whole twenty minutes of it? It's late, Adam. You should probably get some sleep."

"Dunno that I'm all that tired." He set his bowl down, finished with his food, and gave her a look of promise.

Holly tossed her hair, a flirty look on her face. "Did you have something in mind, then? Want to watch a movie? Maybe do a crossword together?"

"I can think of something we can do together, but it's not a crossword."

A sly smile curved her mouth as she picked up his bowl and headed for the sink. "Wrap Christmas presents, then?"

That threw him for a loop. Christmas was coming, wasn't it? And he hadn't gotten her anything yet. Ugh. He needed to get away from the ranch and buy her something in town. Something that would make her smile. Something that would make her eyes light up. Trouble was, he barely had time to breathe, much less plan ahead for a damn holiday.

But he wanted to get her something. He glanced at the tree Sage and Jason had set up in their living room before heading off on their vacation. There was only a scatter of presents underneath it, and it felt a little . . . empty. He wondered what Holly would like. Last week he would have said cookbooks and a set of bowls, but now he wasn't so sure.

He just needed to do something to make her smile again. To let her know that she was loved and that he had her back.

The realization hit him like a ton of bricks. Was he in love with Holly? This fast? It seemed insane to think about, and yet . . . it felt right. In fact, it felt so right that he wondered why he hadn't seen it sooner. Hadn't he always tipped her a dollar just because he knew it got on her nerves? Hadn't he deliberately picked fights with her because he loved to see her eyes flash with irritation?

Was Carson right and they were acting like children? Was this like him pulling on her pigtails to get her attention?

Because now that they'd gotten over their bickering and become something more . . . he was happy. He was happier than he'd ever been. Holly in his arms felt right. He loved coming "home" to her. The sex was amazing. He liked the food, sure, but more than that, he loved her smile and laughter. He liked her smart wit and casual observances. He liked how she listened to him, and he liked listening to her. And when she was sad, all he wanted was to make it better for her.

Wasn't that what love was? Caring for someone else? Wanting them to be your partner in everything? Maybe he was insane for falling for Holly that quickly, but did it matter? People fell in love in less time.

When you knew, you just knew.

He moved behind her, wrapping his arms around her waist and pressing a kiss to the side of her neck. "I was thinking of something other than Christmas presents, though I do admit my idea involved a package of some kind."

She snort-giggled in that way he adored, and his heart swelled again. Yeah, he loved this frustrating, incredible woman. He loved her, and he wanted nothing more than her smile, always.

"Is it . . . a big package?" Holly teased back.

"I've been told it's quite impressive."

She laughed again, turning in his arms and gazing up at him. "Maybe you should show it to me so I can see just what I'm dealing with."

"I think that is an excellent idea." He leaned in and brushed his lips over hers in a light kiss, then moved along her jaw, kissing toward her ear. Her hand moved to the back of his neck and she clung to him, sighing with pleasure as he kissed and teased her earlobe. Holly had delightfully sensitive ears and she made the most erotic sounds when he touched them. He teased one ear with his tongue, then whispered, "Wanna do it on the counter here?"

"This is Sage's kitchen," she protested.

"I won't tell if you won't."

"It feels wrong," she admitted. "I'm not sure she'd want us having filthy sex on her counter."

"Is it gonna be filthy sex, then?" He arched an eyebrow, pretending to be inquisitive. "We should go to the shower, then."

Her eyes lit up. "I think shower sounds good," she breathed. "Very, very good."

Holding hands, they raced toward her room and the en suite bathroom there. The moment they got inside, Adam pulled at her clothes before she could turn the water on, and they kissed frantically. As if they'd been separated for weeks instead of hours, they undressed each other hastily, hands tearing at clothing. By the time they got into the shower itself, Adam had his hand between her thighs, stroking her softness. Damn, but she was wet for him. He groaned. Was any woman ever as perfect as this one?

He hauled her up by the hips, bracing her against the tiles.

"We . . . we haven't even turned the water on," Holly panted as she wrapped her legs around his hips.

"Don't care." Adam's mouth fastened on hers hungrily even as he pushed into her. She was hot and wet and so damn tight that it nearly made his eyes cross with need. He groaned as he thrust into her, loving the whimpers she made, loving the way her nails dug into his skin as she pulled him closer. She wanted him just as badly as he wanted her.

The sex was as frantic as it was hot. He pounded into her, loving the gasps she made as he claimed her body.

Holly rocked against him, trying to increase the friction, and when he changed the angle slightly, it allowed him to rub her clit as he pumped into her. She came moments later, crying out, and he followed her quickly, pressing her against the tiles and caging her in his arms as he shuddered his release.

It was good—it was always good with Holly—but it wouldn't be enough. Something told him that he'd never get enough of her. The thought wasn't alarming, either. In fact, he rather liked it. Falling for Holly didn't make him feel panicked or uneasy. Of course he'd fallen for her. She was easy to love—sweet, giving, smart, and sassy.

Holly tapped a finger against his arm. "Water?" She asked, a hint of amusement in her voice. "Since we're already naked and in the shower?"

"Right. I'm on it." He wasn't, though. Instead, he kissed her again, savoring the feel of her soft mouth under his, the way she yielded instantly as if she'd never wanted anything else in life. Adam supposed he couldn't kiss her for hours on end, though. She'd want to sleep at some point, and he had to wake up early. So he kissed her again, slid free from the warmth of her body, and turned to fire up the shower.

For a few minutes, they were quiet, taking turns under the spray and then washing each other. He scrubbed Holly's back for her as she leaned against him, her expression sleepy contentment. He loved holding her like this, feeling her relax against his chest. It felt as if he was doing his part in shielding her from the difficulties of the world. And he wanted to do more. He needed to restore that joy to her face, and not just through sex.

And he knew just the way to do it.

"Caleb helped me today. I told you that, right?"

"Mmm." She sounded drowsy. "Did he help you catch up?"

"For the most part. But he did ask about you. Amy has a staff Christmas party at the school the day after tomorrow and he wanted to know if you would be interested in baking a cake for her. He said he'd pay double the regular rate because he knows it's short notice. Amy's had a cold and hasn't felt up to baking something."

"Poor Amy. I've met her." Holly's wet hands trailed over his skin. "She's nice. I'm sorry she's not feeling well."

Adam was sure she was pleasant enough, but he was far more interested in Holly. "Should I tell him you'll contact him, then? Do you want his number?"

She pulled away from him, her mood turning cool. He watched as Holly opened the glass door to the shower and stepped out. "Tell him thank you but no."

That wasn't the reaction he'd anticipated. "Why not? You love baking." He didn't point out that she had a lot of free time at the moment and needed the cash. He knew her well enough to know that would hurt her feelings. "And you're so damn good at it, too."

"Hmph." Holly shook her head, picking up a towel and rubbing at her hair. "I can't take a job making cake for money, Adam. It won't work out."

"Why not?"

She turned and gave him an exasperated look. "You know why not."

"I don't, actually. I thought making cakes was what you wanted to do. That you love baking more than anything." He turned off the water and stepped out of the shower. She automatically handed him a fresh towel and they dried off, standing together. It was an oddly cozy moment, and one that he kinda liked sharing with her. Funny how he'd never thought that watching his lover towel her skin off could make him so damn happy, but it did. He just liked watching her. Liked being near her.

Holly shook her head at him, wrapping the towel around her body. "I choke when there's too much on the line. I can't risk making a cake for someone and having it turn into absolute garbage. I'd be so embarrassed I'd never be able to show my face in town ever again. Tell him to ask the bakery. Maybe Geraldine can whip up something for him. Or tell him to go to the grocery store in Casper."

It made no sense. Surely she didn't doubt herself that much after that stupid baking contest? "But you make cakes for me. All the time. Amazing cakes."

"Why are you pushing this so hard? Adam, I can't, okay?" She frowned at him, her pretty features full of frustration. "I humiliated myself with the cake contest at the Winter Festival. Everyone in town laughed at me. The dumb dropout waitress trying to compete with legit bakers. And look what I turned in." She shook her head again. "If I keep shoving terrible cakes at everyone, my dream will never happen. Tell him I appreciate the pity order, but no, thank you."

He stared at Holly. She really thought it was a pity order? She thought Caleb and Amy wanted a cake because they felt sorry for her? Hadn't Becca gushed over Holly's baking for the party? Hell, hadn't he told her how incredible each treat she baked was? He'd probably put on ten pounds in the last two weeks because of her delicious food, and he didn't care. It was amazing, and he was going to be sad when Sage came back and started cooking for them again. It wouldn't be the same.

Did she not understand just how good she was at this?

"Carson's daughter loved your cookies, didn't she? And

your sister, she asked you to bake more for her, didn't she? You told me that," Adam argued.

"Adam, I can't!" Holly sounded distressed, her eyes full of frustration. "You don't understand. No one thinks I'm anything in this town. I can't afford to mess up again or they'll never see me as anything at all."

"This is all over that damn cake in the cooking competition?"

"Everyone in town laughed at me," Holly insisted, her eyes shiny. "They *laughed* at me. I thought I was good at something and the universe just proved me wrong all over again."

Ah, hell. This *was* over that damned cake. He wished he'd never touched it. He'd had no idea how much it had meant to her, and now he was going to have to confess his shitty actions because she needed to know the truth. It was long past the time that he needed to tell her, and he wanted to come clean. More than that, he wanted her to stop doubting herself so much. It wounded him to see her so miserable. "They weren't laughing at you," he insisted. "It was just a mistake."

"It wasn't—"

"There was nothing wrong with your cake, Holly." He tried again. "I swear there wasn't."

She shook her head. "You don't get it. The judges spit it out. People refused to taste it. I tried it and it was nothing but salt when it was in my mouth." Her expression grew heartbroken. "It was my big chance to make something of myself and I must have mixed up the ingredients. I just—"

"It wasn't you," he said again. "You weren't the problem."

"Well, no one else baked my cake," she retorted, irritated. "You can call it what you want, but I'm still the fuck-up."

"It wasn't you," Adam said calmly. "It was me."

She opened her mouth to protest and then paused. Tilted

her head and studied him, and then frowned, as if she couldn't quite figure him out. "What are you talking about?"

"You weren't at fault. I was mad at you after the whole peanut butter and jelly sandwich thing and I came into the kitchen and saw you had all the ingredients in bowls in the fridge. And I might have made a few . . ." He rubbed his forehead. "Creative additions to your recipe."

Holly blinked.

Stared at him.

He watched as her eyes widened in horror as she realized what he'd done. Her mouth opened, her jaw dropping. "You sabotaged me?" she whispered.

God, now he felt like the biggest jerk in the world. The look of hurt and betrayal on her face was killing him. "It was childish. I know. I was just . . . mad and not thinking. I figured you were making the cake for Carson. It was petty, I know." The more he talked about it, the stupider he felt. What kind of grown man sabotaged a cake? Him, apparently. "I thought you were playing games with us, trying to make me feel bad, like my ex did. I didn't know you were entering it into the contest until you showed up with it the next day and then I just couldn't say anything."

"You fucked me over?"

"I didn't know!"

"And you still let me enter it? You couldn't have warned me?" She put her hands to her forehead. "You couldn't have had your giggle otherwise? You let me present that cake like a smug asshole to everyone in the town so they could laugh at me!"

Adam hadn't realized that was how she was going to view it. "I should have said something. I didn't realize you'd think it was embarrassing—"

"How could I not?" she wailed. "Do you know who the

judges were? They were the owners of the two nearest bakeries that I've been trying to do side work for, for months now! Do you know how stupid I looked when I showed up with the world's nastiest cake and tried to ask them for baking jobs?" Holly spread her hands in front of her, glaring at him. "Do you know how stupid I felt?"

He crossed his arms over his chest. "Well . . . now I do."

"How could you?"

"I didn't think it was a big deal," he admitted again, and the words felt lame coming out of his mouth. "It was just a cake."

"Just a cake? Do you know the doors it could have opened for me if I had impressed the judges? Do you know what it could have done for me to have everyone in town talking about what a good baker I am? Do you think it might have helped to have a side gig like that to fall back on when, oh, I don't know, *my place of work burns to the damn ground*?" She drew herself upright, that look of horror still on her face. "I can't believe I slept with you! I can't believe I'm having casual sex with a man who deliberately screwed me over!"

Adam bristled. Not only at her accusing tone, but at the whole "casual sex" thing. "Is that what this is? Casual sex?"

She put her hands to her forehead. "Does it matter? Don't change the subject—"

"It matters to me," he retorted.

"Oh, real great," Holly huffed. "Coming from someone who's explicitly said he doesn't want a relationship at all. And you think women can't be trusted?" She shook her head at him. "Maybe you're the one that can't be trusted, Adam. How could you?"

"We were enemies," he said flatly. "It's not like I thought we'd end up in bed together. It was just a petty moment and I'm sorry."

"A petty moment," she echoed, staring at him. "A petty *moment*. You deliberately messed up my cake and then let me present it to everyone in town. You let me make a fool out of myself and then you never said anything?" She gasped. "We've been sleeping together and all this time you never told me? Oh my god, Adam. How can I trust you after this?" She looked utterly floored. "I thought you had my back. You, of all people, I thought I could trust." She shook her head. "Looks like I'm a bigger idiot than I thought."

It was just a damn cake, for crying out loud. Why was she making this about their relationship? "I messed up," he said again. "Can we move past this, please? It's in the past and I'm trying to help you—"

"Maybe I don't want your help," she snarled at him. Holly stormed out of the bathroom and looked around the bedroom. She grabbed his strewn clothing, gathering it in her arms, and flung it into the hallway. In the next moment, Hannibal raced to grab his discarded jeans, no doubt thinking it was a game. Holly turned to glare at Adam again. "Hey, guess what? It's a good thing you aren't into commitment, because we are absolutely done here. Get out of my room."

"Holly," he began, frustrated. She was dumping him? Over a cake? "We need to talk about this—"

"I have absolutely nothing to say to you," Holly told him, and went into the bathroom and slammed the door behind her.

He stared at the door, still holding the towel over his hips. How had this become his fault? He knew it was childish to mess up her cake, but was it really something to break up with him over? He glanced down at Pumpkin in her bed, and the dog just wagged her tail slowly, as if she, too, was reluctant to acknowledge Adam.

With a sigh, Adam headed into the hall to retrieve his clothing. He'd talk to her tomorrow, then, when she'd had time to process things and realize he hadn't meant any harm.

The next morning, he found a sack lunch on the doorstep to his cabin.

Peanut butter and jelly.

CHAPTER TWENTY-FOUR

Holly punched the dough on the counter, imagining it as Adam's head. His stupid, stupid head.

It had been almost a full day since he'd confessed his dirty secret and she was still furious. It wasn't just that he'd sabotaged her cake. It was that he'd had the nerve to sit there and say nothing while she made a complete ass of herself in front of the entire town. To think that she'd slept with him! To think that she'd been developing feelings for him!

She felt doubly stupid now. He'd fooled her repeatedly. Here she'd thought he wasn't too bad a guy. That maybe she'd see if he was interested in casually dating—even if it wasn't all that casual on her end—even after Sage and Jason returned and Holly no longer cooked for them or temporarily lived at the ranch. It wouldn't kill her to take things slow, right? She'd figured she could date Adam for a while, see where things led, and if she got her heart broken, so be it.

Yeah, well, she'd gotten her heart broken, all right. She

punched the dough again and glanced over at the oven. Her fruitcake was baking and smelled rather good, even if she said so herself. Not that she was a big fruitcake fan. In fact, she wasn't sure that anyone was a fruitcake fan.

Which was why she was baking it for Adam.

Was it passive-aggressive of her? Sure. So were the peanut butter and jelly sandwiches she was going to flood him with for the next while. Since she was hired to make dinners, she was going to make dinners, of course. She was trying to think of the least appetizing things she could possibly make him. Liver and onions? Olive loaf? Something loaf for sure, she decided. With Brussels sprouts.

And beets. Definitely something with beets. Beet loaf?

She snorted with amusement and punched the dough again. The bread she was making was for her, because when she needed to let out her aggressions, baking was the way to go. Baking always made her feel better, and after days of abstaining because she felt so low and worthless, it was good to have projects in the kitchen again. Her sourdough starter was showing signs of life, she had a cake—however fruity—in the oven, and dough under her hands.

She'd get through this. She would.

It freaking hurt, though. Every time she thought about Adam, she felt a fresh wave of betrayal. She imagined his face, smug with amusement, as she brought the world's worst cake to a damn bake-off. He'd known it was awful and he'd said nothing, just driven her into town without a peep. And then he'd had the nerve to be nice to her. And he was her date at Becca's party.

And damn it, she'd fallen for him.

That felt like the biggest betrayal of all. If he'd just been regular jerk Adam and had sabotaged her cake, she wouldn't care nearly as much. She'd be angry and humiliated, of course, but not surprised. But because she'd fallen for him—and fallen into bed with him—she felt betrayed. And sad. Really, really sad.

For the first time since Polly had left—maybe even earlier, to before, when her parents were alive—Holly hadn't felt alone. She'd felt like she had a companion, a partner, someone that understood her and listened to her. Someone that rubbed her feet and made stupid jokes when she was having a bad day. Someone that taste tested all her recipes and watched out for her when she got drunk. Someone that had her back.

Maybe that was what hurt the most. Holly had thought Adam had her back, and instead, he was just laughing behind her back.

Hot tears threatened to roll down her face again and she paused, wiping her face on her shoulder. She wasn't going to cry over Adam Calhoun. She wasn't. She was going to think about those one-dollar tips and not the way he smiled at her when she woke up, like she was perfection. She wasn't going to think about the way he always put her feet in his lap as if she was the only one that had had a long day. She wasn't going to think about his laugh, or the way his breath hitched when she touched him.

Holly was never going to touch the bastard again.

She punched her fist into the dough once more. He'd let her doubt herself for weeks. He'd let her cry over that cake repeatedly. He'd let her feel stupid and useless and made her question her skills, and the entire time, he'd known there was nothing wrong with her ability to bake. Nothing at all.

And now that she knew the truth . . . she still worried about whether she was any good or not, and wasn't that the freaking saddest thing of all? That Holly still had no confidence in herself?

She needed to stop this shit. Today. She wasn't the type to mope. She was the type to pick herself up and move on, because the world wouldn't allow her a chance to wallow . . . even if she very much wanted to wallow. She glanced around at the kitchen, at the variety of baking projects in various stages of completion.

Yeah, she wasn't going to save these for Adam. Fuck Adam.

And then she burst into tears again, because fucking Adam was part of the problem, wasn't it? Adam had been wonderful up until last night, when he'd shown his true colors. She should have known it was too good to be true between them.

A few hours later, Holly had her freshly baked bread wrapped up in cheesecloth and two delicately iced loaves of fruitcake boxed up. She'd contemplated leaving the fruit-cake for him and then figured he didn't even deserve that. With her luck, he'd be the one person in the world that loved fruitcake. So she packed up her baked goods, put a sweater on her fluffy little dog, and drove into town.

Immediately, it felt like a bad idea. There was an enormous, charred hole in the cluster of buildings downtown, right where Wade's saloon should have been. Seeing it made her feel worse, and Holly parked her car and stared morosely at the burned-out ruin for a long moment before forcing herself to get out. With Pumpkin tucked under one arm, she picked up one of the cakes with her other and crossed the street, heading for Becca's salon.

Her friend was inside, which wasn't much of a surprise—Becca was always inside, working. She was just as much a workaholic as Holly was, but Becca ran her own salon and loved to sit and just talk for hours with her customers. Today, someone was seated getting her ends trimmed. She had dark hair and a full figure. Holly had seen her around town but never ran into her much—the local accountant. Not that Holly ever had enough money to need an accountant.

But Becca beamed a wide smile at Holly. "Well, hey there! Happy holidays to you!"

"Happy holidays," called the woman in the chair, her hands moving under the bright pink cape.

"I thought I'd bring you a present to say thank you for inviting me to the party the other day," Holly lied. I mean, as excuses went, it was a perfect one, wasn't it? It made a lot more sense than "rage baking." "If you don't like fruitcake, I've got a loaf of cinnamon bread out in the car."

"Are you kidding me? I'll eat anything you bake." Becca set down her scissors and made grabby hands at Holly.

"Is it weird if I say I love fruitcake?" asked the other woman, giving them a sheepish look. "I used to eat it to spite my mother and now I actually just like it."

"Knowing your mother, that is absolutely not weird," Becca told her, and then gestured to Holly. "This is Layla. Layla, Holly."

"You work at the restaurant, right?" Layla asked, smiling.

"Used to," Holly said, and it was hard to keep the smile on her face. "Now I'm just baking to burn some time." She held the container out to Becca and hesitated. "Would it be weird if I asked you to taste it and tell me what you think? I'm having a crisis of faith."

"Not weird at all." Becca took the container from her and smiled at the little dog tucked under Holly's arm. "You want a treat for that one? I've got my Alaska's treat jar freshly refilled."

Holly took one of the baked bone-shaped cookies, feeling a little smug when Pumpkin sniffed it but didn't seem all that interested. The treats she made for her dog were much better. She squeezed the Pomeranian tight as both Layla and Becca took a slice of fruitcake—god, why had she made fruitcake of all things?—and chewed. She bit her lip so hard it stung, waiting.

Becca looked over at her, an expression of surprise on her face. "I think I love it."

Holly let out a huge breath. "You do?"

"Yeah, and I don't think I've ever loved fruitcake before. This is amazing. Did you say you had another in your car? Can I buy it from you?"

Layla shoved her entire piece in her mouth and raised a hand. "Wait, no, I want to buy it. Jack will love that."

Holly felt as if she could breathe again. "You're not saying that to humor me?"

"I'm not humoring you," Layla said. "I will absolutely fight for another piece of that cake." She pulled her hands out from under the cape, revealing the knitting needles she had under there. "And I'm prepared."

"We'll buy everything you have, regardless," Becca said, smiling.

"Oh, I couldn't sell it," Holly protested. "You can have it for free. I just needed someone to taste it and tell me it was good."

"Why wouldn't you sell it?" Layla looked confused. "It's ten times better than anything I've bought at the bakery here, and god knows I'm there far too often."

Holly considered for a moment, then decided to spill the whole sordid story. "It started with me getting hired to cook and look after the house while Sage and Jason are gone. Adam has always been kind of a dick to me, and we butted heads. He made a crack about not wanting anything but peanut butter and jelly sandwiches so that's what I made him for a week straight. He got mad about it, and apparently he sabotaged the cake I brought for the baking competition." She crossed her arms over her chest. "And he didn't tell me about it until last night, after we'd had sex."

Layla clutched at the arms of the barber chair as if her hair had just blown back.

Becca stared at Holly, frozen. "I . . . think we missed a few steps in there," Becca said. "You guys were fighting and then you slept together? Was it hate sex?"

"Oooh." Layla leaned forward. "Was it hot?"

Becca smacked her on the shoulder and turned her attention back to Holly. "I don't understand. You say you guys were enemies but you were both really cute together at my party. I thought you were dating."

"That . . ." Holly paused, not sure how to explain it. "That night we went as friends, but we turned into something more the next day."

"I was at the party," Layla mused. "And I vaguely remember seeing you with a tall, hot guy that looked at you like he wanted to eat you up. That's your cake saboteur?" When Holly nodded, Layla's expression fell. "So I shouldn't ship it, then?"

"Ship . . . it?" Holly echoed.

"Never mind." Layla tapped one of her knitting needles on her lip. "So, okay, let me get this timeline straight. You guys hated each other, and he sabotaged your cake without you knowing. Then you went to Becca's party as friends, and then you fell into bed together and you . . . just found out about the cake sabotage yesterday? Do I have that right?"

Becca's eyes lit up. She straightened, her gaze intent on Holly. "Oh. Who bent first?"

"What?" Holly said.

"Who gave in first?" Becca asked, speaking slower. "You

know. You both were hating each other, and then something changed. Who gave in first?"

"I . . . I don't know," Holly admitted. She thought back to the days after the Winter Festival. She'd been so down, so defeated. She hadn't wanted to bake anything . . . and then Adam had shown up and flattered her, and told her about his birthday. "I think he did? He asked if I'd make a cake for his birthday . . ."

Holly trailed off as Becca jumped and raced over to her cash register. She pulled out her ledger and flipped through it, then made a squealing noise. "He was here, you know!" At Holly's blank look, Becca continued. "I thought this sounded familiar to me, and I checked my records. He was here the day after the Winter Festival, and he was quizzing me all about you, Holly." She clutched the book to her chest, a dreamy expression on her face. "You think maybe he felt bad and wanted to make it up to you?"

Layla oohed. "I bet it wasn't even his birthday!"

Becca squealed again, acting more like a schoolgirl than a married woman with a child.

Holly frowned at both of them. "Well, if it wasn't his birthday, it was just another thing he lied about."

"I bet he was trying to get on your good side," Becca gushed. "He felt guilty and he liked you and so he decided to romance you instead."

"No," Holly protested. Even as she did, though, it felt a little weak to her. They had become friends after the birthday cake, hadn't they? If not fast friends, they'd certainly called a truce at that point and began to talk to each other in a civil manner. And she'd nursed him while he was sick, because she'd felt bad for him being so helpless and ill. "This doesn't change anything!"

"Doesn't it?" Layla gave her a dreamy look. "I mean, he's cute. And he was clearly head over heels for you at the party. Watched you like a hawk and scared off anyone that looked as if they wanted to talk to you."

"He did?"

Layla nodded. "Oh yeah. Jack was laughing about it because he said Adam looked utterly flummoxed every time a guy looked in your direction."

She didn't remember that. Then again, she'd been drunk that night so she didn't remember a lot. Just Adam hovering over her with an amused smile on his face as she acted like a fool. Adam gently steering her away from people. Adam taking her out on the dance floor when she wanted to dance, even though he seemed rather miserable about it.

She didn't know what to think. It didn't make up for the fact that he'd let her make an idiot of herself in front of the whole town. Not by a long shot. He could have talked to her, damn it. He could have said something. Instead, he'd let her suffer for weeks, and she wasn't ready to forgive that.

No matter how much Becca and Layla gushed about him.

"It doesn't change the fact that he sabotaged me," Holly said. "Or the fact that he let me bring my cake into town and make a fool out of myself in front of everyone. If he really liked me, he could have stopped me at any time. The fact that he didn't just makes me feel stupid." And even more stupid than that, she'd been happily sleeping with him, all the while knowing he wanted no strings attached. She'd been fine to take things a day at a time, to see where it led, and if it led nowhere, she knew to expect it.

That was the worst part about this—she hadn't expected sabotage from him. And she couldn't forgive it.

* * *

It was hard to finish his day without Holly's warm smile at the end of the night.

Adam had a long day of work, and when he finally headed toward the main house, he found the door locked and the lights off. There was a note posted on the door, directing him to a bagged lunch left on his doorstep. Hannibal whined and scratched at the door, clearly expecting to be let in for dinner and treats, and it was hard to turn him away.

It was hard for Adam to turn away, too.

He supposed he deserved that, given that he'd sabotaged her cake. He deserved to eat peanut butter and jelly until she forgave him. He knew that, and he was okay with that. But he missed talking to her. He just wanted to see if she was okay, if she'd baked anything that day—which always seemed to put her in a good mood—or if she was still down over her job. He wanted to apologize to her. He hadn't thought the consequences through, and he hadn't realized how much it would hurt her.

He felt like he'd lost something he hadn't even realized he wanted.

So Adam turned around and went home, ate his sandwich, and went to bed, wondering if Holly was crying herself to sleep. God, he hoped not. He almost hoped she was over him quickly, just because he didn't like the thought of her being in pain. It tore him up.

One day turned into the next, and the peanut butter and jelly remained for lunch only. Dinner turned into the usual repertoire of deliciously cooked food—roast and potatoes, shepherd's pie, freshly made chicken enchiladas—but Holly never made an appearance. She left the food for him carefully packaged in a labeled container on his doorstep, and locked the door to the main house every night.

It was clear she didn't want to talk to him. It was clear she was done.

Adam hated it.

One stupid mistake against his (then) enemy and he'd lost the best thing that had ever happened to him. He felt like he'd lost his best friend and partner. After two days of her not answering, he'd tried texting her, too, only to have his messages ignored. So he'd sent her one final message.

ADAM: When you're ready to talk to me . . . I'm here.

He wanted to tell her that he missed her, but he felt like that would be emotional blackmail. He didn't want Holly to get back together with him out of guilt. He wanted her to be with him because she wanted to genuinely be with him. Guilting her would only make her feel shitty, and she had enough on her plate. He was at a loss.

It didn't help that Carson wasn't on his side, either. He'd woken up one morning to a new text message from the older man.

CARSON: You're a good ranch hand, but damn, you're stupid.

ADAM: Gee . . . thanks.

CARSON: Why'd you fuck with Holly's cake? You don't shit where you eat, son.

ADAM: It's a long story . . . and I'm sure she already told it to you.

CARSON: Yup.

CARSON: You hurt her feelings bad, you know. You let everyone laugh at her. It's more than just the cake. It's that you humiliated her in front of the town.

ADAM: I didn't know it was going to be in front of the entire town!

CARSON: Am I wrong or were you the one that drove her?

ADAM: You're not wrong. I should have said something, but what could I have said at that point?

CARSON: Try "Hi Holly, I added salt to your cake because I'm a childish idiot, don't serve it to anyone"?

ADAM: Fine. I admit it. I messed up. That's what you want to hear, right?

CARSON: Yup.

CARSON: She needs to hear it, too.

ADAM: I've tried. I've really tried. I keep trying to talk to her and she shuts me out. I don't want to push too hard because I don't want her to feel trapped, but she won't even give me a chance.

CARSON: Would you give you a chance?

ADAM: Yes.

CARSON: Then you're stupider than I thought.

ADAM: Is there a point to this conversation?

CARSON: Yeah. You still don't get it.

Adam glared down at his phone. Why did Carson think he knew Holly better than Adam did? It was ridiculous . . . and it was starting to really irritate him. How could he fix what was wrong if no one would tell him the problem?

ADAM: What is it I don't get, o wise expert?

CARSON: You said your ex-wife cheated on you, right?

ADAM: I don't see what this has to do with anything.

CARSON: Hear me out. Where did you used to live?

ADAM: Norfolk, Virginia.

CARSON: So after you got out, why didn't you stay there?

Adam gritted his teeth. Why, indeed? He hadn't wanted to stay in Norfolk because everyone he knew was Navy. His entire social circle was Navy buddies, and the gym was full of Navy. He'd go to the damn supermarket and run into someone in uniform. And it got on his nerves after a while, because it was all a reminder of the fact that he'd been cheated on while serving his country. And when he'd run into the guy at a bar, he knew it was time to leave.

He was tired of being "that guy that got cheated on." He was tired of the sympathetic looks everywhere he went, like he was some sort of idiot for not realizing Donna's unhappiness earlier. So he'd left and gone as far away as he could.

But he wasn't about to text all that shit to Carson, who was already acting smug and annoying.

ADAM: I had reasons.

CARSON: Yeah well, let's think real hard about this. Holly grew up in this town. She hasn't left. In everyone's eyes, she's still a dropout. She has to work twice as hard as everyone else to be taken seriously.

CARSON: And you shit all over that.

Hot guilt rushed through him. He hadn't thought about Holly's situation in town when he'd done it. To him, she was just that pretty but annoying waitress. Then again, he hadn't grown up here. He knew that she was sensitive about being seen as a dropout. Becca had mentioned the same thing, so clearly it was on people's minds. It was crazy, really. Couldn't they see how smart she was? How driven? How caring?

ADAM: Why's everyone hung up on her education? She did it to take care of her sister. You'd think she'd get a lot more credit for that.

CARSON: You'd think. But in a lot of people's eyes, she's nothing but a waitress. She feels like she's got something to prove.

ADAM: And let me guess, all I proved is that what they think of her is right?

CARSON: I don't think it, and you don't think it, but everyone else thinks it.

ADAM: Then they're all idiots.

CARSON: Agreed. So you'd better fix it. I don't like her sad.

ADAM: You think I like it? She won't even talk to me. How can I fix it if she won't even talk to me?

CARSON: I don't know, but you'd better figure it out.

Adam wanted to pitch the phone away in disgust. It was just like Carson to text him a long-ass lecture that ended with no useful information, just griping. Hadn't he done that all month with the ranch? It was like he didn't trust Adam to handle anything while he was gone. He knew it came from a good place, but . . . he also didn't want to hear it.

He knew he'd hurt Holly. He knew she was embarrassed.

The question was . . . how did he fix it? That was the part he had no answer to.

All he knew was that he needed to have Holly back in his life again. He'd only been a few days without her and it felt like the longest year of his life already. There was no joy in a world without Holly's bright laughter and sly wit. He was going to get her back, damn it. He just had to figure out how.

CHAPTER TWENTY-FIVE

That evening, after he finished mucking the stalls in the barn, he headed for his cabin and collapsed on the bed. It had been another long day, and he felt like everything was getting away from him again. Jason had texted to check in on things, as he had several times over the last month, and Adam didn't complain. What could he say? *I need you to come back because the cattle are a real pain in my ass and doing cattle stuff? That number 34 is constantly having to get retrieved out of deep mud? That I have to keep caking them because there's not enough protein in their shit and I can't keep them at the weight they need to stay at in order for the calves to be fat and healthy for the spring? That one of the horses twisted a leg and the vet will be over tomorrow? That the fences keep falling down and the Gator needs maintenance and we're low on hay bales and and and . . .*

It was all normal stuff. It was all things that could be handled on a regular day with the three of them working together. Except Jason wasn't around, and Carson was visiting his daughter, and it was practically the holidays and so Adam didn't feel right about calling up the Watsons over at the Swinging C and asking for more help. So he did what he could and handled all the immediate problems and tried not to worry about everything else. He made sure the animals were healthy and fed and all accounted for. Everything else could wait for a while.

Hannibal jumped up on the bed next to him and began licking Adam's face, whining with excitement.

He sputtered, pushing away Hannibal's muzzle with a chuckle. "What's gotten into you?"

The dog whined again, then bounced off the bed and raced toward the door. He waited by it, tail wagging, and Adam's heart sunk. Did he think they were going to the main house to visit Holly? Adam got up from bed and glanced out the window. The lights were on in Holly's room, but he didn't think she'd want to see him. A quick check on the porch showed him that she'd left his meal there, just like normal. Yeah, he was still in the doghouse.

He sighed heavily, picked up the tray, and set it on the small table in his room. "Come away from the door, boy."

He unpacked the food, noting half-heartedly that it was chicken strips and homestyle fries, along with reheating instructions. He was too tired for that, so he just grabbed one and started chewing, and offered one to Hannibal. He wasn't all that hungry. Not really. Food kinda depressed him lately, because he knew the only reason that Holly was feeding him at all was because she desperately needed the money the job brought. As if she worried he'd somehow complain to Sage and stop her from getting a paycheck. That stung, of course. He'd never do such a thing.

Adam ended up giving half his food to Hannibal, who

scarfed it down. There were two cookies inside the dinner kit, one for him, and one shaped like a bone with Hannibal's name written on the Saran Wrap. He stared at his cookie for a while. He wasn't sure if the sight of it made him feel better or worse. She was baking, at least. That made him happy. He didn't like it when she was sad and miserable.

But did it mean that she'd moved on past him? That she was utterly done with him?

There was a red envelope below the container of food that Adam hadn't noticed at first. His heart thudded at the sight of it. Was Holly . . . sending him a card? But when he saw the postage marks in the corner, his hopes sunk. It was from Iowa.

His brother.

With more than a bit of annoyance, Adam opened the card. He wasn't exactly on good terms with Mike. Ever since Adam and Donna had divorced, Mike had been difficult. He'd been full of advice, all of it nothing Adam had wanted to hear. He'd offered for Adam to "come home" to the farm repeatedly, but it was the last thing Adam had wanted. Mike had married his high school sweetheart and they'd had kids right away. Mike had taken over the farm when his dad had gotten sick, and it was a smooth transition when Dad had passed on. Mike had always known what he wanted. He'd never suffered from a crisis of faith.

He was also quick to tell Adam what to do, and Adam had always resented it. He was sure his brother's Christmas card was full of all kinds of shit advice he didn't want or need, but he pulled it out of the envelope anyhow.

Instead of some insipid reindeer picture or a Santa illustration, it was a family photo. The entire family was huddled into the picture in front of the fireplace. He recognized that fireplace—it was the one in the living room of the old farmhouse. Mary—his sister-in-law—was seated on the floor with their youngest in her lap. The little girl was in twin pigtails and the two boys stood next to their mother, gaps in their wide smiles. With a hand on each shoulder of the boys, Mike stood over them, but his gaze was on his wife, seated in front of him.

His brother had such a look of utter pride and happiness on his face as he gazed down at his wife that it wrenched something inside Adam. His brother was getting older, his hair sprinkled with gray and his waist a little thicker. Mary looked more like a mom than the fresh, apple-cheeked blonde he remembered.

But they were all so damn happy.

Adam stared at the picture for a long moment and then opened the card. It had been signed by everyone, from Mary to little Shelby. Underneath, his brother's cramped, tight writing crept across the bottom of the card.

I know you don't like to need anyone. I get it. But if you ever need a family, you know where we are. —Mike

It was . . . not preachy. Not demanding, like Mike's normal notes were. It was nice.

Adam flipped the card closed and stared at the picture again. Instead of his brother and his wife, he imagined Holly as the one seated by the fire, a kid in her lap, and Adam as the one gazing adoringly at her.

He wanted that so damn bad he could taste it.

It wasn't like this with Donna, he realized. They'd gotten together before he'd shipped off and it had never been excessively romantic, at least on his side. Maybe that was why she hadn't felt the need to be faithful. He'd left the

Navy to be with her, but looking back, that was more about him than her. He'd been tired of his life in the military and had wanted a change. He was gutted when he found out she was cheating, but it hadn't hurt his heart. He'd felt betrayed, but he hadn't pined over her. He didn't ache to see her again.

But knowing Holly hated him? Felt like he'd betrayed her? It was like a hole burning through his heart, an ache he couldn't quite shake. It may have happened fast, but he knew he'd feel this way about her a year from now, or a dozen years from now.

Holly had felt right. Being with her had felt like the missing puzzle piece locking into place. It had been easy, and fun, and just . . . made him happy.

Like Mary made his brother, Mike, happy. He wanted that happiness. He wanted that partner in his life. And he wanted it to be Holly.

He tossed the card down on the bed and stormed out of his cabin, heading for the main house. Hannibal barked and bounded at his feet, excited. Adam knocked at the back door, but there was no answer. He tried calling her phone. Texted her.

She didn't pick up. Holly was still avoiding him.

Adam stared at the door in frustration. He could break it open, he supposed. Force his way into the house and make his pitch . . . but he doubted she'd listen.

He'd just have to figure out a way to make her listen, then. He needed a plan.

Rubbing his goatee thoughtfully, Adam turned around and headed back to his cabin. He needed a plan to win his woman back. A plan to show her just how much he cared, how he thought she was smart and wonderful and perfect.

And he knew just who he needed to pull in.

Immediately, the idea unfurled in his mind, and he knew it was perfect. With a grin, Adam picked up his phone and started to text, then paused, glancing at the clock. It was late.

Okay, he'd text in the morning, then . . . but he didn't have much time to waste. Christmas was just around the corner, and he intended on giving Holly the perfect gift.

Holly stared out the window, a mug of hot cocoa cradled in her hands, and tried not to feel sad and depressed. Big, fat snowflakes tumbled from the sky, and the ground was blanketed in fresh white powder. Inside it was nice and toasty warm, and she had the fireplace going. The kitchen was full of delicious smells, her dog was curled up on the couch, and *It's a Wonderful Life* was playing on the television. It was a lovely Christmas Eve day.

Except for the fact that Holly was completely and utterly alone.

She'd expected this, really. She knew Polly wasn't coming down from university. They'd talked again yesterday, the conversation brief. Polly had plans to go out with friends for Chinese food on Christmas Day and then would dive right back into her studying. She couldn't talk long, though, and had ended the call quickly. All their calls seemed to be shorter and shorter lately, which made Holly feel sad. She knew Polly had a life of her own, but Holly was rudderless at the moment and wanted nothing more than to have someone to lean on.

She hated that she missed Adam. She still felt betrayed and alone. She'd given him her trust and he'd crapped all over it. But even so . . . she still missed him. Missed his big warm body in bed next to hers, missed seeing him through the day. Missed stolen kisses and laughter and small touches. Missed sharing bits about her day. She ached to hear his laughter and to see him scoop up her small dog and lavish attention on Pumpkin.

She just missed . . . him.

And she missed him far more than she missed Polly, which felt like a betrayal. Like there was something wrong with her for being completely bereft and miserable because she'd broken up with Adam—her fling—more than because Polly wasn't coming down for Christmas. It didn't help that he was just across the way, in his cabin, and she had to make food for him every day. It didn't help that she could look out the window most days and see him on horseback, or walking around with Hannibal at his heels, or working on the farm equipment. She could ogle him from afar as much as she wanted, but she didn't trust herself to have a conversation with him.

Holly was pretty sure it would be nothing but tears on her side, and she didn't want to break down like a fool. She wanted to hold on to her anger. Her embarrassment. Her indignation.

Well, okay, she wasn't really all that angry anymore. Talking with Becca and Layla yesterday had taken a lot of the sting out of the wound. Becca was convinced that Adam had regretted his actions, and Holly kind of wondered about that, too. It would explain his overnight turnabout, attitude wise. And from what she knew of Adam, he wasn't vindictive. He had a weird sense of humor, sure, but he was never nasty about it. Hadn't Carson been bugging him via text for weeks now about all the stuff he wanted Adam to do while he was gone? She thought about his patience with those, and how even when the texts bothered him, he still did as Carson asked because they were friends.

So that meant either she was wrong about Adam's vindictiveness when it came to her cake, or she'd judged Adam wrong all along and he was a worse person than she—or anyone in town—thought. And she suspected that wasn't the case . . . but it still made her sad. She'd trusted him and he'd humiliated her in front of everyone she knew.

Holly supposed that was the part that was hardest to forgive. How could you fall for someone—be with someone—who didn't support you? She could forgive a lot, but not that.

She sipped her cocoa and stared out the window at the snow. Even though she'd known she'd be spending Christmas here at the ranch, alone, she wasn't prepared for how isolated she felt. Holidays were for spending time with family. For sharing the joy of the season. For reconnecting.

And she had no one to reconnect with. Maybe that was why she was so low.

Well, today, she was going to make it all about her, Holly decided. She was making her favorite cake—a crumbly cinnamon coffee cake—because this day was about her. She was whipping up a big pot of macaroni and cheese to share with Pumpkin, and she was going to sit in front of the fire, watch holiday movies, and maybe give herself a pedicure. It was a day of self-care, she decided, and headed upstairs to put on a charcoal face mask that she'd been saving for such an occasion.

Holly had her hair bound up in a towel and was dressed in her ugliest sweatpants and oldest T-shirt when the doorbell rang. She stared at her reflection in dismay, wiping her hands off. She'd just put the last of the charcoal mask on her face and she had visitors? Seriously?

Didn't they know it was Christmas Eve?

Oh lord, what if it was carolers? What if it was someone feeling sorry for her and wanted to invite her to a get-together of some kind? She'd just die of embarrassment.

The doorbell rang again, and her dog barked with excitement. Holly groaned, scooping up Pumpkin before heading toward the door. "I guess we can't pretend to not be home, right?"

She headed for the front door, peering out the window as she did. Her vision was blocked by the wreath that Sage had covering the glass, but she could just make out what looked like an ice cream truck—the big, boxy vehicle with the speakers on top that played music and had the window on the side.

What in the ever-loving heck was an ice cream truck doing here? She frowned, her face tightening as the charcoal mask did its thing, and tried to peer at who was at the door. All she could see were jeans and boots, which could have been anyone, really.

The doorbell rang again, impatient. And then again, and again. Pumpkin yapped right in her ear, giving away her location and making her half-deaf.

Holly moved to the door and stared through the peephole. It was a man on the porch, and his back was to her as he gazed out at the ice cream truck. The peephole glass distorted his form, but on his head was a familiar baseball cap . . .

And her heart lurched.

Oh god. It was Adam. She bit back a whimper, clutching her dog closer. What was he doing here? Why was he trying to talk to her today of all days? She closed her eyes for a moment, steeling herself, and then opened the door.

Adam turned around, his gaze moving over her hungrily. It made her blush, seeing how avidly he drank in the sight of her, despite the fact that she looked like a damn slob. "Hi," he said, dragging his focus back up to her face. "Missed you."

That was her greeting? That he missed her? Holly's face flushed. "What are you doing here?" The words came out tight . . . because her face was freezing up, thanks to the mask. It was hard to move her lips to speak. "Why do you have an ice cream truck?"

He took a step forward, pulling Pumpkin from her arms and cradling the dog in his. The Pomeranian wriggled with excitement, licking at his chin. "I came to apologize." He put a hand on the excited dog's back, trying to calm her, a smile curling his mouth. "I know you're not as happy to see me as this one is, but I thought you needed to hear the words anyhow."

He . . . was here to apologize? It made her even more flustered. Did he miss her, then? Adam had said he wasn't looking for a relationship, but maybe . . . she didn't want to allow herself to hope.

"I fucked up," Adam said bluntly. "I can't describe it in any other way. I fucked up and I should have said something before you took that cake into town, but I didn't realize how big of a deal it was to you. I didn't realize it would embarrass you in front of everyone. I wasn't thinking. I made a petty decision and once I realized it, I just made things worse by not saying anything. I didn't realize the repercussions it would have on you. I should have thought it through. Hell, I shouldn't have done it in the first place. All I can say is that I'm sorry and I get why you were so upset at me. I understand if you never want to speak to me again."

Holly blinked. His expression was completely and utterly earnest, and she believed him. He couldn't have known how stupid she would feel in front of the whole town because he hadn't grown up here. He didn't know. To him, she was just a waitress. She wasn't the local good-for-nothing dropout.

She was just Holly to him. She'd never had anything to prove to him because he'd never asked for it. They'd gotten off on the wrong foot in the beginning, but it was because of their personalities, not who she was. The realization of that was . . . soothing. It went a long way toward making her feel better.

"You really hurt me with that," Holly said eventually. She'd taken a moment to compose her thoughts, and the longer she took to respond, the more worried he seemed. It was that worry on his face, the way he kept watching her, that decided her. It was important to him that she not be upset . . . because she was important to him.

That realization was like a balm that soothed away the last of the hurt.

"I know." He scratched at Pumpkin's ears, a look of sheer frustration on his face. "I'd give anything to take it back, but I can't. So that's why I'm here with your Christmas present. I can't fix what's happened in the past, but I can try to make amends for it, if you'll let me."

"Amends?" She didn't understand. "By . . . bringing an ice cream truck?" She smiled, though it probably looked weird given how tight her face felt. She touched the charcoal mask, but it was hard on her face, too late to wipe off. "I mean, I like ice cream, but maybe not that much?"

His eyes flashed with excitement. Adam reached for her hand and pulled her forward, onto the porch. "It's for you. And it's not an ice cream truck. It's a cake truck. Or a pie truck. Or whatever you feel like baking that day truck."

Holly looked over at him in surprise. "W-what?"

"I've been thinking about you a lot over the last few days." The tops of his cheeks were pink, as if he were flushing. "It sounds goofy to admit it, but I just . . . I wanted to fix this. Even if you never speak to me again, I wanted you to know that I believe in you and that you're as smart and clever and brilliant as anyone I've ever met. I wanted you to realize that. And I thought about how you've approached all these bakeries and no one wants to work with you. You keep going to them and so I figured . . . well, what if you didn't have to? What if the customers could come directly to you?" He rubbed his goatee and then set Pumpkin down on the steps. The dog immediately raced toward the ice cream truck, no doubt smelling cookies or whatever it was that the truck had on it.

He watched Pumpkin race away with a smile on his face, and that smile warmed Holly's heart. It distracted her, that gorgeous smile of his. It made her think of nights in bed together, his hand tracing patterns on her bare back. He took her hand, leading her to the edge of the porch. Flustered by his touch, she looked around for his dog. "Where's Hannibal?" she asked, surprised to see his shadow wasn't nearby.

"In the truck with the driver." He glanced over at her, that wicked smile curving his mouth again. "Are you changing the subject?"

Changing the subject? When he was standing so close to her and she'd forgotten how good he looked? How good he smelled? How his big, strong hand felt as it touched hers? When he was smiling at her in that way that made her feel so damn special and seen, and here she was in a mud mask and old sweats and he still made her feel beautiful with just the way he gazed at her?

"I can't remember what we were talking about," Holly confessed, her gaze sliding to his mouth.

"The truck is for you," he emphasized again, giving her fingers a light squeeze. "Because I want you to be a success. If you can't get the bakeries to notice your food, you start a food truck of your own. You park it on Main Street and sell cakes and pies or whatever you feel like. You can do food deliveries if you want. You can do whatever you want, and I'll help out in whatever way I can."

Holly stared at him, her eyes wide.

A food truck.

No, a desserts truck. The moment it hit her, she realized what a genius idea it was. She could set up in one town in the morning, then drive over to another town in the afternoon. She could have a menu of things she'd baked, or she could take orders and deliver them. She could go to the customers, instead of looking for ways to get others to take a chance on her. She could run her perfect little sweets shop out of a truck and drive as far as she needed to get to the customers.

It was so damn smart. Painted Barrel wasn't big enough to handle more than one baking shop, and neither were any of the towns nearby. But if she could hit all of them . . . she just might be able to do it.

Her lips parted.

"Here," Adam continued, releasing her hand. He fished in his pockets. "Before you say you can't do it, I wanted to give you this list. I talked to Becca for . . . things." He paused. "And she wanted me to ask you about doing some more baking for her. One of the customers in her salon asked the same thing. The lady at the inn asked, too. The guy that gave me the lead on the truck wants a birthday cake for his kid. Wade wants your bread. Everyone I talked to thinks you're amazing, Holly. They want you to bake for them." He took her hand in his and pushed the list into it. "The only one that thinks you can't do it is you."

"An ice cream truck," she stated dumbly, still staring at it. "Those can't be cheap."

"It wasn't," he admitted. "But I wanted you to have it."

Oh no. She had no money to spare. Holly looked over at him, eyes wide. "How do I repay you?"

A funny expression crossed his face. "You don't. It's a Christmas present."

"Adam, it's too much—"

"It's not," he said softly, and took her hand again. He gave it a warm, gentle squeeze. "It's a gift. I wanted to get this for you. I wanted to show you that I believe in you, even if you don't believe in yourself." He squeezed her hand again. "Because I think you're the most beautiful, funny, smart, and amazing woman I've ever met . . . and I want you to realize that, too."

A lump formed in Holly's throat. "Oh, Adam."

"The biggest mistake I made was causing you to doubt yourself." He held her hand higher, rubbed his fingers over her knuckles, and then kissed them softly. "And that kinda kills me. If you don't want to be with me, I get it. But I need you to realize that you're talented, no matter how you and me turn out, all right?"

Hot tears slid down her face. "You're going to make my mud mask melt," she said, sniffling.

"You mean this isn't natural beauty I see before me?" Adam teased.

She laugh-sobbed. "I'm having a spa day to pamper myself." Holly swiped at her nose with her free hand. "I figured since . . . since I was alone today . . ." She shrugged.

A stricken look crossed his face. "Am I bothering you?" There was a quiet note in his voice, a careful one. "Should I go?"

"No!" She reached out and grabbed his shirt. "No . . . I want you to stay."

They moved closer as if drawn together, and Adam gazed

down at her, his expression thoughtful. "I guess I wanted to ask about you and me, too, if I'm being selfish."

"It's not selfish," she protested, her heart fluttering. God, she loved the way he looked at her. She reached up and ripped the towel turban off her head, letting her hair flow over her shoulders. "You . . . you should definitely ask about me and you."

"How are we?" he murmured, voice low and husky. "Me and you?"

"I don't know. How do you want us to be?" Holly didn't want to be the first one to speak up. She was afraid of sticking her neck out and getting hurt again.

"I want us to be together," Adam said. His hands moved to her waist, pulling her against him. "If it's not what you want, tell me and I will leave you alone. But I wanted you to know that I miss you and I'm crazy about you. That's not my stomach speaking, either—I will happily eat peanut butter and jelly every day for the rest of my life if I get to eat it at your side."

She sucked in a breath. "That sounds . . . very much like a commitment, Adam."

"It does." His expression didn't change. "Did you not want one?"

"I thought you didn't want any kind of commitment. Not after your divorce."

He gave her a rueful look. "I thought so, too, and then I met you. And I realized that I'd be an idiot if I let you get away from me. I'm willing to try the commitment thing again if you're willing to give me a chance."

It sounded good, and yet . . . Holly hesitated. "I really like you, Adam. And I like us together. But . . . you need to have a stronger reason to be with me than just sex and good times. I need you to be with me, even in the bad times. Even when it's not fun. I need a life partner, not a bed partner."

He adjusted his baseball cap, shaking his head. "I'm fucking this up, aren't I?" He took a step toward her and cupped her face, heedless of her stupid mud mask that was even now cracking all over her skin and making her face hurt with how tight it was. He gazed deep into her eyes. "Holly. I want to be with you because I love you."

Her knees grew weak. "You do?"

"I do." Adam kissed her gently. "It's not because you're an amazing cook or because you're fantastic in bed. You are. But it's the small things I miss about being with you. I've gotten used to mornings with you. Hearing you laugh. Watching you yawn through a TV show. I miss your cold feet on my leg and sharing a shower with you. I miss your smile." He kissed her again. "Those are the moments I want."

"Oh, Adam." She was melting into a puddle, an absolute puddle.

"Though I'm not going to lie," he whispered against her lips. "I do like the sex a lot."

She giggled as he leaned in to kiss her. Her arms went around his neck and then they were kissing, kissing, kissing. Holly's breath stole from her throat as his hands roamed over her back. It felt so good to be back in his arms, so very right as their mouths met and tongues brushed against each other. She loved the soft groan he made as he conquered her mouth, and she clung to him.

When he finally pulled away, his gaze was hot on hers. "Merry Christmas, beautiful." He brushed a finger over her face and she felt a chunk of mud mask fall off.

"Merry Christmas, Adam," Holly breathed. "I love you, too."

His smile was brilliant. He took her hand in his again and kissed her knuckles. "Want to take a closer look at your present?"

Excitement bubbled up inside her. Holly bounced, holding his hand. "Yes!"

A look of uncertainty crossed his face as he led her forward. "I don't want you to feel obligated," he began. "You can always take the deed and sell it and use the money for a start-up in some other way—"

She reached out, putting a hand over his mouth. "Hush. I'm admiring my present."

They walked the short distance out to the gravel parking lot in front of Sage's ranch. The ice cream truck was still running, and the closer she got, the more Holly fell in love with it. It was boxy and old, sure, but she could paint it a cute lemon yellow with pink ribbon. She could put a sweets menu on the door, or heck, she could do a whiteboard and change the menu as often as she liked. The truck looked big enough to hold plenty of trays of baked goods, and the possibilities were endless.

She could see herself in it, and the smile on her face grew wider and wider. Holly looked over at Adam, ready to thank him again. He was smiling, too, but in a strange, watchful way. As if he was waiting for something.

The window on the side of the ice cream truck opened and a familiar face appeared. Her sister, Polly, leaned out of the truck, a bright smile on her face. "What'll it be?"

Holly's squeal of delight was earth-shattering.

CHAPTER TWENTY-SIX

A few hours later, he sat in the kitchen with Holly and her sister, Polly, watching the two women, a cup of coffee in his hands. The cattle were taken care of—he'd raced through the majority of his work that day with the help of Caleb and Jack from the Swinging C, because they'd known he wanted to celebrate the evening with Holly. They'd agreed to help out and Holly was even now baking them a cake as a thank-you. Polly stirred a cheese sauce in a pan and chatted with her sister, both of them talking nonstop ever since she'd arrived.

Polly wasn't what he'd expected Holly's sister to be. He knew she was away at college and Holly thought she was brilliant. It was strange to see them standing next to each other, though. They had similar builds, but Polly was leaner and slightly taller. Holly's hair was long and loose, her face mask scrubbed off and her smile bright. She was utterly beautiful. Polly was cute enough, too, he supposed, with the short bob of hair framing her face, but he liked Holly's stubborn chin and the sparkle in her eyes. Polly was a little more calm and reserved, her expression thoughtful.

Holly was also arguing with her sister as she pulled one of the cake layers out of the oven. "I don't like it, Polly. I want you to be able to concentrate on your studies. I want you to be able to go out and have fun with your friends. I want you to have a life!"

"And you think I can't do that as a teacher's assistant?" Polly gave her an exasperated look. "Mr. Stemmons asked me because he thinks I can help the other students. That I've got a good handle on biochem and being a TA will look great on my résumé. And best of all, the school will pay a large chunk of my tuition if I TA in the spring."

"Yes, but—" Holly began.

"But what?" Polly insisted. Okay, he'd thought Holly was the stubborn one of the two, but the mulish look on Polly's face was one he recognized very well. "This is the answer to all our problems. Or are you sitting on ten grand I'm unaware of to pay for my classes?"

Adam choked on his coffee. "Ten . . . grand?" he asked between coughs as the women looked over at him. "A semester?"

Holly gave him an exasperated but affectionate look as she set the cake on a cooling rack. "That's after all the financial aid. I wanted Polly to go to the best school we could afford."

"We," Polly retorted. "You mean 'you,' as in, 'you work yourself into the ground.'"

Holly frowned at her.

"Look, I'm going to TA next semester, and there's nothing you can do about it," Polly said, her hand on her sister's shoulder. "So get used to the idea."

"I've never met anyone as stubborn as you," Holly said.

Adam choked on his coffee all over again.

They both turned to look at him.

"Sorry. Sorry."

Holly's lips twitched and she turned back to her sister. "I just . . . if you want to just go to school, I understand. I'll find the money."

Polly shook her head at her older sister. "I want to help out, you know. Being a teacher's assistant is something I can do that won't interfere with my studies and it helps take care of tuition. Just because you *can* shoulder all the burdens doesn't mean that you should, all right? I worry about you, too."

"If you're sure . . . I just don't like the thought of you feeling like you can't count on me." Holly turned and looked at Adam again.

He gave her an innocent look. "What?"

"Just waiting for you to spew coffee again." She grabbed the coffeepot and refilled his cup. "Or do you have anything to add?"

Adam shrugged. "If your sister wants to try to work to pay for classes, why not let her? If her grades slip, then you two can reexamine things over the summer break, right?"

Polly brightened. "A man of logic. Listen to him."

Holly gestured at Adam. "This man? Are you sure?" She put a hand on his forehead. "Maybe he's sick again."

Adam just grabbed her hand and nibbled on her palm, making her blush.

The women talked for hours, and Adam was content to sit nearby and eat all the cake Holly tossed in his direction. They eventually migrated out to the living area, and the dogs basked by the fire while Adam sat with Holly's legs in his lap, rubbing her feet while she and Polly chatted. Before they knew it, the clock was striking midnight and the women were yawning.

"I'm going to call an official end to the day," Adam said, setting Holly's feet down. He took her slippers and put them on her feet. She looked ready to fall asleep where she was, her eyelids heavy. "Time for bed, ladies."

"Oh, I don't have a bed ready for you, Pol." Holly sat up, frowning. "I just kept talking instead of getting you set up in a room."

"I can sleep in your room if you're spending the night with Adam," Polly said with a shrug.

Holly froze.

Polly just rolled her eyes, languidly getting to her feet. "Oh, come on. We're all adults here. I'm not judging."

"I can't believe my baby sister just said that to me," Holly said, pretending to be offended. "What are they teaching you at that college?"

Polly snorted and sauntered out of the room. "I'll get my bag from the truck."

It left Holly and Adam alone together. She looked over at him, suddenly shy, and it occurred to Adam that maybe she didn't want to sleep in his bed. Maybe she needed more time. "If you want to sleep alone, I can go sleep in Carson's cabin," he offered. "I don't want you to feel trapped with me."

She was quiet for a long moment and then got to her feet, standing in front of him. Holly studied his face, strangely quiet, and then put her hand on his chest, right over his heart. "I guess the question I should ask is where do you see us going?"

"What do you mean?" He thought he'd made that pretty clear, but maybe she needed more from him.

Holly gazed up at him. "Where do you want me tonight? I need you to be specific. Because I want to be with you, but . . ." She shrugged. "You've never invited me to stay in your cabin before. I thought it was one of those things where you needed your space."

His space?

Adam laughed, shaking his head. "I had my space for the last week and I absolutely hated every moment of it, beautiful. I want to be with you. I want you in my bed. I don't care if it's in my cabin, or in the barn, or if you want me to take you into the kitchen and we dirty up the countertop like I promised you before." He moved closer to her, sliding a hand to the back of her neck. "The only reason we've never made it out to my cabin before is because it's a lot further away than your bed."

"Oh." Her cheeks pinked. "So, what you're telling me is that you're a man of little stamina—"

He growled, grabbing her by the waist and slinging her over his shoulder. "I'll show you stamina." He turned . . . and saw Polly standing there with her overnight bag on her shoulder, a smirk of amusement on her face.

"Please, don't let me interrupt," Polly said.

Holly squirmed hard on his shoulder. "Oh my god. Adam, put me down!"

"Nope," he drawled, and winked at Polly. "It's bedtime. You want Santa to come, don't you?"

"I am so not stepping into that joke," Polly teased. "Good night, you two. Okay if I keep Pumpkin with me?"

"Works for me," Adam said, and tapped his hand on Holly's sweatpants-covered butt. "You?"

She made an indignant sound.

"That's her saying it's fine." He grinned at Polly and then slapped his hand on his leg. "Come on, Hannibal. Time for bed."

Holly continued to make indignant noises as he carried her out of the main house and into the snow. The cabins were a decent walk away from the main house, nearer to the barn, and before he even got halfway there, she was squirming on his shoulder. "Put me down. Please!"

He patted her ass again and gave it a little bit of a rub, just because he could. "You going to make any more cracks about my stamina?"

She huffed, punching at his back. "You can show me your stamina in bed, but if you don't put me down, I'm going to puke all over the place."

"Fair enough." Adam set her down, grinning. He felt light as air tonight. Happy. Like everything was right in his world once more, now that Holly was back in it. He held his hand out to her. She took it, shivering, and stepped closer to him. Automatically, Adam put his arm around her shoulders, hugging her against him. "Let's get you over to my place so I can show you just how much I missed you."

They raced over to his cabin, because it was cold and snowy out, and neither wanted to spend a lot of time outdoors. As they approached, he noticed a tray on his front porch. She must have put that there just before he arrived with Polly. "Let me guess, peanut butter and jelly?"

Holly gave a little sigh. "It's Christmas, so I took pity on you."

"Oh?"

"It's a pie full of onions." At his look of horror, Holly broke into giggles. She nudged him with her shoulder. "It's ham and some stuffing. I didn't feel much like cooking for myself but I thought you should have something nice on Christmas, even if I was mad at you."

"And were you mad at me?" he asked softly.

She bit her lip, thinking. "I don't know. I think I was more sad than anything. Sad that you weren't the person I thought you could be. Sad because I still liked you and missed you despite all of it."

He felt like an ass. "I'm going to make it up to you, Holly. I swear I will."

Holly gazed up at him as they stood on his porch, her eyes shining in the moonlight. "The fact that you believe in me so much takes a lot of the sting away, you know. I don't think I've ever had anyone that believed in me like you do."

"I will always be your biggest cheerleader," he promised her, and he meant it.

"Because you love me?"

"That, and because I think you're amazing," Adam admitted. "And I feel lucky that you even speak to me."

She gave him a playful look. "If you'd have tipped me more than a dollar, I'd have spoken to you a lot sooner."

"Then I'm an even bigger fool than we both thought," he teased back, opening the door to his place. Inside his cozy cabin, the heater was humming, and most of his dirty clothes were in the hamper. Thank god. It was only a slight disaster instead of a major one. "Uh, give me a moment to straighten up."

"You forget I've seen your place before," Holly told him, stepping in after him. Hannibal barreled past both of them, heading for his food dish.

Right. She'd taken care of him when he was sick, because she was a good, kind person whom he didn't deserve. "Sure."

Holly sat down on the edge of the bed and yawned hugely. "How did you get my sister here anyhow? I meant to ask but there was just so much to talk about . . ." She lay down on one side of the bed, tucking her head against her arm and gazing up at him sleepily. "Not that it isn't the best Christmas present ever, because it is."

"I knew you were down and it was my fault. I figured even

if you hated my guts and hated the truck, I could at least bring your sister in to brighten up your Christmas." Adam moved toward the bed and took one of her feet in hand, pulling off one of her snow-dampened slippers. He liked to take care of her, liked to know that she was looked after. It felt like his job, a pleasant duty he'd taken on because he loved her and wanted her to feel cherished. He'd make sure she felt cherished every damn day for the rest of his life. "I got her number from Becca and bought her a ticket out here."

Holly tried to sit up, alarmed. "Oh no, how much did it cost? Christmas fares—"

He shook his head. "It was a present, and I won't hear anything about it."

"Oh, Adam." Holly's voice was a soft, tired sigh. "You're far too generous."

"Me? I'm just thanking my lucky stars you've decided not to hate my guts."

"I couldn't hate you," Holly said drowsily. "I love you."

She said the words in a small voice, as if she was half-afraid he'd mock her over it. *Never*, he vowed silently. She was his. He loved hearing her say that, and he wanted to hear it again. Louder. Enthusiastically. It would be his new goal in life, he decided, right after being her biggest cheerleader. "I love you, too, beautiful. Do you want to stand up so I can take these pants off you, or do you want to sleep in them?"

"Sleep in them?" Holly gave him a puzzled look. "You don't want to have sex?"

Oh, he wanted sex more than almost anything . . . but he also didn't want to presume. "I'm letting you set the pace, beautiful. You tell me how you want tonight to go."

Holly sat up, her hair falling over her shoulders as she gazed up at him. Her hand went to his belt, and then she slid it between his legs, rubbing against the denim-covered bulge there. "I want sex," she told him in a husky voice that made him instantly hard.

"Thank fuck," he groaned.

She chuckled at his response, stroking her hand up and down his package. "I missed you," she told him again. "Didn't realize how much I'd miss you."

"That's my line," he managed, though it was hard to think about joking when she had her hands all over his cock.

"We're allowed to miss each other," Holly said in a soft voice. "Just . . . don't pull any stunts like that ever again, all right?"

"Never," Adam swore, and he meant it. It wasn't about his pride. It was about the fact that he'd hurt the woman he loved so deeply. "I still need to make it up to you."

Holly gazed up at him, her fingers stroking over his bulge. "What did you have in mind?"

"How about I show you?" He gestured at the bed. "Lie back for me."

She tilted her face and stared up at him. "You mean to tell me that you're going to try and beg forgiveness by going down on me?"

"Did you have a better plan?"

Holly squirmed, breathless. "Not at the moment."

He nudged her shoulder and she leaned back on the bed, her gorgeous legs just begging to be touched. He tugged her jeans off her, then skimmed a hand up one leg, fascinated by how soft she was. "How about I start with that and you can tell me later if you have more ideas."

She shivered. "Okay."

Adam tugged at her panties, easing them down her legs with reverence. She was so damn beautiful. He told her that, too. Told her in half a dozen ways as he kissed his way back up her calf, grazing his mouth over her smooth skin.

He told her how much he'd missed her as he kissed her knee and then moved up her thigh. With gentle hands, he pushed her thighs open and felt her quivering underneath his touch. He leaned in to taste her.

"Dog," Holly said suddenly.

That broke him from his reverie. He looked up. "What?"

She nodded over at the side of the room, a smile playing on her lips. "The dog is watching us."

Oh. Right. "Give me two seconds." He closed the dog into the bathroom and practically raced back to the bed, where she remained spread and waiting for him. Her hand was between her thighs, and she was touching herself as she gazed up at him. It was the hottest damn thing Adam had ever seen, and he groaned as he dropped to his knees before her. "I'm the luckiest man alive."

Holly whimpered with need, and the sound was the most beautiful thing he'd ever heard. He cradled her legs, sliding them over his shoulders, and settled in.

He was going to be here for a while, he decided.

And he was. Adam took his time, relearning every inch of Holly's body as if she were absolutely new to him. He tasted her everywhere. He licked her everywhere. He sucked and nibbled and caressed every bit of skin. He savored his woman, just like he savored a perfect bite of her cake. All the while, Holly clung to him, her hands on his head, the breath panting out of her as he made love to her with his mouth.

It took her a long time to climax, but Adam didn't mind. He loved taking his time with her, and when she finally quaked around him, her thighs clamping against his ears, her sheath gripping his fingers as he worked her from inside, everything felt right in his world again.

Murmuring words of love, he kissed his way back up her body, then got to his feet and undressed.

She watched him with a hungry gaze, as if she couldn't get enough of the sight of him. Holly reached for him as he moved back over her, running her hands all over his body. "Mine," she whispered, her gaze fascinated as she ran her fingers down his arm. "All mine."

Damn. There was nothing hotter than his woman being possessive. Hungry for her, his body aching, Adam moved over Holly, kissing her as he fit his hips against the cradle of hers. She was warm and wet and ready for him, and he rocked against her, rubbing his shaft against her folds, reveling in the feeling of her underneath him.

"Want you, Adam," she panted. "Inside me." She gripped his ass, dragging him against her. "Quit being such a tease."

It broke his control, her demanding. He loved that, and it made him wilder for her than ever. With another drugging kiss, Adam pushed into Holly, claiming her. She moaned against his mouth, eagerly lifting her hips to meet his thrusts. When he finally came, he collapsed on top of her, stars dancing at the edge of his vision.

Holly sighed, the sound one of utter contentment. Her hands traced over his back as he lay atop her, trying to catch his breath. "I love you," she said again. "I hope you don't get tired of hearing that."

Never, Adam decided. *Never ever.*

They stayed up late, making love once more before finally collapsing into sleep. Adam woke up before dawn with Holly in his arms, his body curled around hers, and Hannibal at the foot of the bed, and he felt a deep sense of contentment.

Unfortunately that deep sense of contentment didn't feed the cattle, which meant he needed to get out of bed soon. He rubbed Holly's arm lightly, watching her sleep, lingering for just a little bit longer. To his surprise, she rolled over and smiled up at him, her eyes shining.

"Merry Christmas," she said, beaming.

"You should go back to sleep." He leaned down to kiss her. "It's before dawn. Sorry if I woke you up."

"You didn't," Holly promised. "I was just thinking."

"About?" His hand slid down to cup one of her breasts. Maybe he could linger in bed a little longer . . .

"Profiteroles," she said. "I think I'm going to make some today."

"Prof-what?" he echoed, pausing.

"Profiteroles. Cream puffs. I think I'm going to make some today." Holly smiled up at him dreamily. "I feel like baking. I want to bake everything." She reached over and patted his waist. "I hope you're ready to eat some sweets."

"Already did, last night," Adam teased. "Or . . . wait, you mean baking?"

Her groan at his joke was utterly delightful, and Adam decided maybe he had a few more minutes to spend in bed after all.

It *was* Christmas.

EPILOGUE

One Year Later

Holly fiddled with her scarf, trying not to seem too anxious.

"You look beautiful," Adam reassured her as he drove, not taking his eyes off the road. "My brother's not going to care about your clothing."

"I care," Holly retorted. "I want to look good for the inevitable photos." She flipped the mirror down in the car and checked her lipstick and smoothed her hair. This was her first chance to meet Mike and Mary, Adam's brother and his wife. They'd been invited up a half dozen times in the last year once they'd found out that Adam and Holly were in a committed relationship and had moved in together, but the timing had never been quite right. Adam couldn't leave his job for extended periods of time and Holly had her own business to run. With the Christmas holidays, though, they were stealing away a week of time to visit family.

Or at least Adam's family. Polly was staying at university through the Christmas holidays again, but she'd been down for Thanksgiving with her new girlfriend, so Holly couldn't complain. Polly was happy, and Holly had liked Esme immensely—she was exactly the quiet, thoughtful, study-absorbed type that would be perfect for her sister. For Christmas, Holly had sent them a deluxe tray of macarons in every single flavor that her Baked-to-Go truck offered. She had the same sitting in the back seat for Adam's family, along with a fleet of gingerbread men, a fruitcake, and a yule log. Holly glanced backward, checking the boxes of baked goods again, as she had over and over for the long drive out to Iowa.

"Do you think we brought enough stuff, Adam?" Holly fretted. "We could stop by a grocery store and pick up some ingredients and I can make them a cake once we arrive—"

"Hol." Adam glanced over at her, chuckling, as he turned down a country lane, snowy fields on both sides of the road. "Babe. You've made more than enough. They'll be eating sweets for weeks to come."

"Not if your brother eats anything like you," she teased back, putting her hand on his thigh and squeezing. "They'll be gone in two days."

Adam just grinned over at her. "Is it my fault if you're talented?" He patted his waistline, where he swore he'd put on a few inches in the last eight months, ever since Holly had moved in with him. Holly thought he was full of crap, because he still had washboard abs despite the fact that he ate like an absolute maniac. "This is a holiday," Adam told her, as he had repeatedly on the drive. "I want you to relax and enjoy yourself."

"Well, the same goes for you!"

He gave her a sultry look. "Beautiful, I always enjoy myself around you."

And now he was making her blush. She squeezed his thigh again, a promise for later. Lord, how was it possible that they'd been together for a year now and he still made her get all red in the face like a schoolgirl? She kept waiting for things to change between them, waiting for the other shoe to drop, but being with him got better and better every day. Holly felt so lucky. Ever since that Christmas Eve when they'd gotten back together, Holly had stayed with Adam in his cabin. When Sage and her family returned, Holly had continued to stay at Adam's place, and once her lease ran out on her apartment, she didn't renew it. He insisted she move in with him.

Now they were both squeezed into his tiny cabin, and if it was packed with their stuff, neither one of them minded. They'd talked about renting a place in the future, but right now it was easier for her to run her business with one less rent payment.

And business was booming. She'd launched officially in February, just in time for Valentine's Day. She'd needed a kitchen to bake her goods and had rented one in a tiny town over, where a restaurant had folded, and gotten the licenses to run her business through her food truck. Wade's saloon had been quick to rebuild, but Holly had declined when he offered her her job back, even though that had been terrifying. She wanted to give her sweets business a chance to work, though, and she couldn't do it while waitressing.

Business had been slow at first, as she'd tried to figure out what items enticed people to buy when they were on the fence, but she'd settled into a menu that sold briskly and had two offerings—Street Sweets and Weekend Meals. Her Street Sweets were anything from cookies to cupcakes to more delicate treats like macarons or slices of light, buttery cakes. Once a week, she took orders for take-and-bake entrees—from casseroles and pastas to brisket. On Sundays, she drove her deliveries out to families who didn't want to cook through the week.

Business had been so brisk that she hired an assistant to help her bake—a girl fresh out of high school who was taking a gap year before heading to college. Tina drove the truck when Holly was busy baking, and she helped Holly deliver on the weekend. Everything had exceeded Holly's expectations and she was looking at purchasing a second truck and expanding outward in the spring.

But that was in the spring. For now, she was concentrating on family time. Holly glanced over at Adam as he turned the car down another country lane. He'd been so incredibly supportive of her business, letting her borrow money to get her truck "wrapped" with her logo. She couldn't count how many nights he'd driven out to the kitchen to bake with her when she was working late, just so she wouldn't have to be that much later. He was thoughtful and caring and had bragged about her business to everyone he met. Heck, when the local paper had interviewed her and given her business a boost, Adam had emailed the other nearby newspapers and suggested they feature her as well—and her business had exploded afterward. He really was the best, and she loved him more every day.

"We're here," Adam said, and for a moment he looked incredibly nervous. He parked the car in front of a big, yellow farmhouse with a wraparound porch, and stared at it.

Aw. She gave his thigh a pat. "It'll be all right, babe. It's just your brother and his family. There's no need to be anxious."

"Right." He adjusted his baseball cap repeatedly—a sure sign he was nervous—and then smiled at her. "Shall we go?"

She nodded, and they got out of the car. The air was cool and crisp, but not nearly as bitter cold as it was in the Wyoming mountains. The snow here wasn't nearly as thick, either, but the yard boasted a few rough-looking snowmen that had seen better days. Holly glanced up at the house and the Christmas garlands that were woven through the railings on the wooden porch and the wreath hung on the door. It looked festive and cozy.

As she watched, the door opened and the family poured out—first the three kids, then the woman, who must be Mary, and then Mike, who looked like a broader, more dad-like version of Adam. She found herself smiling at them and waving as they headed toward the car, and her gaze strayed back to Adam.

He still looked nervous.

Holly beamed at the children, who raced up to them, and laughed when the little girl threw her arms around Holly's waist. "Oh, what a greeting!"

"Merry Christmas!" the little one called. "Did you bring us cookies? Uncle Adam said you'd bring cookies!" Well, cookies were always a great icebreaker.

Holly giggled. "I did. Can you help me carry them?"

The children helped her clear the back seat of the baked goods, and then there was a flurry of hugs and greetings. Mary was warm and sweet and Mike reminded her of a teddy bear. Some of Adam's nervousness seemed to ease as they headed inside, and Holly admired the charming little house with the big Christmas tree next to the fireplace, stockings hanging from the mantel. "Your home is lovely."

"Thank you," Mary said, and then paused. She looked over at her husband, smiling.

Puzzled, Holly followed her gaze and saw Mike was looking at Adam . . . and Adam was sweating again. He watched her, a funny look on his face, and she bit her lip, worried. She wanted to pull him aside and ask if everything was all right, but the kids were screaming about the gingerbread men and there was chaos everywhere. Mary gave them an apologetic look and tried to shush the children, but it was no use.

Holly moved to Adam's side, wondering if he wasn't feeling well. "You okay?"

He nodded, and then his phone rang. She expected it to go to voicemail, but Adam got even more flustered, grabbing the phone and clicking on the screen repeatedly. "There we go," he finally said, and held it out to Holly.

Curious, she took the phone and glanced at the screen. Polly was there, with her girlfriend squeezed into the picture. They both waved. "Video call!" Polly said. "Happy holidays! Adam wanted to get everyone together even if we couldn't be there!"

"Oh! This is wonderful. Happy holidays!" Holly couldn't stop smiling. She gave Adam a warm look. He was always so thoughtful.

Her boyfriend only adjusted his baseball cap again, swallowing hard. As she studied him, Mike reached over and snatched it off his brother's head, grinning, and Adam turned red. He cleared his throat. Paused.

And then Adam dropped to a knee in front of Holly.

Holly nearly dropped the phone in shock. "W-what—"

"Wait! Hold us out!" Polly screeched from the video call. "We can't see!"

Mary hustled forward, beaming, and took the phone from Holly's numb hands, maneuvering so she could get the entire picture. Holly didn't move. She couldn't stop staring at Adam. Her handsome, wonderful Adam, who was on a knee in front of her in front of their families . . . and who looked so nervous he might throw up.

"Yes," Holly said immediately.

Adam swallowed hard, then managed a half grin. "You didn't even let me ask yet."

"Unless there's something else you're planning to ask while on your knees, then I already know my answer."

His grin grew broader, and he held a small ring box out to her. "This has been burning a hole in my pocket for the last week. Will you do me the honor?"

She took the box from him with trembling hands, and snapped it open. It was a simple band, a lovely platinum without any design on it. It looked plain, but Holly sucked in a breath. Hadn't she griped last week that her assistant Tina had gotten dough into all her jewelry and how simple was best? He'd paid attention. It wasn't the ring for everyone, but it was perfect for Holly. "Oh, Adam," she breathed. "It's amazing."

"Since I couldn't put a stone on it, I got it engraved," he told her, grinning.

She squinted at the inside of the ring. ONE PART HOLLY, ONE PART ADAM. MIX WELL. HAPPY EVER AFTER.

It was a recipe.

Stupid, silly tears poured down her face as she laughed and laughed. "This is the worst recipe ever!"

Adam chuckled, too, getting to his feet. He moved toward her, his arms going around her waist. "It's the inside of a damn ring. What do you expect?"

She just laughed even more as he slipped it onto her finger, and they kissed. She didn't need a recipe to make their relationship work. Some things you just knew by heart.

"Is that a yes?" he asked between kisses, smiling.

"Yes," Holly said, and everyone cheered.

Keep reading for a
sneak peek at Jessica Clare's
magical romance,

GO HEX YOURSELF

When I pull up to the location of my job interview in Nick's borrowed car, my first thought is that I've made a mistake. I peer up at the ominous-looking building, a black-brick brownstone tucked amongst several more brightly colored neighbors, and consult my phone again. No, this is the right place. After all, there's only one Hemlock Avenue in the city. With a worried look, I glance up at the building again, then find a place to park that's not too close and not too far away. I check the parking lot lines to ensure that I'm perfectly within my space, and then re-park when I'm not entirely satisfied with how close I am to the yellow line. It takes a little more time, but it's always better to be precise than sloppy.

Ten minutes later, I'm down the street with the freshly fed meter running, and I've got my CV in hand. Am I really going to interview at someone's house for the assistant job? I'm a little uneasy at that, but it's for a gaming company, and those sorts of people are notoriously quirky . . . I think. I check the address one more time before I move up the steps and ring the doorbell, smoothing my skirt with sweaty hands. Up close, the building seems a little more imposing, with dark burgundy curtains covering every single window and not letting in a peep of light. The stairs have an ornate black iron railing, and even the door knocker looks like something out of a horror movie, all vines and animal heads.

Someone has a goth fetish, clearly.

The door opens, and I'm startled to see a woman about my age in jeans and a T-shirt proclaiming her favorite baseball team. Her hair is pulled back into a bedraggled ponytail and she's not wearing a stitch of makeup. She's also about twenty months pregnant, if the balloon under her shirt is any indication.

"You must be Regina," she exclaims with a warm smile, rubbing the bulge of her stomach. "Hey there! Come on in."

I'm horribly overdressed. I bite my lip as I step inside, painfully aware of the clack of my low-heeled pumps on the dark hardwood floors. I'm wearing a gray jacket over a white blouse and a gray pencil skirt, and I have to admit, the feeling that I'm in the wrong place keeps hitting me over and over again. I don't normally make these mistakes. I like for things to go perfectly. It's the control-freak in me who needs that satisfaction. I researched what one wears to an assistant interview, so I don't know how I flubbed this so badly. I want to check the ad one more time, but after rereading it over and over for the last three days, I know what it says by heart.

SPELLCRAFT EXPERTISE WANTED
Assistant required. Excellent pay for familiar.

I mean, I've been a fan of the card game Spellcraft: The Magicking since I was a teenager. I have thousands of dollars of cards and even placed second in a local tournament once. Sure, I was playing an eight-year-old . . . but he had a good deck. Heck, I've even brought my favorite deck with me in my purse, in case they think I'm bluffing about my love for the Spellcraft game.

So am I qualified? Fuck yeah, I am. I can be an assistant to someone who works for the Spellcraft: The Magicking company. It's kinda my dream job. Well . . . my dream job is actually to work on the cards themselves, but I'm not experienced for that, so being an assistant would be the next best thing. But I'm smart, I'm reasonably educated, I'm good with spreadsheets, and I'm excessively, excessively organized.

(Some might say "obsessively" but I ignore haters.)

I smile at the pregnant woman, suspecting she's the one I talked to on the phone. "You're Lisa?"

"That's me!"

I hold out my CV, tucked into a fancy leather-bound folder. I pray that the nice packaging will hide the fact that my detailed CV is kinda light on office jobs and heavier on things like "Burger Basket" and "Clown Holding Sign in front of Tax Masters." It's all about enthusiasm though, right? I've got that in spades.

Lisa takes the folder from me with a little frown on her face, as if she's not quite sure what to do with it, and then gestures at the house. "Want me to show you around Ms. Magnus's house? She'd be the one in charge day-to-day."

Er, that's kind of odd. Why do I need to know about my employer's house? Maybe she's just really proud of the place? But since I'm interviewing, I paste on a smile. "That'd be great."

Lisa's smile brightens and she puts her hands on her belly and begins waddling through the foyer. "Follow me."

I do, and I can't help but notice that the interior of the place looks much larger than the exterior suggested. Inside, the ceilings are incredibly high and the rooms seem airy despite the dark coloring. The walls are the same burgundy red, and several of them are covered in reproductions of ancient Roman murals. "Your boss must like Roman stuff."

"Oh, she's Roman. All the big names are," she calls over her shoulder.

"Ah." Funny, I've researched the game and thought the CEOs were from Seattle. Maybe she's an investor? Who just likes to talk about the game? That might be kind of fun. My enthusiasm brightens as Lisa shows me through the living room and the modern, elegant kitchen. She heads down a long hall and looks over at me again. "This way to the lab."

"Lab?" I echo. "Oh, you mean office?" I beam. "It's so charming that she calls it a lab."

"What else would he call it?" Lisa opens a large, symbol-covered door, and I think Ms. Magnus must be a huge nerd to decorate her office like this. When we step inside, though, I'm a little stunned. There's a large desk, all right, but instead of a laptop and paperwork there are beakers and bottles. An old book is spread out on the table, and the walls are lined with jars and even more books. The ceiling is hung with what looks like dried herbs.

It's an absolute nightmare. Every iota of my organization-loving heart cringes at the sight of this. It's clear that Ms. Magnus needs me. I'd never let a place of work get this disorganized. The books are all over the place, there's no computer to be seen, and stacks of loose paper everywhere.

It all needs a guiding hand, and that's what I do best.

Guide. Or . . . control. Whatever. I'm good at this kind of thing.

"So this is the lab," Lisa chirps. "I hope you're up-to-date on your herbs, because a lot of Dru's favorite spells are plant-based. She's not like her nephew at all, who prefers the more physical sort of casting." Her cheeks turn red and she rubs her belly. "That's the sort of thing that got me into this kind of mess."

"Sorry, what?" I ask, stepping inside and peering at a jar that really looks like it's got a pickled frog in it, of all things. These props are really amazing. It looks like something out of a Harry Potter scene, except there are no cobwebs or sorting hat, and I'm definitely not at Hogwarts. I poke another jar, but it just looks like it has wizened berries of some kind in it. "This place is amazing. Does she use these props to help her get in the mood? Sort of like method acting?"

"Method what?"

I turn to look at Lisa, and as I do, I suck in a breath at the sight of a glowering god standing in the doorway to the room. The man there looks . . . intense. He's impossibly tall, with broad shoulders that would put a linebacker to shame. He's dressed in a black suit with a black shirt underneath, complete with black tie, and his hair is dark and just brushes his collar. The long, solemn face is unsmiling, his expression stern, but his mouth is full and pink and shocking against the paleness of his skin.

"Who are you?" he asks bluntly, ignoring Lisa and looking right at me.

"Hello," I chirp, extending my hand and moving forward. "I'm Reggie Johnson, here about the job. I'm such a big fan of . . ."

The tall man gives me an up-and-down look and then

dismisses me as if I'm unimportant. He turns to Lisa and holds out a piece of paper. "I need these books from the library. Today. And did you file those requests I asked for?"

"I'll get to them," Lisa says tersely. She rubs her belly and glares at the man, who glares back.

Well, this is awkward. I tuck my hands back down to my sides and glance between the two of them. I truly hope that this isn't going to be my boss, because yikes. Hot but pissy.

The man casts another imperious look in my direction and then points a finger at Lisa. "Get it done, today." He turns on his heel without acknowledging me, and then he's gone.

Lisa sticks her tongue out at his back. "Such a dick."

My mouth has gone dry. "Is that . . . Mr. Magnus?" If so, my boss has a stunningly handsome (and stunningly dickish) husband.

"Sure is."

I divert my attention to what looks like a stack of bills shoved under a book and my hands twitch with the need to clean up. "Does Mr. Magnus work for his wife?"

Her eyes widen, and then she chuckles. "Oh no. That's *a* Mr. Magnus, but he's not married to Dru. He's her nephew, and between assistants himself, so I'm having to fill in." She leans toward me confidentially. "No one likes him. Can't keep anyone in his employ."

My smile returns. "I'm good at multitasking." I'm also a huge suck-up.

Lisa snaps her fingers and then pulls out her phone. "While I'm thinking about it, I had a few questions for you."

"Oh, of course." I read a book last night on interview questions one would expect at a fast-paced job, so I'm more than ready for this. I do wonder when we're going to get to the sit-down part of the interview, but maybe Lisa's just doing introductions before I meet her boss. That makes sense, and I give her a practiced, I'm-very-interested look. "Ask away."

She flicks through her phone screen with her thumb. "Any allergies, food or otherwise?"

"No." Weird, but maybe I'd be in charge of getting coffee or grocery shopping or something. Some assistants do that, don't they? "Do you need to write this down? Should I take notes for you?" I dig in my purse, pulling out a notepad and pen. "I'm happy to do so."

"Not necessary." Lisa taps something on her phone and I'm pretty sure I hear game music. She stares at the screen for a moment and then looks back at me. "Star sign?"

Getting weirder. "Taurus."

"Ah, a hard worker, and stubborn." She dimples, nodding. "She'll like that. Tauruses are great employees. Very easy to work with."

"Thank . . . you?"

"Too bad Mr. Magnus is a Cancer. Very moody." She makes a face, still locked onto her phone. "Here we go. Any particular crystal affinity?" She gestures at one of the shelves, and I notice for the first time that there are rows and rows of crystals of all shapes and sizes in glass containers. Not in any sort of order, of course, but I'm sure I can help with that, too.

"Um, I don't think so?" This is definitely verging into weird territory. I'm starting to get a little uneasy, but I glance around the office again. Maybe this guy is some kind of new age hipster who needs inspiration to work on the game? "What do crystals have to do with the position?"

"A lot. Blood type?"

"Is that really important?" I ask finally, resisting the urge to show my frustration.

"Not necessarily," Lisa admits. "But Ms. Magnus likes to know."

"I'm an O."

"Wonderful." She types with her thumb. "Any physical ailments? Do you work out at a gym? Eat healthy?"

I'm torn between pointing out that those are extremely inappropriate questions and just answering, because I really want the job. "I count macros," I say after a long moment. "For my nutrition." And because it feeds my obsessive need for control to hit the numbers perfectly.

She tilts her head. "I guess that's pretty good. Come upstairs with me and I'll show you into Ms. Magnus's personal offices."

I follow behind her, glancing backward at the "lab" we're leaving. If that's not the office . . . *Nope, Reggie. Don't ask questions until they mention the pay. You've had weird jobs before. As long as it pays well, you can put up with weirdness.* I paste a smile on my face and follow Lisa's slower steps down the hall and toward the stairs. As we cut through the house, I glance over at the kitchen. Mr. Magnus is in there, with a glass of water in front of him on the counter. He's leaning over it and staring intently in our direction, practically scowling.

I can't help but notice that the kitchen is in complete disarray, with dishes on the counter and several cabinets hanging open. Maybe he hates the mess as much as I do, and that's why he's cranky.

"Just ignore him," Lisa continues. "He doesn't like strangers. Remember. Cancer sign."

Right. Moody. That fits him. I cast a brilliant smile in his direction and I'm pleased when he gives me a startled look and turns away. I could swear he's blushing. Suck on that, Magnus.

We head up the stairs and I swear, the second floor feels bigger than the first. There are two halls, both of them lined with doors, and a high ceiling with a crystal-covered chandelier above the stairwell. I gaze around me in awe as Lisa leads me past a glorious-looking library filled to the gills with all kinds of old books. There are portraits on the walls, most of them old, and I realize that the Magnus family is old, old money. No wonder they're eccentric. Lisa heads toward a pair of double doors and opens them. "Just have a seat and I'll let Ms. Magnus know that you're here."

"Thank you," I murmur and step inside.

She turns and goes to leave, and then pauses in the doorway. "Actually, before I go, I should give you a bit of a warning about Ms. Magnus." Lisa gives me an apologetic little look. "She can be a bit of a . . ." She hesitates, clearly choosing her words.

Oh boy. Here it comes. "Hardass?"

Lisa clears her throat. "Dingdong."

I blink.